Condottiere

Book 6 in the Sir John Hawkwood Series

By

Griff Hosker

Condottiere

SWORD BOOKS

Published by Sword Books Ltd 2023

Copyright ©Griff Hosker First Edition

The author has asserted their moral right under the Copyright, Designs and Patents Act, 1988, to be identified as the author of this work.
All Rights reserved. No part of this publication may be reproduced, copied, stored in a retrieval system, or transmitted, in any form or by any means, without the prior written consent of the copyright holder, nor be otherwise circulated in any form of binding or cover other than that in which it is published and without a similar condition being imposed on the subsequent purchaser.
A CIP catalogue record for this title is available from the British Library.
Cover by Design for Writers

Contents

Condottiere i
Prologue 3
Chapter 1 7
Chapter 2 17
Chapter 3 27
Chapter 4 37
Chapter 5 46
Chapter 6 54
Chapter 7 63
Chapter 8 71
Chapter 9 81
Chapter 10 92
Chapter 11 104
Chapter 12 118
Chapter 13 128
Chapter 14 140
Chapter 15 150
Chapter 16 159
Chapter 17 167
Chapter 18 180
Chapter 19 190
Chapter 20 199
Chapter 21 212
Epilogue 228
Historical note 233
Other books by Griff Hosker 236

Real People Used in The Book

Sir John Hawkwood - Captain of the White Company
Giovanni d'Azzo degli Ubaldini - Italian warrior and member of the White Company
King Richard II of England
King Charles VIth of France
Pope Urban V[th]
Pope Urban VIth - Bartolomeo Prignano Cardinal Gil Álvarez
Carrillo de Albornoz – Papal envoy and general
Robert de Genève - Cardinal, papal legate and general, later Pope Clement VIIth, an anti-pope
Alberico da Barbiano – Captain of the Company of St George
Queen Joan (Joanna) I - Queen of Naples, and Countess of Provence and Forcalquier
Louis of Anjou - heir to the throne of Naples
John II - Marquis of Montferrat
Amadeus - Count of Savoy, known as the Green Count
Bernabò Visconti - Lord of Milan and Duke of Milan
Ambrogio Visconti - his son and leader of the Company of Ambrogio
Ettore Visconti - an illegitimate son
Rodolfo Visconti – a legitimate son
Donnina Visconti - an illegitimate daughter and later wife of Sir John Hawkwood
Gian Galeazzo Visconti - son of Galeazzo Visconti and Duke of Milan
Francesco 'il Vecchio' da Carrara – the leader of the Paduan council
Francesco 'il Novello' da Carrara – his son
Bartolomeo Cermisone da Parma - the commander of the Paduan infantry
Pellario Griffo - Chamberlain of Pisa
Giovanni Agnello – Merchant and doge of Pisa
Geoffrey Chaucer - poet and diplomat
Ivan Horvat - Ban of Macsó
Facino and Filippino Cane - Veronese nobles

Prologue

I am Sir John Hawkwood, leader of the White Company. I have been a warrior my whole life and began fighting for England and King Edward before the Great Plague took so many English villages. War is my life. That life changed dramatically when I married Donnina Visconti, the illegitimate daughter of my former ally, Bernabò Visconti the ruler of Milan, the most powerful state in Northern Italy. Life changed but not in the manner I anticipated. Soon after my first daughter, Giannetta, was born I had a falling out with Donnina's father. My father-in-law was the most unscrupulous man I had ever known and I had known some villains. He was happy to promise payment and then withhold it. He tried that with me when I recovered his wife's dowry. He learned to his cost that was a mistake. I simply held on to the dowry. I always believed that my men, my White Company, should be paid. The result of the discord was that I entered the service of Florence and the long relationship with Visconti ended. I still smile at that for I had been the enemy of Florence for many years and I think they hired me and my men simply to avoid me attacking them. It was a measure of their distrust that they would not let me or my men enter the city of Florence. We lived without. On the positive side, we were allowed to work for any other city-state so long as it was not an enemy of Florence. That suited us.

Condottiere

The change in my life came because of Donnina. She was seventeen when we married and if I was Giovanni Acuto to the Italians, John the Sharp, then my wife showed that she had more keenness to her than any other woman in the land. She was clever. She took the news that her father and I had parted company with a philosophical shrug, her father had used her, as he had used all his children, legitimate and illegitimate, and there was no affection between them. Instead, she set about making us financially secure. William Turner had been my bookkeeper for many years but he had married well and now lived in Pisa. Florence and Pisa were enemies so whilst William could continue to manage my books, he was too far away for me to use for my own finances. Besides that, his wife and I did not get along. I was a soldier and all that I knew of money was that it was there to pay my soldiers and to ensure that we ate well. Donnina took charge of my finances. She had me write to King Richard of England. I was of some use to the young king as I kept him informed of events in Italy. My wife wanted the young king to ensure that the coin from my English estates was paid to me directly. She began to invest our money so that we would become richer.

I had been lucky.

We were given a house outside of Florence but it was not grand enough for Donnina. She used our money to buy a larger plot of land and had a house built. The fact that she was pregnant with our second daughter, Caterina, did not slow her down and she harried and harangued the bemused workmen until Casa Donnina was finished and she was able to furnish it in a grand manner.

My personal life was perfect. My professional life, however, was changed. My success had also brought success to my men and Giovanni d'Azzo Ubaldini, my right-hand man, was persuaded to take command of the Paduan army. His loss was a great one but I understood why he took the job. He had lived in my shadow for many years and yet I knew that he had almost as much skill on the battlefield as I did. There was no animosity in our parting and we remained friends. It was the loss of his companionship that hurt. It was exacerbated when Sir Edward and Sir Thomas, both long time comrades, along with Sir Dai all left my service to return to England. Sir Edward had been Ned of Lincoln and I had knighted both him and Tall Tom. They stayed with me for some months after our victory but their full purses and the thought of a life in England was too great a lure and they left the company. Dai and Robin had been with me for a long time and I had thought they would stay forever. While Robin, the commander of my archers, was happy to do so Dai, who had been my squire, also chose to head back to England. As with all those who had fought with me there was no acrimony but I felt disappointed. Others left to join other companies as we had no prospect of war for a while. Some men crave such things. The men who remained on our books were the core of my lances and archers, my officers. The result was that I was left with fewer senior leaders in whom I could confide. It was left to Robin and the new captain of my men at arms, Michael, to be my close companions. Even then it was not as close as it might have been as they had their own homes. They were close but I no longer saw them every day. My world became a world of women. The only men in the house were the servants. My home was Donnina's. She understood why the men had left but she also knew that my name would draw men to the white banner of my company when we needed them. She lavished the money we saved on their pay on Casa Donnina and the hall became a small palace.

Condottiere

Northern Italy 1379

Chapter 1

Politics in Italy were complicated. This was not England where one man, King Richard, ruled it all and while lords might conspire against others, there was no open war. Italy had many city-states, some huge, like Milan and Florence, and others small like Lucca and Mantua. I knew why Padua had hired Giovanni d'Azzo Ubaldini, the Venetians were making war on the Genoese and Venice coveted the lands around Treviso which belonged to Padua. To keep Venice from taking Treviso, the da Carrara family had to ally themselves with Venice in times of war. The war between the two pre-eminent masters of the sea was nothing to do with Italy but with islands and lands in Greece. Padua was an ally of Venice and while the war was largely fought at sea, the victories of the Hungarians and the loss of Dalmatia had hurt Venice. Giovanni was hired as insurance against a Genoese attack by land. Bernabò Visconti was not averse to taking advantage of distractions and Milan might try to gobble up Paduan land if Genoa sent men overland to Venice. Giovanni was more than capable of hiring men to protect Padua and ingratiate himself with Venice. Florence just watched on, an interested spectator. Genoa was a rival to all the other city-states and since the demise of the Pisans, the seas were ruled by Genoa and Venice. This war was a bloody struggle for control of the seas. Florence had no ships and they would watch. My sharp sword would be kept sheathed. The Doge of Florence would await the outcome and then, if things were aligned, like the stars, then my company might be used to take advantage of the situation. This meant that my pared-down company had no war to fight and we haemorrhaged more men every day as they left to join other warring companies. Many joined Giovanni.

My men and I still trained every day but the company was slimmed down. We were like men who had once eaten well but now looked skeletal. The pension from Florence was not enough to maintain a large army. I still had English archers and more than a hundred lances. A lance was made up of a man at arms, his squire and a foot soldier. Other companies often had an archer or crossbowman in each lance but I had been an archer and I was English. I knew the benefit of a massed band of archers. It was one reason for our success. They were expensive to maintain but the ones who had stayed with me were the best in Italy. What we needed was a paymaster and the Venetian-Genoese war was fought by others. Florence did not want to be dragged into this titanic struggle between two monsters, each of which could swallow Florence if they so chose.

Donnina and I were close. Some thought that was remarkable for she was more than thirty years my junior, but Donnina had the mind of a mature woman and she understood me better than any man or woman alive. She was a practical woman and had hired a wet nurse for Caterina, and Giannetta, my elder daughter, was whisked away when we ate so that the two of us could enjoy good food, fine wine and intelligent conversation. She was the daughter of Visconti and, as such, was keenly attuned to the politics of Italy. We did not speak of mewling children but how best the company could make more profit. My estates in England brought an income but the effect of the plague that had devastated the land all those years ago was still being felt. My Romagna estates should have brought more money into my treasury but my falling out with Bernabò Visconti meant that some of those who owed me an income withheld it, knowing that they had the support of the Lord of Milan. I was not afraid of Visconti but now was not the time to test my strength. I needed him to be under attack from others.

Donnina showed that she had news from places further afield than Pisa and Florence when she said, one evening as we ate slow-cooked veal, "Hungary is a place where you could earn money, John."

"Hungary? That is far from here."

She smiled, "Yet Charles of Naples has just claimed the throne of Hungary. One side or the other will need lances and we are well-placed to supply them."

Shaking my head I said, "Lutz von Landau and I parted on poor terms and he will support one of the combatants. I would rather he was fighting elsewhere."

"You do not think that you can defeat him?"

I sighed and wiped my mouth, "Fighting an army made of citizens is one thing but fighting against another band of mercenaries is quite another. I think I am a better general than von Landau but our men are more equally balanced."

"Your archers give you the edge."

"And two of my leaders have left. Other archers have returned to England too. King Richard needs an army to defend his crown from those who might take it." I could see where she was going with her argument. "I agree that we need another employer but we need to be careful whom we choose."

That seemed to make her think, "Florence still wishes to have both Pisa and Siena as her lands."

"Pisa is nothing. She is a spent force. She will fall soon enough but I would not be the one to crush her." I was not a sentimental man. The bank we had built and which stored our coins was in Pisa. I wanted a Pisa that lay hidden.

"The rest of Italy sees you as a tough man but I see a gentler side. Siena then?"

"The Doge of Florence does not wish me to enter his city and so until he seeks me out then my hands are tied. When the Florentines want to hurt Siena then I will go to war again."

Donnina was relentless, "Then let us actively seek an employer."

I knew she was right but William Turner had been the one who had secured the contracts for us. Since he had married into the Pisan nobility, he had grown comfortable and we had become distant, largely due to his wife and her antipathy towards me. I nodded, "Then Michael and I will ride to Padua and speak with Giovanni. He is still a friend and he has an ear for these things."

It was my inactivity and what she saw as my indolence that Donnina did not like. So long as I was doing something then she was happy. She beamed. "Good. I have plans for the next treasure that you fetch."

"We have no employer yet."

"You shall have one for who would not choose the captain who brings such success?"

I rode the next day to speak to Michael. I knew I should have knighted him but as three of the four men I had knighted had left me I was loath to lose another. Michael did not mind. I had taken him under my wing when he was a boy and he had profited from our association. As he said, many times, he would have had no life had I not given him one. He would be forever grateful. He had hired two Italians and he was with the two of them, Sebastian and Luigi, in the orchard in his garden. He had a small farm with horses and fruit. The two Italian warriors were young but he had seen that they had skills. He would keep paying them from his own income until they had shown that they were worthy enough to join the company. We had a good reputation and only needed proven warriors. He had hired them himself and both were like he was, without a family. They were little more than youths but Michael saw the raw clay that he could mould into warriors like himself. I had made men of both Dai and Michael. I was a little flattered that he was trying to do the same as I had. There were advantages to them being Italian. Although both Michael and I were fluent in Italian, neither of us looked Italian. Our skin and hair marked us as different. The two young men could hide in places where Michael and I would stand out. I had won as many battles through tricks and cunning as I had through strategy and martial skills.

They stopped their sparring when I strode into the garden. Michael had only one servant. She was the old woman who cleaned and cooked for him. Her own family was dead and I think she saw Michael as a son she might have had. She had opened the door for me, curtsied and then scurried back to the kitchen.

Michael beamed as he greeted me, "Sir John, what brings you here? Work?"

"In a manner of speaking. Lady Donnina thinks that we should be earning money and I intend to ride to Padua to speak to Giovanni."

He nodded and handed his sword to Sebastian. Luigi fetched him a towel and he dried the sweat from his face, "She is right, my lord. We have been idle too long. More men are leaving each day to seek new paymasters."

He was right but I did not enjoy the implied criticism. "I would have you come with me." I nodded to the two young men, "Have these two men horses that they can ride?"

"Of course, my lord."

"Then they can come with us."

"Who else will be coming with us?"

"I will see Robin. Perhaps he tires of the women in his life."

That made Michael laugh, "He will never tire of that but more than making love he craves action and adventure. He will be ready for the journey."

His words confirmed my own thoughts, "Be at my home by Prime. I will provide the sumpters."

Sir Robin lived just a mile or so away. He lived close enough to his archers and they trained most mornings. He then indulged himself in the afternoon. He liked women. His house had a couple of men to watch his horses and tend his fields but his house was filled with women. He was not the marrying kind and the women in his life had the same attitude towards lovemaking as he had. So long as they were paid, either for their work or their services, they were happy. He never forced himself on any woman and they chose to live with him. When they had enough of Robin's money they left. There was always a ready supply of new ones to take their place. It was a comfortable and mutually beneficial arrangement for them all.

I caught him and the one hundred archers who remained just before they finished at the mark. They took their work very seriously. One reason why Robin had bought the old farm was the land. There was a long meadow. There were too many rocks for it to be of any use as arable and so he kept a few cows on it. He and his archers would pen them while they used the meadow for practice. It was eight hundred paces long and he had permanent marks set up. The finest archer in Italy, he had a critical eye and was able to correct potential flaws in the men he led. My archers had been the one constant in my time as captain of the company and they had never let me down. That was due, in no small part, to Robin's leadership. The archers were all English and they knew me. When I had fought at Crécy then I had been an archer. My huge frame reflected my youth as King Edward's archer. I might no longer draw a bow in anger but the practice had given me a muscled upper body.

Robin beamed, "Have you come to draw a bow, Sir John? We have an easy one for you to pull here." I could see that he was in good humour and I sensed that he intended to have fun at my expense.

I snorted, "I can pull any bow that you give me, Robin Good Fellow." I used the nickname of Puck, in jest.

He grinned and said, "Hob, fetch me my old bow and let us see if our lord and master still has what it takes."

I could have refused but that was not in my nature. I nodded and took off my cloak. It had been a week or so since I had exercised with a bow and Robin was quite right, I could not have drawn his best bow, not at full draw, at least. The other archers all unstrung their bows. It was clear that the work for the morning was over and they had priceless entertainment before them; the humiliation of Sir John Hawkwood.

It was an older bow that was brought and Robin strung it for me. He made it look effortless. I picked an arrow from the ones stuck in the ground by Robin's feet. They would be the best arrows for they were his. I nocked it when he handed me the bow. I smiled, "Which mark?"

There were marks every fifty paces up to the ones at the far side of the meadow. I guessed that the last one had to be more than four hundred paces from us. Few men, without a following wind, could hit a target that far away but Robin liked to stretch and test his men.

He nodded to the standard one, it was two hundred and fifty paces from us, "That one will do, I think." He grinned, "Unless you wish to use the one we give to the boys." He nodded at one a hundred paces from us.

"Your first choice will do."

Holding the nocked arrow and bow in my left hand I licked the forefinger on my right hand and held it up. The wind was coming from behind me. There was an air of hushed anticipation as I drew back the bow. I felt my shoulders begin to complain as the string neared my ear. I kept pulling and then, when I thought I could pull no more, I released. When I had been younger, little more than a youth, I had spent hours each day at the butts. It had been many years since I had done so but my hands, arms, shoulders and eyes all remembered their training. I watched the arrow soar into the air. I would have been happy if it had landed close to the mark but the gods of the bow must have been with me. I struck the pole holding the mark at head height. The strike was halfway down the pole. There was a cheer and applause.

Robin grinned and winking at Hob said, "Well if this had been a battlefield someone would have a sore knee, still, it is not bad for a knight with manicured hands."

That made them all laugh. Shaking my head I joined in with their laughter. I handed the bow to Hob and then nodded at Robin, "Come, we need to talk."

"Dismiss the men and release the cows, Hob."

"Aye, Captain." Robin was a knight but none of the men gave him that title. Robin preferred the one he had earned.

"Tomorrow, I ride with Michael to Padua." He cocked an eye. "We need to find an employer. William is, well, distracted and I will seek the advice of Giovanni."

He gave me a cheeky grin, "Lady Donnina wishes to buy something?"

"Perhaps but the men need a war and the company needs payment."

"I have enough for my women and I have men who make cheese for me."

I laughed out loud, "Robin of Wakefield, a cheesemaker?"

"An honest profession and I like cheese."

"As do I but I enjoy being a warrior more. If you wish to stay and eat cheese then…"

"I did not say that. The diversion might be interesting. I will come."

"Bring your bow and be at my hall by Prime."

My shoulders felt as though the torturer had been at me with red hot pokers.

Donnina was delighted at my decision. She was an eminently practical woman. When she had been chosen as my bride, by her father, she had agreed to it not for any lovelorn reason but because she knew that I was the best chance she had of a life as good as that she had enjoyed as the daughter of her father's former concubine.

Ajax was getting old but my horse and I were comfortable with one another. I had my ostler groom him and feed him the choicest of foods. "I will need a good sumpter too. Have one readied for the morning. It will need to carry weapons, food and blankets."

"Yes, my lord, Mary is the strongest. All will be ready."

"We leave at Prime and I will brook no delay."

I believed that I was a good master who paid well and treated his servants well but woe betide any who did not meet my high standards. Thus far none had endured my wrath.

I took my sword to the blacksmith, "Put an edge on that." I also handed him a stiletto and a rondel dagger, "And those."

"Yes, my lord."

He was a good enough smith but I did not use him to make either weapons or armour. I paid for the best and knew that when I went to war my body would be well protected. That meant going to Florence and, in former times, Milan. My plate and mail were the best and I did not need a new suit. For this journey, I would not wear armour. I needed to dress comfortably. The weapons were there in case they were needed but I hoped that they would not be. I would travel without marks of either my rank or my name. We would be cloaked and cowled. I would let Sebastian and Luigi negotiate for the rooms we would use and I would pay with silver and not gold. When a man paid with gold it attracted the creatures of the night who might seek to take it and it would mark me as a man of means. Silver suggested a lower-ranked man. Nor would we wear spurs. I did not need them to ride and being marked as a knight merely increased the cost of most things. The people we met might think that we were swords for hire but I wanted no one to recognise me as Sir John Hawkwood, Captain of the White Company and confidante of dukes and doges.

As I lay in bed, Donnina in my arms, she said, "Take any contract you can. Your men need the work and the family needs the money." She patted her belly, "There will be a third child soon."

"Good, then our blood will continue for more generations."

I kissed her and closed my eyes. Now that my first daughter, Antiochia was married to Sir William Coggleshall I could expect my first grandchildren. One of my sons was a monk and I doubted that his loins would keep my blood going but John, my firstborn and now in England raising his own company, might.

My mind was restless and I was, I confess, more than a little excited. I woke early and slipped from the bed. My wife had created a house for comfort as well as luxury. There was a chamber next to the bedchamber where I could dress without disturbing her. She was eminently practical. I disrobed and glanced at my frame. I was not yet a Bernabò Visconti with a belly reflecting my comfortable life and fine table but I was no longer the lean yet powerful archer who had fought for the King of England. I patted my stomach and reflected that a few days of riding and the vagaries of the food from inns would help me regain some of the muscle I had lost. I knew that the visit to Giovanni might just be the first stage in a long journey. He would be the oracle that I would consult but like the ancient heroes of Greece, the oracle might send me elsewhere. Donnina knew that and she would not be over-worried by an extended journey.

The servants were up already and, when I entered the hall, I heard the whispered voices as they scurried from the kitchen with food. They knew my tastes and my habits. Carlo the steward would be harrying them along to fetch the delicacies I liked. In truth, they were hardly delicacies. I still enjoyed the oat porridge that I had eaten when growing up and when I had been a young archer. Augmented with fruits and honey it was always the first thing I ate. However, I was a lover of fried ham. The Florentines and Pisans were always bemused that the ham they enjoyed, just cured, would be fried for me. I liked it crisp and served on freshly made bread. The baker would have been up before Lauds to ensure that the bread was brought at the perfect temperature. The eggs I liked were always poached and I was particular about their presentation. I liked runny yolks and a seemly appearance. The serving and devouring of my porridge seemed to be the perfect time to make my eggs.

Sophia placed my porridge, fruit and ale on the table, curtsied and scurried back to the kitchen. Carlo bowed, "I will have food prepared for your journey, Sir John. How many men will be with you?"

"There will be just four and they like my tastes."

He looked relieved. He would know exactly what to pack: a ham, the hard cheese that I liked, a jar of honey, figs, five loaves, a wineskin and an ale skin. Such rations would enable us to ride all day without seeking out an inn. I wished us to be hidden for as long as possible. Whilst not going to war, I would be leaving the safety of Florence and my company. The world was a dangerous place and the most perilous part was that through which we would ride, Northern Italy.

Chapter 2

Donnina arrived just as I was about to leave. I had eaten well and felt replete. I had heard the horses of my companions as they had clattered into my courtyard. She smiled, "They are punctual. Have a safe and profitable ride, my husband." She stood on tiptoes to kiss me. She knew how to kiss and I was grateful once more for the decision of the Lord of Milan to marry off one of his daughters to me. It had worked out better for Donnina and me than for her father.

Carlo had already had the sumpter packed and Ajax was pawing the ground for he was eager to ride. I had not used him for a long journey for some time and I knew that I would not take him to war again. My four companions all bowed as my wife emerged, wrapped against the morning chill. "Watch over my husband, Robin and Michael. He is the one who will put the food on the table."

Robin nodded, "I have done so these fifteen years or more, my lady."

We had said our farewells in the house and I mounted without further ado. I donned my riding gloves. They were made of good hide and were excellent protection for my hands. My sword hung from my belt and my sharpened smaller weapons were there also. Upon my head, I wore a simple but comfortable hat. It came down around my ears and, allied to my cowl, would hide my features should I need to be secretive. I saw that Sebastian led one sumpter and Luigi had taken the reins of Mary, the other. I spread my cloak so that it covered the rear of the saddle and Ajax's rump.

"Let us ride."

The five of us clattered through my gates. They would be closed once we had left. I had half a dozen old men as guards. They had served in my company and each had endured minor wounds. They were fed and paid better than they would have been in the employ of another. Sir John Hawkwood rewarded loyalty and was one reason why fewer men had deserted me in this time of unemployment.

Robin nudged his horse next to mine, "Which way?"

I shrugged, "It matters little for we have to pass enemies whichever way we go. I would ride as far as we can before we stop. I have supplies and we can use streams to water the horses. I aim to stay this night in Monghidoro." He nodded. We had not raided the walled town and as it lay at the top of a steep ascent with inns where we could stay it seemed an appropriate choice. It was a long ride, more than forty miles, but we had good horses and, on a campaign, we might travel further. We knew the roads close to our homes well and were able to take less well-travelled ones. They did not slow us and by their use, we would be able to be beyond the land of Florence before anyone knew we had gone. We would avoid the castles when we neared them. I had learned, over the years, that the less others knew of my plans the better chance I had of survival. The two Italians rode at the rear just behind Michael but I knew that while Robin and I spoke, he would be looking for any danger to us. I turned to the two Italians, "Do not use our titles while we are on the road. If you must give me a title then make it master. Do not use, Sir John or Sir Robin."

They chorused, "Aye… Master."

I smiled, they would do.

We were travelling through forest as well as over mountains and the road twisted and turned, dipped and rose. Trees gave shade and then in places where winter storms had wreaked havoc or men had hewn trees for timber, we found ourselves in bright sunlight. As we rode Robin and I spoke. The hiring of archers was Robin's domain. I hired the lances and men at arms but they would only manifest themselves when they knew we had a contract. Active service with the White Company meant full purses and victory.

"The Pope would always hire us, Master."

I shook my head, "Our last experience with a pope was not a good one and we know the mettle of this one who rules Rome." There were two rivals and one of them was the man who had ordered the massacre at Cesena. He lived in Avignon. I had been blamed but my men had not taken part in the slaughter of the innocents. That had been a papal decision. "Besides, the papacy is a poor employer. Genoa or Venice are engaged in a war and one of those might suit us."

Condottiere

"It might mean fighting against Giovanni."

"And that is why we make this visit. It is to sound out the waters. There may be others too. My wife suggested Hungary."

Robin shook his head, "The Hungarians are wild and unpredictable, Sir John. No matter which side we joined we would still fear a knife in the back. I know that the Neapolitans have entered that nest of snakes but trust me, it will not end well for them. Besides, we do not know the country. Verona might hire us but as they are enemies of Padua and Mantua, once again it would bring us into conflict with our old friend." He took out a piece of dried venison from his satchel and began to chew. He offered me one but I shook my head. "This way may be the best. Giovanni is a friend and he will give honest advice and sound intelligence to us."

We had all learned to trust each other. Condottiere like Paer and Sterz had betrayed us. We did not trust von Landau and English condottiere like Sir John Thornbury had left Italy for England. My leaders and my men were the only ones I would truly trust.

The horses were weary when we reached the road that twisted up to the village of Monghidoro and we dismounted. The Alpe were a brooding range of mountains that overlooked the village. I was not so high and mighty as to continue to ride a horse when the walk would save his strength for the next day. Others were hurrying up the hill for night would come soon. There were bandits in these hills. During the day they would stay hidden but any traveller foolish enough to move after dark was asking for trouble. In addition, the ones who reached the village first might have a greater choice of rooms. We were lucky for the others heading up the road had carts, wagons and laden horses. Relieved of their human cargo our horses were spritely by comparison and we overtook the laden merchants. Once we entered the town, I nodded to Sebastian to find us a room. He gave the reins of his sumpter to Luigi and hurried off. I did not know the two youths well but Michael did and he knew that Sebastian would be discreet. My name would not be mentioned although my size might mark me out as Sir John Hawkwood. If my name was known then the price would rise. Sebastian would negotiate a price and then, if I was recognised, so be it.

We stopped in the square where there was a trough. The horses drank while we waited for Sebastian. He returned with a beaming smile. I have secured us two rooms," I saw him about to mouth *'Sir John'* and I shook my head, He corrected himself, "Master. One chamber is a large one and can accommodate the three of you. The antechamber will suffice for we two."

Michael said, "And the horses?"

"There is a stable but that has cost almost as much as the rooms."

I smiled for he had done well, "That matters not. Food?"

"Wholesome rather than grand I fear."

"Wholesome is good so long as they do not charge us for richer fare. Lead on."

It was a good choice for it was not large and noisy nor was it mean and squalid. The stables were small which explained why they charged so much. The innkeeper looked to be a shrewd businessman and, as I later discovered, the inn was not his only source of income. He kept a flock of sheep and goats and, like Robin, made his own cheese. The two of them hit it off as they spoke of the problems of cheesemaking. The room where travellers ate was surprisingly large. We discovered that the food, while simple, was also of good quality and regular travellers used it. I was happy with the choice made by Sebastian. There were three beds in the room and they were slightly bigger than many we had used. We would be comfortable.

After changing out of my cloak and discarding my gloves and hat, we descended to drink and dine. Robin went to order both and to continue his discussion with the innkeeper. While we sat Michael and I scanned the faces that we saw. I had looked for any familiar faces all the way through the town. We had served with other companies and not all of our partings had been peaceful. I had bloodied the noses of many men, mainly Germans and Hungarians, and my eyes sought any that might represent danger. Michael did the same and I knew that Robin, despite his animated conversation, would be vigilant. The men I saw were Italians. None had the look of a warrior. You can always tell a warrior. In my case and Robin's, it was our build. We had the lopsided look of an archer, Robin more so than me.

Many had scars and all of them had flitting eyes. The ones we saw were travellers who came for food or locals who could not be bothered to cook for themselves. Monghidoro was prosperous. It belonged to Ferrara but the lack of a castle meant that it would not be fought over. It straddled the main route from Florence to Venice and was frequented by merchants. Those who lived in Monghidoro did well from travellers and it was reflected in the men we saw. I relaxed.

The food, when it came, was good. Neither Donnina nor I were slaves to fabulously presented food. When it was offered, we enjoyed it. Her father would have stormed out of the inn for the food was too plain for him. I found myself smiling at the thought of Bernabò Visconti travelling such a road and staying in the inn. When he travelled it was in comfort. He no longer rode very far. He would also only travel if he thought he was going to stay in a place which suited his expensive tastes. His son, Ambrogio, was also a condottiere and he would have appreciated the food but he was unlike his father. Bernabò was a unique man. He had the power of a king but he was just a duke. I knew that he had not achieved, in his life, all that he wished. He had married off his legitimate children to nobles and princes but none had, as yet, achieved a crown. I think it was that ambition which kept him going. I was just pleased that he was no longer in my life. Our acrimonious parting meant that I doubted he would seek to use me again. I knew that I had been used, some might say overused by the manipulative spider who spun his webs and plotted in his Alpine home. I did not resent it for I had benefitted and I knew that I would not have the power I did, not to mention my wife, but for our association. As I pushed away the empty platter, cleaned by the last of the bread, I reflected that this journey was a necessary one for it was the first where I was freed from the Visconti fetters. My new life would begin with whatever contract I managed to procure.

I had the ability to sleep whilst on campaign and the bed, even though it was smaller than the one I was used to, allowed me to sleep well and I woke refreshed. I knew that we might need another two or three days to reach Padua but by leaving early we gave ourselves, if the road and weather conspired in our favour, to do it in two. The frugal side of me knew that if we did so then we could save the expense of an extra night in an inn or a monastery.

There was no town watch and there were no gates around Monghidoro. That meant we were spared the scrutiny of sentries and guards but I knew, as we left the town, that we were being watched. I saw no one taking undue interest but the hairs on my neck prickled and my feelings were confirmed as we headed up the pass. Robin said, "Someone was watching us."

I nodded, "Aye, and they were good for I saw them not."

Luigi's voice came from behind us. He had heard my words, "I saw no one. How do you know, my lord?"

I shrugged, "To survive as long as Robin and I have you need to develop such senses."

Robin did not look around as he did not want to alert any to our suspicions. The road was beginning to descend and twist and turn as it headed towards the plains close to Bologna. Any watcher skilled enough to stay hidden from us would most likely be at the side or ahead of us if they intended us harm. We both knew that we had some time. If the watcher intended us harm, he would have to get ahead of us. He would need to bring others. There were five of us and we were armed. I said to Sebastian, "How far until we are out of the mountains?"

"Perhaps twenty miles, Master."

That meant any danger would come in the next sixteen or so miles. I looked to the Alpe to our left. The mountains here were high but there would be trails known to locals that could take an attacker ahead of us. They might have to thrash horses to do so but if any wished to do me harm then it would be worth it.

"And how many villages on this road we have chosen?"

Sebastian did not answer immediately. He was thinking, Michael had chosen his men well. "Perhaps ten."

"Then the attack, when it comes, will be between two. Let us hurry for we may be able to get well ahead of them."

Luigi said, "How do you know that we shall be attacked, Master?"

Robin snorted his answer, "We were watched and recognised. Sir John Hawkwood is a prize worth risking danger. There are many men who would like to take the Captain of the White

Company as a hostage. Keep your eyes to the sides and your hand on your weapons."

Michael added, "If we are attacked then forget the sumpters. We can always recover them later."

The journey along the twisting mountain road became tense. All conversation ceased as we pushed our horses and watched for danger. Despite the fact that we were generally descending there were still gradients we had to ascend. I knew that our horses would be tired once we had reached the plain. My plan to make the journey in two days was already in tatters. That would only be possible with a steady and measured gait.

We reached the first village of Monterenzio without seeing anyone, but as we watered our horses at the trough in the centre of the tiny village, I saw that there were roads and trails that entered from the left and the right. An attacker could have already got ahead of us.

Robin knew me well and he saw my worried frown, "Not yet. We rode hard and they will not yet be ahead of us." He nodded towards the slopes to the east and west of the road, "We are easily spied from above. The next time we pass through trees we will stop so that I can string my bow."

As we mounted, I said, "You are right."

His bow was our secret weapon. His bow case was on the sumpter and would not have attracted undue attention. An Englishmen might have known what it was but the Italians preferred the crossbow. Robin could string the bow and hide it beneath his cloak, hanging from his cantle. Our opportunity came just three miles later. The road passed between high trees and rocks had tumbled down the slopes to make ambush almost impossible. We halted and I said, "Feed the horses while Robin prepares." We were pushing our animals hard and a handful of oats would help them to recover. Robin took his bow from the case and the string from his hat. He made the stringing of the bow look easy but I knew it was not. The string might be spoiled by being kept taut for so long but a bowstring was a cheap alternative to a dead man. His arrow bag would be a giveaway too and so he jammed three arrows in his belt. That done, and the bow secreted, we mounted and headed down the road.

It was another eight miles before the ambush was sprung. We had passed through the handful of houses that made up Noce and the road twisted to the left. As we turned a blind bend, Ajax neighed and I knew that danger lay ahead. There were eight men that we could see. One held a crossbow and the others had swords and spears. The crossbowman was on a rock and kneeling. He was the furthest from us but at a range of twenty paces, if he used his weapon, he could not miss. The others were closer, perhaps fifteen paces from us. I saw no horses but Ajax's neigh told me that they were close. All the men wore a brigandine, some were leather but most were padded. They were normally worn beneath the armour. I recognised the leader as one of the men who had served with Lutz von Landau. He was a Hungarian.

It was he who spoke, "Sir John, it is some time since I saw you. You have put on weight and look like a merchant."

If he was trying to insult me, he failed, "You have the advantage of me for I do not remember your name but then again there have been many minions I have seen over the years. Why do you stop us and threaten me with a crossbow?" I smiled, "That crossbow is aimed at me is it not?"

He nodded as he shrugged, "Simple, with no wars my men and I need an income. When I spied you in Monghidoro I saw the chance for a good payday. Visconti, the Pope… there are many who would pay for you to be taken. You are outnumbered and any resistance, Sir John, will result in the deaths of your men and the whole world knows how sentimental you are about those who follow you."

Robin's horse began to snort and rear a little. The Hungarian frowned as Robin tried to control it. I knew that Robin had made the horse do so as a distraction. He was as skilled a horseman as any. I moved Ajax down the slope a little as I drew my sword. I knew that Michael would do the same. The two Italians were an unknown factor.

"Put down your weapons and surrender or I will order Jurgen to begin the killing."

The crossbowman lifted his weapon. I had not stopped Ajax as he continued his descent down the road. Robin seemingly had his horse under control and he reached forward to stroke the animal's neck. I knew what he was doing. He was reaching for his bow and it was my turn for a distraction. I was the one they wanted and that gave me an advantage. They would kill the others first. Indeed, the crossbow was clearly aimed now at Michael who was to my right. I was needed alive, as a hostage for ransom. I kicked Ajax hard and went straight for the Hungarian. He had his sword out but its tip was touching the ground. Even as he raised it the crossbowman shifted his aim and his bolt flew over my head towards Michael. Michael would easily avoid the bolt as, like me, he knew how to do so. I swung my sword as I shifted Ajax to the left. The Hungarian had a hand and a half sword. It was longer than mine but it rose slowly. I swept my sword in an arc as Robin's first arrow slammed into the luckless crossbowman who was busy trying to reload his weapon. Michael and his men had followed me and their swords were sweeping down at the men on foot whose leader I had just killed. A second arrow hit one in the head and the three who had survived our initial attack fled for we now outnumbered them. I was in no mood for mercy and I did not want to keep looking over my shoulder. They had clearly left their horses down the slope and were hurrying to them. I leaned from my saddle and hacked across the back of the first fleeing Hungarian. His padded brigandine merely slowed the blade and it sliced into flesh. Michael took two, one to his left and one to his right. The ambush could not have gone better for us.

"Did the bolt hit anyone?"

Robin laughed, "Not even close!"

"Collect the weapons and purses. Michael, fetch their animals. They will pay for our accommodation this night."

Sebastian was clearly shaken by the ambush. Robin had said that the bolt was not even close but it had flown over the Italian's head and worried him. "Will there be more attacks on this road, Master?"

I shrugged, "Perhaps. These men were not enemies of mine. They were opportunists who saw a chance to make a fortune. They gambled and they lost."

Their purses yielded some coins. Their weapons would be a source of income for we could sell them as we could their horses. The Hungarians had abused their horses in their haste to get ahead of us and would not fetch as much as they might. However, having lost nothing in the encounter, this was all profit.

We did not stop until we reached San Martino which lay on the plain. It was a large village and there were inns and, most importantly, a horse trader. We arrived in the late afternoon and he was happy to take the sumpters and ponies of the ambushers. He also took the weapons off our hands. He would resell them at a profit to men who were more desperate than we were. They did not bring us a fortune but enough to pay for two rooms, stabling and food for us. The purses we had taken were also an unexpected gift. We had been lucky but, then again, I had learned that a man makes his own luck. Had I not had a skilled archer like Robin nor such a good swordsman like Michael with me, then it might not have ended as well as it had.

Chapter 3

We reached Padua without further incident. If nothing else the attack had shown the two Italians that we could take nothing for granted and war was always just a crossbow bolt away. Padua was a walled city and we were both questioned and scrutinised before we were allowed to enter. Luckily Rodrigo, one of the Italians who had left Florence to serve Giovanni as a captain, came with the relief guard and recognised me. He berated the luckless sentries, "Do you not recognise Giovanni Acuto, the greatest general in Italy? Mark his face well and that of his companions. Do not hinder them again." The men cowered before Rodrigo's aggressive words.

The bond in the White Company held both ways.

Rodrigo accompanied us to the huge house close to the city walls. "Captain Ubaldini chose this house from those that were offered as it is in a quieter part of Padua. It has enough room for you all."

"How many men does he command?"

He has but one hundred in his company but there are five hundred Paduans, nobles mainly, four hundred crossbowmen and a thousand citizens." I stopped and he shrugged, "Captain Ubaldini knows that is not enough but the Paduans are nervous allies of Venice. We have been ordered to stay close to Padua to defend it should the Genoese come."

I shook my head, "A defensive war is a mistake." Even as I said the words, I saw the opportunity for profit.

Giovanni was delighted to see me. We had been together in one form or another since Flanders and he was the most loyal of men. He had real skills as a commander but always deferred to me. I was flattered. He was close to both Michael and Robin and their greeting reflected that warmth. When men have faced death together then the ties are deeper than blood.

"Sir John, a most unexpected pleasure. You should have told me you were coming."

I smiled, "We wanted secrecy."

He nodded, "I will show you to your rooms and after you have freshened up you can tell me the purpose of your visit." He turned to Rodrigo, "Go to the council and tell them that we have a guest, Giovanni Acuto, and stress that he is a friend."

"Of course, Captain General."

Giovanni shrugged, "They are like virgins on the night before a wedding and fear their own shadows. Verona terrifies them as do both Florence and Genoa. They fear that Verona might ally itself with Genoa and take over the disputed lands."

"They have nothing to fear from me so long as you command."

Maria his wife, although I could not remember the actual ceremony, came from the kitchen. She too beamed, "Sir John, what a delight." She turned, "Alfonso, fetch the hindquarter of boar from the larder." Turning back she said, "Tonight I will fete you. I have waited a long time to do so."

I took her hand and kissed the back of it, "My lady, you grow more beautiful each time I see you."

She snorted but I could tell that she was flattered, "With the beautiful Donnina at your side I doubt that you have eyes for any, Giovanni Acuto, but it is kind of you to say so."

Giovanni had not chosen his wife without the same care he chose his weapons and they had always been perfect together. She had followed him on our campaigns. I knew that Donnina would not do so but Maria was made of sterner stuff and she was always there for the man who, since Flanders, had been my right hand.

That evening we dined with Giovanni. The two Italians had been invited but they had been too intimidated and ate with the soldiers who served the commander of the Paduan army. Maria sat with us while we ate and we chatted about the people they had both known in Florence and Pisa. I was champing at the bit to get to the meat of the matter but I would not sully the conversation with martial words, Maria was too nice a woman to talk of war.

Once we had begun to drink the sweet dessert wine she rose, "I will leave you gentlemen to speak of that which brought Sir John here. I will leave a light by the bed, husband."

Giovanni blew her a kiss, "I will not be far behind you, my sweet, for our guests have endured a long journey and will be tired."

When she had gone, I pushed the glass of wine from me and leaned forward, "The purpose of our visit is simple, old friend, we need an employer. We are losing men and the sword that is the White Company becomes dull."

"I cannot offer you action here, Sir John. I keep my men and the Paduans active but we have not yet had to fight. I do not think that the Genoese will march across Milan to attack either Padua or Venice, their strength lies in their fleet."

I sat back, a little deflated.

He smiled and drank some of the wine, it was called Lacryma Christi, the tears of Christ, and came from Naples. I knew that it was Giovanni's favourite wine. "There is a chance, however, that Venice might employ you. I will send Rodrigo tomorrow to Venice to offer your services. It would be better if the request came from me. Your marriage to Donnina, the daughter of a Visconti, made the Venetians suspicious of you. They seem to trust me." He laughed, "They think that all Englishmen are not to be trusted."

I began to become agitated and then saw the irony. I knew that my countrymen all had the view of foreigners that was the same. "Perhaps so." I drank some of the wine. "And why would Venice employ me?"

"We cannot attack Genoese land but you could. The White Company, as I well know, rarely fails and when you command, alone, then success is guaranteed. Whatever you charged the Venetians they would more than recoup if they were able to defeat the Genoese and take the disputed islands and cities. The loss of Dalmatia to the Hungarians cost them dear. They are not a land army."

Robin nodded, "And we know the Genoese lands and cities well. We could do it, Sir John."

"We would need more men." Michael was eminently practical and had seen, as I had, the weaknesses in the idea.

Robin shrugged, "They will come but we need to think about further work." He downed his wine and poured himself another. "How long do you think this war will continue?"

Giovanni had a mind attuned well to the politics of Italy, "If I was a gambling man then I would say another year or eighteen months. Neither side has yet to deliver a blow that will unseat their opponent. I think that the weight of the White Company might be the deciding factor."

"Then send to Venice and we will enjoy a few days in Padua."

The food and wine had been good and the bed was comfortable. I slept well and Maria laid on a breakfast that would keep me going all day. We went, after Rodrigo had been sent on his mission, to the area where the standing army of Padua was being trained. It was mainly infantry for the nobles, as Giovanni told me, rarely came to train. That was where my company had the edge. My men at arms were not nobles but they were superior horsemen. Their horses might not be as expensive as those of the nobility but the horses knew their job as did their riders. My lances would obey my orders instantly and act as one. It made each man at arms as valuable as four nobles.

Giovanni introduced me to the commander of his infantry, Bartolomeo Cermisone. He was a young man and he had honed his craft serving in other companies. He had never served with my company but Francesco 'il Vecchio' da Carrara who was the effective ruler of Padua, had seen his talent and even before Giovanni was appointed had been raised to high office. I liked him for we had much in common. He too had humble origins, even humbler than mine but he had skills not only with sword and lance but that most valuable of weapons for a soldier, his mind.

Once the Paduans heard that I was to watch them train I was almost mobbed. Had I been in England few would have even heard of me. Poitiers was a long time ago but here my name was known by all. Giovanni and his officers almost had to beat his men to get them to return to their duties. As I watched them train, I was impressed but I also saw the weaknesses. These men were, with a few exceptions, all Paduans. A handful were Provvisionati, professional soldiers most of whom had served in the White Company, but most were just men who had shown skill with weapons. That weapon determined their position in battle. There were crossbowmen, sword and buckler men and spearmen. The difference with the White Company was that my company could all use any weapon. It gave us greater flexibility. My men at arms could fight mounted or on foot. They would use a sword and shield or a two handed sword. They were skilled with all pole weapons. It meant that when I looked at the battlefield, I could choose the best combination to defeat whoever we fought. Giovanni would be restricted in his choices. We enjoyed the day. The women who were married to the soldiers brought us food at noon and we ate it in the shade of trees that had been planted for this purpose on the training ground.

As we walked back to his home, I spoke to Giovanni about the positives and negatives of his army. "If you have to fight another city and they do not have condottiere then you will do well, but a company such as mine…" I let the words hang in the air like a sword about to descend.

"You are right, but yours are the only ones that use the longbow. Since Sir John Thornbury returned to England the only English longbows are to be found in the White Company. I hear that Verona is seeking to employ Lutz von Landau and his company. They might pose a threat. You fought alongside him, as did I, but what do you know of him?"

"He uses Germans and Hungarians. Their horsemen would sweep your nobles from the field as easily as a mother rids the spiders from her home. You would need to use a wall of pavise with crossbows and have the protection of a wall of spears. From what I saw this morning you have the men who could do that but you would merely be holding the enemy. You would not be able to defeat him." I nodded to the high stone walls of the city, "Put your men behind those and you might win for you could make an enemy bleed away their hopes."

He nodded, glumly, "You have the right of it, Sir John. We need horsemen who are as well led as our infantry. They are the nobles of Padua."

"You could lead them."

"Francesco 'il Novello' da Carrara will command them. His father, Francesco 'il Vecchio' da Carrara, is master of Padua." He shrugged, "The son is a sound enough horseman but he is reckless. The nobles adore him and see him as a leader like the

Black Prince. You and I know that Edward was unique and Francesco is not even a shadow of that great warrior. Francesco could win a battle but just as easily he could make a reckless charge and lose it. I remember the story I heard about the first King Edward who threw away the Battle of Lewes when he charged off after fleeing men. It cost him and his father their freedom. Here it could cost us the city."

Rodrigo was away for just a day and he returned before noon the next day with a Venetian nobleman, Agnello Participazio. They had an escort of four horsemen. We were fetched from the training ground and we gathered in Giovanni's hall. That he was a senior figure was clear from the deference shown by Giovanni. The Venetian studied me as I approached. He must have heard of me and I guessed he was seeing if the reality lived up to the reputation.

I bowed and Rodrigo said, by means of a formal introduction, "This is Signior Agnello Participazio and the doge, Giovanni Dandolo, has authorised him to negotiate with you."

I could see that the elaborate introduction was part of the negotiation. The new doge was letting me know that they were the ones in control. I did not mind. I could always refuse a contract which did not suit us.

I bowed, "I thank the doge for sending such a distinguished nobleman for this task. I am honoured."

I had learned that Italians loved flattery. It cost me nothing and the smile on the Venetian's face told me that my decision was the right one.

He waved me to a seat and Giovanni waved over a servant with wine. "I have heard of your exploits, Sir John, and I wonder why you seek employment." He sipped the wine and nodded his approval.

I decided on honesty, or a version of it at any rate, "I am here with two of my men at arms because it has been some time since my men drew swords. The White Company is a weapon best left unsheathed. I came to Venice because I know that the Genoese are a threat to the landward side of the Republic. I can do something about that."

He nodded and then frowned, "I like your words, Sir John, but you should know that Gian Galeazzo Visconti made similar overtures." He leaned forward, "We later discovered that he had said the same to Genoa."

The young nephew of Bernabò was an ambitious and cunning young man. I nodded, "But I am not a Visconti."

"Yet you married one."

I smiled, "You are a well-informed man and you must know that my wife and I have been ostracised by the Visconti family. I am Sir John Hawkwood and I have never failed to deliver that which I promised."

"The Pisans say you abandoned them."

"The Pisans did not obey my instructions and I abandoned no one." I let the room fill with silence, I was not going to justify my actions. If he did not wish to employ me then I would take my men and we would raid Verona and Mantua. Both were plums which could be plucked. However, I believed that the Venetian was going to offer me a contract.

He finished the wine and studied my face as though I might add to my explanation. When I did not, he opened his hands and said, "Venice would like to hire the White Company for six months. We would have you raid the Genoan cities and towns that lie to the east of the port. For that, we will pay you forty thousand florins."

I looked at Robin and then Michael. Both had inscrutable expressions on their faces. We had played this game before. Usually, it was William Turner who played the game but I knew how to do it too.

"That is enough as a retainer but keeping a company in the field is expensive. We would need two thousand florins a month as well."

That would take the pay to over fifty thousand. He needed some negotiation room and the figure gave him that. "Let us say fifty thousand as a payment. It will save the trouble of sending coins each month."

"That will be acceptable and we start when?"

It was his turn to smile, "I will have the money brought here and you can begin immediately."

The Venetians were good businessmen and the contract was drawn up, witnessed and signed before he left. That evening Giovanni said, "Such a large amount of money will draw every bandit in the north of Italy. I will send twenty of my men at arms with you as an escort." I cocked my head and he smiled, "It will cost you just a thousand florins. Let us say it is an agent's fee."

He was right and I thought to be generous, "And if they have to draw swords then I will double it."

"No matter what your enemies say of you, Sir John, you are an honourable man."

In the end, we had no extra coins to pay out for the journey was free from incident. We had fewer choices when it came to sleeping and had to spend one night in a barn but the gold was safe. I think the sight of the mailed men at arms put any bandits off. They might have guessed that the men were guarding treasure but there was little point in risking life and limb to try to get it. There would be easier targets on the road.

The guards stayed a night in my home before returning north and I sent a rider to William. He was still the bookkeeper for the company and he paid the men.

Donnina was delighted about the contract and was able to add information about the region and the powers who ruled there. Having fought in Montferrat I had some knowledge already but as I had learned, you can never have too much information. She told me that the doge of Genoa was Nicolò Guarco who had ousted his predecessor, Antoniotto Adorno. The former doge was exiled and lived with Gian Galeazzo Visconti. That told me all that I needed to know. Milan was ready to take control of Genoa once the time was right. Would my attacks help the Visconti?

I was not certain how William felt about Donnina. He was certainly intimidated by her and he may even have resented that she had an imperious way about her but he always deferred to her. When he arrived, with just a servant for company, the three of us sat in the small room I used when planning an action. He was still a good bookkeeper and he made the allocation of funds to my men easy.

"How many more men will you need, Sir John?"

His question was a good one. Donnina had no idea, of course, and she leaned back as I stroked my beard. There were piles of coins on the table and I used them to illustrate my thoughts, "Archers are the rarest of beasts and as many as I can get. Robin is already scouring the land for them. I do not think he will find above twenty. We will need horses for them all. I intend for my company to be mobile. As for the lances…" I tapped a small pile of coins I had made, "We have a hundred lances but that will not be enough. We need at least double that number." I made another pile of coins. Each lance represented three or, in some cases, four men. The term lances really represented the number of mounted men at arms.

William made the piles ordered once more. That was his way. He liked neatness and order. I saw Donnina smile as he did so. He nodded and said, "There are men in Pisa who would happily join you and ships arrive each week so…."

I interrupted him, "We do not have weeks. We have seven days. This will be where I conduct the business. Return to Pisa, by all means, and spread the word but I need you here to deal with the contracts. I will have Michael go into Florence and do the same there."

"Do we tell them where the company will be campaigning?"

I snorted, "Of course not. Only a handful will know. All that they need to be told is that the White Company goes to war and soon. That will be enough."

Donnina frowned, "My cousin, the Duke of Milan, will think you go to make mischief for him when you march north."

I smiled, "And that will reassure the Genoese. When we fall on their cities it will come as a real surprise. We have been given free rein by Venice to keep all the gold that we can take from the Genoese. Our purpose is to make them draw in their horns and have men here and not in the Adriatic. That is why we are only paid for six months. The doge and his advisers hope to have victory in their grasp in that time."

William rose, "Then I will send my man back to Pisa on the morrow. My wife will need to know I am kept here on business and the warriors of Pisa can be alerted."

I nodded, "Hopefully, men will come sooner rather than later. We have but seven days."

"Of course." His manner told me that he was not happy about the extra work. Whilst peace had not suited my company, he was delighted with the opportunity to use his time to make money for himself. He was now one of the richest men in Pisa and one of the most influential. I had little sympathy for him. He owed all his success and money to the White Company and to me.

Chapter 4

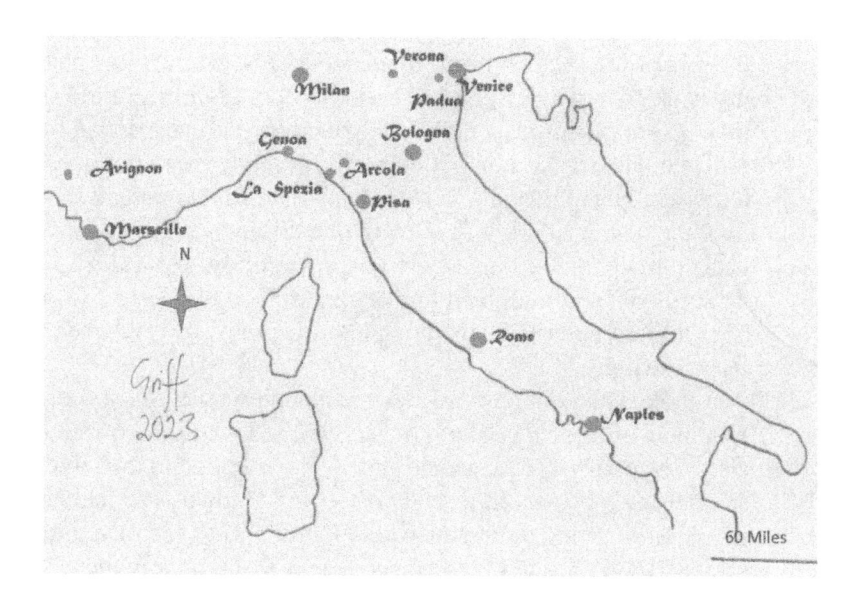

It took just four days to swell my ranks. Robin found fifty archers and that was more than I had anticipated. Many archers had heard of our success and found that other mercenary bands did not appreciate archers or know how to use them. I think that some of those who joined me had deserted but I did not care. They were English and would join the backbone of our company. We were also lucky to find another one hundred and fifty lances. One hundred of them were English. Since Sir John Thornbury had returned to England to enjoy his money, we were the only English company in Italy and Englishmen liked to have an English leader. The other fifty were largely Italians. Some came from the company led by Ambrogio Visconti, Bernabò's son. He was not a bad leader but not as good as I was. He had sometimes lost and when men heard that I had a contract then they flocked to join me.

By the end of the week, the men were gathered and we prepared to leave for the north. William had stayed with us for he was needed to organise the men and to pay them their stipend. I had hired an Italian, Gianluca, to be my servant and bodyguard. He had come to the muster but had come alone. He was a swordsman and had no horse. That did not worry me. He had plate armour, a good helmet and his weapons were the best. It was when I saw him sparring that I gave him more money than the others who had no horse. I needed a good warrior to watch my back. When I saw his skill that was enough for me and I paid him as though he was a lance and gave him a horse. Michael was relieved. He had been my bodyguard for many years but now he led my mounted men at arms. A man could not do both. I handed over the responsibility of ensuring that all my war gear was packed to Gianluca who seemed happy to do so. He was a solitary man and not given to idle chatter. He was perfect for me. That task completed I began to gather the maps I would need for the campaign.

I looked at the maps and saw the place I would attack. I had fought at La Spezia before now and whilst I was not worried about attacking it for a second time, I had decided to take the smaller town of Arcola first. It was a walled town but I had no intention of trying to take its walls. I would use deception and trickery to get inside the town. With that as a base, my men could raid the land around and draw the Genoese to battle. Their navy was a formidable one but they relied on others to do their fighting for them on land. Their crossbowmen were the most formidable element to their army but as their best men hired themselves out, I was not particularly worried about them. Robin and my archers would be more than a match for them.

The night before we left, I dined with my wife, Robin and Michael. I went through my plans with them. "We cannot hide our movements. William has left to tell the Pisans that we will be passing through their land. Once we have passed through, I have no doubt that word will be sent to Milan and the Visconti will know we are on the march. It will only be when we attack Arcola that they will know that Milan is safe and Genoa is our target."

Robin nodded and sliced a chunk of cheese to pop into his mouth, "And the Milanese will attempt to profit from our attack."

Donnina smiled, "Of course, it is our way. That can only help the Venetians, can it not?"

"And us. If the Visconti take the Genoese towns close to them then that means there will be fewer men to face us." I was not a fool. Some, like Sir Andrew who had briefly served with me, liked to believe that we fought for glory. We did not. Our success came from victory and I would do anything to achieve that. If the Milanese profited from our efforts, then I might be able to use that when I sought another contract.

By the time the two officers had returned to their homes, we all knew what we had to do. The men would only be told what they needed to know.

The first two days of our journey north were spent training the new men in the way we marched. They learned that we had archers at the fore and at the rear. We had no baggage train as such, although I had four servants leading sumpters with my own needs. Each man was given the responsibility of taking his own supplies. We paid for whatever we needed: food, fodder, beds, anything that was required. Some companies were like a plague of insects, stripping what they needed as they travelled. I had learned that paying for what we required was safer and meant that we had fewer enemies to worry about. Once we struck the Ligurian coast then we were in lands that would be patrolled by Genoa. Robin chose his best scouts to range ahead of us and warn us of any threat or danger. I knew that the only danger came from being spotted and the Genoese alerted. Who knew what spies lived in Padua? We left the coast and turned northeast to head through Lucca and Monsagrati. It added to our journey but the Luccans liked me and made us welcome. That was worth the detour and it added to the illusion that we were headed for either Milan or Montserrat. Both places would fear me and prepare for a chevauchée by the White Company.

I left the company as we headed through the mountains and went ahead with just Gianluca, Sebastian and Luigi. Both Robin and Michael had tried to dissuade me from such an action but my mission was crucial to the success of our raid.

"Bring the company slowly and I will negotiate with Lord Malaspina."

I headed for the castle at Fosdinovo. Opizzo Malaspina was lord there. The Malaspina family ruled the land south of Milan and east of Genoa. They were not as powerful as the Visconti family but they had good castles that controlled the passes. If my plan was going to succeed then we needed their cooperation. I was convinced that I could persuade Lord Opizzo that it would be in his interests to allow us to pass through his lands.

His town was not a large one nor was his castle but both had a good position, precariously perched on the mountainside. They could easily bar the progress of any army, even the Milanese one. When I viewed it, close up, I knew I had made the right decision. If we headed through this valley then I would easily be able to take Arcola. Any other route would give them a warning.

It was clear, as we neared the castle, that the only professional soldiers were the ones guarding Lord Opizzo. When we reached the castle, I recognised one of the five men wearing the livery of the Malaspina family. He had fought in the White Company six years earlier. He bowed and said, "Sir John, this is an honour. Is Lord Opizzo expecting you?"

I shook my head, "No, Antonio." I left it like that and he nodded.

"If you leave your men here in the courtyard my men will entertain them and I will escort you to his lordship."

My three men looked at me and I nodded my confirmation. I took off my cloak and handed it to Gianluca. "See to the horses first."

"Yes, my lord."

It was a cosy castle and very compact. The bailey was little more than a cobbled yard. Stairs took us up a narrow and easily defended stairway to what passed for a Great Hall. I doubted that more than twelve could dine at the table. "If you would wait here, Sir John, I will fetch his lordship."

It was almost noon and I wondered where he could be. If I was back in Florence then I would have been up for hours and ready for food. It took some time for Lord Opizzo and Antonio to return. I smiled and bowed, "Lord Malaspina, thank you for seeing me."

He waved away Antonio and gestured for me to sit at the table. He did not offer to summon a servant for food or wine. It did not bode well. He was a blunt man and came to the point immediately, "I do not know what has brought the infamous English man, Giovanni Acuto, to my humble castle but if you come to seek employment then I have to say that we cannot afford you."

I was relieved and I shook my head, "There is no need to seek employment, my lord, for I have a paymaster. I come here as a courtesy only. My company is along the road and we wish to pass through your lands. I know that my company has a certain reputation and I wanted no one to be fearful of our passing. We will pay for food, grazing and beds. All we seek is your permission."

He looked relieved too but then he frowned, "You wish to make war on a neighbour of mine?"

"The Malaspina family and its lands are safe from the White Company."

"But what of the Visconti? Genoa? Do you wish to harm your former employer, Monserrat?"

I merely smiled and said, "We journey through your lands, my lord, that is all."

"And if I was to tell my neighbours that you are here, that would not spoil your plans?"

"You may tell whom you wish, my lord, but I might point out that two of your neighbours are like wolves and they are hungry. It is no secret that the Lord of Milan wishes to be the King of Lombardy."

"If he tried to take my lands then he would discover that we would be harder to swallow than he expected."

I shrugged, "And that is why I seek your permission, my lord. Yours is a peaceful land and it would be a shame if it was subjected to the privations of war."

It was a threat but a veiled one. Having seen the defences, I knew how easy it would be for me to take the town. I think that Lord Opizzo saw that too. He might tell Galeazzo Visconti that we were in the mountains but only after we had left.

"And you will pay for all that you consume?"

"Of course, we have been well paid by our employers."

He chewed his lip as he debated his decision. It was an easy one and he nodded, "Then you may pass through my lands. I will inform my guards and the townsfolk. When will your company pass through?"

"By the time I reach your gate, they should be heading towards it."

His mouth fell open. He realised that my visit was just that, a courtesy. He had no idea that there were mercenaries within attacking distance of his lands.

We spent two days in Fosdinovo and the lands of Lord Opizzo. Travelling slowly meant we conserved both men and animals. We ate well and the horses were rested. Our sojourn delayed the news of our presence and meant that we effectively disappeared. As soon as we left his town Lord Opizzo would send word to the Lord of Milan but that suited my purposes. We left and took the road west before turning off, as soon as we could, to head for the coast.

There was an old castle at Battifollo that the Genoese used to guard the crossing of the Magra River. We had to take the castle before we could begin our attack on Arcola. My plan was a simple one. I rode into the town and castle with a hundred mounted men at arms. We galloped in hard and fast. The guards were used to peace. There was no war and when they saw the horsemen approaching, they did not see it as a threat. As with Fosdinovo, it was a small garrison and our arrival was so sudden and unexpected that there was no resistance. We galloped over the lowered drawbridge into the castle before the castellan even knew. Even had he withdrawn into the donjon we would have been able to hold the town and castle.

I did the garrison the courtesy of allowing them to keep their weapons. They were not a real threat for they were men who had never fought in a war and kept weapons that were dull. We made ourselves comfortable in the castle. This was Genoa and we took what we needed from the farms and villages close to the river and the crossing. We did not mistreat the people and my men were courteous but we let them know that we were here on behalf of the Venetians. It was important that they knew we were not a band of freebooting brigands.

It was then that I summoned my leaders to a meeting in the Great Hall. "Tonight we attack Arcola." They all knew that Arcola was a more formidable castle than Battifollo. "Half of the company will stay here with the horses. I intend to send a chosen band of Italians to ride up the road and warn the Arcolans that

Battifollo has fallen." I saw the faces of some of the men. They thought I had lost my mind. I smiled, "Do not worry. By the time our men are inside the town and castle, the rest of us will be hiding in the woods outside the town. The gates will be opened in the middle of the night and we shall take the town without the need to assault its walls."

Richard of Shrewsbury asked, "Why tell them that Battifollo has fallen? We could still use the men inside the town."

I shook my head, "We need the men in the town and castle to be trusted. The last thing they will think is that the White Company is outside. The men I have chosen will say that the castle of Battifollo has fallen to Milan. They will send word to Genoa and the first that they will know of the White Company is when we begin to raid the lands between here and La Spezia."

I saw understanding on their faces. Robin and I, along with Michael had chosen the ten Italians who would be our version of a Trojan Horse. Sebastian and Luigi would go with them. We had taken some of the jupons from the garrison at Battifollo to give credibility to their story. They would be the only horsemen who would ascend the two miles to the castle.

We headed out of Battifollo in the middle of the afternoon. The Italians came with us and they were the ones who used the road. The rest of us filtered up through the woods that bounded the town. The trees clung to the hillside like drowning men to a piece of wreckage. Once we were in position, just a hundred paces from the gate and the walls, we waited. Francesco, who led the Italians, had been with me for ten years. He had stepped seamlessly into the place vacated by Giovanni d'Azzo. The men with him were a mixture of new men and others who had served with me for some time.

I was close enough to see them as they galloped up to the gates and I saw the play-acting from Francesco. He kept turning, fearfully, in his saddle and pointing down the road to the river. He was giving the sentries the impression that the Milanese were hard on their heels. They were admitted and the doors slammed ominously shut.

We waited. It was always hard waiting for we had to be vigilant and yet we could not move. The bells from the churches in the town marked the passage of time. The smells of cooking food made us all realise how hungry we were and still we waited. When silence descended, we became more alert. We heard the guards as the captain of the night watch passed by them. They were also vigilant and they were watching the road. That was another reason I had concocted this plan. The walls would be manned while the gate, below the walls, would only have a couple of men to ensure its safety. The garrison would need eyes on the walls. Francesco and his killers would have just a handful of men to deal with and we knew where the rest would be, on the walls.

It was a mark of their skill that the first we knew of their success was when the gates opened and a light was moved from side to side. It would be hidden from the walls. Robin and his archers broke from cover first and their shadows were seen from the walls. Not knowing that the gates were already opened and assuming that this was an attack, the alarm was sounded. With shields held before and above us Michael and I led the men at arms to the gates. A few bolts were sent in our direction but in the dark, the crossbowmen were aiming at shadows. None of my men were hit and then the foxes were in the henhouse.

The castellan had manned his walls with his warriors and while my archers sent arrows from inside the town, Michael and I led our men at arms up the stairs to attack the sentries. Where we could, we accepted surrender but there were many brave men in Arcola and they fought us. We had shields and they did not. We wielded swords and they had pole weapons. We were professionals and they were men hired to guard the walls. My sword was bloodied but within half an hour of the gates opening the town was ours. The assault on the castle came next and thanks to the majority of the guards manning the walls, the ones left to defend the castle were fewer in number. I raced with twenty men at arms along with Michael and his men. We reached the gates to the castle just as the last of those fleeing the walls of the town tried to close them. Francesco was with me and like me was a big man. We threw our plated bodies at the gates before the defenders had slipped the holding bar into place and we knocked the men attempting to do so to the ground. Our swords were quick and the four men died. We held the gates open for Michael and the others to race inside. The bailey was a bigger one than the one at Fosdinovo and the castellan ran at us to drive what looked like a handful of men, from his castle.

The castellan fell to Michael as he tried to lead his bodyguards to drive us back. Michael had great skills and the castellan died along with eight of his bodyguards. The garrison, now leaderless, surrendered. Arcola and Battifollo were ours and we could begin to earn the money Venice had paid us.

Chapter 5

I left just twenty men to hold Battifollo and brought the rest into Arcola. This time the surviving soldiers were disarmed and held prisoner. We found the treasury and took that. We could now begin the real work. This would be an old-fashioned chevauchée. I divided my men into three groups. One would guard the town while the other two would raid the land that lay around the stronghold. Robin, Michael and I would each lead one group. It meant one day in three would be a rest day and that would keep both us and our horses fresh.

It was Robin and I who led the first two raids. If the Genoese thought that we would head for their towns then they were in for a surprise. We raided the farms and villages that had no defences. That way we laid in supplies without risking the lives of my men. The White Company was now pared to the bone. Most times we did not need to draw weapons. The sight of more than a hundred horsemen, half of whom wore gleaming helmets and plate armour, was enough to send most people fleeing to woods and churches. We took their animals and food. We searched their homes and found the pots of gold. We took money from churches in the form of bribes to leave their relics alone.

On the second day, I stayed in Arcola and I studied the papers we had found there as well as apportioning the treasure we had found. It was while I was thus occupied that a rider arrived from Lord Malaspina. He sought an audience with me, "My lord was visited by the Lord of Milan. He wished to know your whereabouts. My lord told him."

I nodded. It had been obvious to me that we had been followed to Battifollo and that it was men from Fosdinovo who had followed us. Lord Malaspina was playing both sides off against the other. I did not mind. Galeazzo Visconti would not interfere with me. He might try to ambush us on the way home and take our gold but I would ensure that he did not. "Tell Lord Malaspina that I appreciate the information. We are still friends."

The relief on the envoy's face told me that I had been right.

The three of us, Robin, Michael and I dined together each night. Thanks to our raids the food was good. I told them my theory that there might be an attempt to ambush us on the way home. Robin smiled, "That is five months away, Sir John, and I am sure that you will have devised a plan to circumvent that."

"Of course. The main problem we will face is that the Genoese will only endure these raids for a short time and then they will do something about us."

Michael had grown as a warrior and it was he who saw the solution, "They will try to oust us from here and as we raid each day then we shall know when they are coming. Our men are more than capable of defeating whoever they send."

"And what if they seek to ambush one of our raiding parties?"

"We would know that they were close."

Robin shook his head, "They know this land better than we do. I will tell my archers that each day ten of them should scout a mile or so ahead of the main column. That way we will have a warning."

The attempted ambush came during the second week. As luck would have it, I was leading a raid in which we had burned the fishing ships from a coastal village and the smoke was still spiralling into the air some five miles behind us when the archer scouts galloped in. We were heading back to our stronghold with laden sumpters. Ned and Hob reined in, "Just up the road, Sir John, there is an ambush. A hundred men wait around the bend two miles up the road."

Ned pointed through the trees, "It is where the road twists around a sharp bend. They have crossbowmen waiting and there is a phalanx of men with spears in the road." He shrugged, "We were seen and they will be expecting us." My scout archers carried their bows in their cases. The Genoese would just see two scouts.

"Is it possible for archers to flank them?"

Hob shook his head, "They have chosen well. There is a drop on one side of the road and they occupy the high ground."

"Have the archers take the sumpters back to Arcola. You archers can get through trails and paths that we cannot."

"But Sir John, how will you get through the ambush unharmed?"

"Through surprise. Now go."

I turned to Gianluca. As well as being my bodyguard he also acted as a deputy. Even seasoned men at arms were happy to take orders from the veteran. "We will walk our horses to this ambush. I intend to make them wait for us. They will see the smoke from the village and think that we are hurrying to our stronghold. I want the men to mount on my command and then we charge through the ambush as the sun begins to set."

"Yes, my lord." Nothing came as a surprise to the Italian and he went about his business, calmly telling the others what we would be doing. There were just fifty of us but everyone had plate armour and a good helmet. We began to slowly walk our horses along the rising road. The mile markers we saw were a reminder that this road had been built by the Romans. Walking our horses helped them to recover a little quicker and also made us less easy to see and hear. We stopped half a mile from the bend. If they had someone watching for us, we were hidden by the trees that rose from the rocks. How they found purchase there I do not know. I saw that the smoke from the burning ships was almost gone and the sky behind us was darkening. Our temporary home lay six miles to the west and the sun would be setting behind the ambushers. I took out some dried venison to chew and poured water into my helmet for Caesar to drink. I had left Ajax at Casa Donnina and Caesar was a good horse. Others did the same. I was trying to time our charge well. It was a couple of hours since our archers had reported to us. Waiting men become nervous. Arms that hold crossbows ache. Eyes and ears imagine sounds. When Caesar had finished drinking, I put the helmet on my head and climbed into the saddle. I drew my sword. I let my shield hang from my guige strap so that it protected my left leg. The men needed no command and they mounted. Gianluca placed his horse next to mine and he and I were flanked by two more of my men. We had twelve lines of fours and two men at the rear. I waved my sword and we moved up the road to the bend. The drop to our left became more pronounced and severe as we neared the rock that jutted from our right. They had chosen well.

The sentry who saw us was atop the rock and his cry of alarm was the signal for me to spur Caesar. He leapt forward and

Gianluca and the other two men struggled to keep up with me. As I turned the bend, I saw that we had achieved surprise. The phalanx of spearmen had tired of standing with spears at the ready. Some had leaned against their spears while others had laid them down. Others were making water or emptying their bowels. Standing in the hot sun is not easy. The wait had been a wise move. Similarly, the crossbows were not aimed at the road. The heavy crossbows were on rocks and had to be raised and aimed. Neither was a quick action. As we appeared around the rock, they raised them but the speed of our attack would take us too close to their spearmen for them to hurt us. A phalanx of spearmen can stop horsemen. Horses do not like to approach a hedgehog of steel but these were not a solid phalanx. Some had risen and were standing shoulder to shoulder but others were hurrying back to the positions they had occupied when my archers had seen them. I leaned forward with my sword. I was aiming at a determined-looking spearman who wore a leather brigandine and, on his head, had a kettle helmet. He was liveried. Caesar was a big, powerful warhorse. He had snapping teeth and when his jaws opened, the spearman was distracted just enough for the spear to waver and I was able to slide my sword into his throat. His death created a hole and I exploited it. We burst through their first men and when some fell over the drop to our left others simply fled up the slope to the safety of the trees.

The spearmen had been accompanied by horsemen. It had to be a lord and his oathsworn. They had dismounted and were now racing to get to their horses. Our charging mounts made the horses panic and barely four managed to mount. The rest, the lord included, took to the trees. The four men were now trapped ahead of us. We had to keep going to secure our escape although the setting sun helped to hide us from the crossbows. The four men took a trail to our right while the rest of their horses kept racing ahead of us. When darkness fell, we slowed and I checked on my men. We had lost none although three had been hit by crossbow bolts. I pointed to the horses ahead of us, "Gianluca, have the horses gathered. They are an unexpected treasure."

Robin and Michael were waiting at the gatehouse to the town when we rode in. Michael said, "We were worried."

"Why? We knew where the Genoese waited and our men have skill."

I dismounted and walked with the two of them up to the castle. Robin said, "This will happen again."

"I know."

"Have the archers used many arrows yet?"

He shook his head, "Barely half a dozen. We have achieved surprise with every raid."

"Good, for when they come in force, they will be our secret."

Michael said, "I am not sure what you mean."

"I think that what the Genoese have seen are our men at arms. The archers look like light horsemen and their bows are in their cases. When they attack us here, and they will do so soon, they will not expect archers. I plan on keeping our archers hidden."

The Genoese gave us another four weeks before they decided that they had endured enough of our raids. Perhaps they had a problem mustering enough men, I do not know. I think that we were more annoying than a real threat but we had destroyed a number of villages and our control of the river crossing stopped land trade. They had gathered an army to take back their town. Michael and his men spotted the mailed column as it marched from La Spezia. Their fluttering flags and glittering armour marked their progress. Unlike my company, the Genoese could not mount all their men. They had far more men on foot than on horses. The crossbowmen were accompanied by pavesiers. Michael told us that he had seen more than a hundred provvisionati but the bulk of their infantry were the levy. Their horsemen were nobles and their squires. We had a day to prepare and I sat with Michael and Robin to plan it.

We still had a detachment of men guarding the river crossing but we had more than enough archers to man the walls and gatehouse. They would remain hidden behind the stone crenulations. I would lead three hundred men at arms from the town to face our enemy. "The last thing I want is a protracted siege. I want to tempt them to our walls so that we can slaughter them with our archers."

Robin said, "It is a risk."

"A slight one and if this was not the White Company then I would think twice. These are our men and they will obey my orders."

Our men who fought on foot would be waiting at the gate. That would be the prize that would lure them close to our walls. Just as we had taken advantage of the open gates of Arcola Castle, so the Genoese would seek to flood into the town as my horsemen fled. What they would not see were the wooden barriers my men constructed overnight. The area behind the town gate would become a killing ground.

We rose well before dawn and each man was fed. The archers moved into position and squatted behind the walls. Squires with javelins would be the defenders that the Genoese would see. The one hundred men on foot waited by the gates and, as the sun rose, I led my men at arms from the town. We had lances and our horses were mailed. The ground upon which we would fight was not a large area. Arcola was on a steep outcrop of rock. The only clear area was three hundred paces from the gates. It was a flat patch of grass, bordered by trees. It was four hundred paces one way and three hundred deep. My men would fill one end of it and I hoped that the Genoese would suspect an ambush from hidden men in the trees. We waited.

It was mid-morning when the Genoese arrived. The light horsemen, favoured by Italian armies, appeared first and two men turned to ride back to the main column. Michael had already given us their numbers and so I was not surprised when the nobles appeared along the road while the levy flooded up between the trees. As the pavesiers set up their pavise I saw the leader of the nobles point to the trees on both flanks and light horsemen headed there to investigate. We were clearly outnumbered and only a fool would charge.

My men were waiting for my command and when I lowered my lance they began to move at the same time as I did. We had caught them unawares and the crossbows were yet to be loaded. As we galloped to cover the three hundred paces to the pavise I heard the panicked horns sound. Some pavesiers fled. The Genoese horsemen formed up but they could not charge because their crossbows were in the way. I pulled back my lance as the crossbowman brought up his weapon. If he had snapped it quickly then he might have been lucky and hit me but he was a professional and he aimed. My lance hit him squarely in the face and Caesar crashed through the pavise. For the Genoese, it was a disaster. Their most potent weapon was destroyed by my pre-emptive charge. The crossbowmen fled behind their horsemen. I speared one in the back and then shouted, "Retreat, there are too many of them." It was, of course, a ruse but it worked.

As one we wheeled and the Genoese horsemen struggled to make their way through the retreating infantrymen. On the flanks, the militia saw us retreating and as with all such bodies, they took their opportunity to charge after us. We would be rich pickings for men who rarely saw a silver coin. Our plate and horses marked us as rich men. It was a measured retreat. Had the Genoese been led by a condottiero they would have suspected a trick but the nobles thought we were really fleeing and, with little order to their lines followed us. It was like a swarm of insects and both militia and nobles were charging as fast as they could for the invitingly open gates of Arcola.

The first of my men were already at the gates and were making their way through the two open avenues my foot soldiers had left for them. They would dismount and use pole weapons to add to the weapons held by those on foot. Fifty paces from the gates Michael and I wheeled. The twenty men we had chosen the night before also wheeled and we lowered our lances. When we were in a straight line we charged, taking by complete surprise the leaders of the nobles. We crashed into them and unhorsed at least eight. Others were wounded and before they could be rallied and surrounded, we wheeled again and headed for the gates. This time we did enter for the rest of my horsemen had entered, dismounted and were now waiting with a wall of spears and pole weapons.

Our sudden attack had annoyed the Genoese and they followed hard on our heels. Robin chose the perfect moment to order the squires to hurl their javelins and his archers to rise and unleash a feathered storm of death. The enemy were so close to the walls that even an Italian archer could not have missed. The difference was that the English archers sent so many arrows that it sounded like the buzzing of angry hornets and men fell in great numbers. The only safe avenue of escape seemed, ironically, to be the gates and they were funnelled into it. There they were met by spears, lances, pikes and poleaxes. Riders were knocked from their saddles. The militia who made it were simply slaughtered and within a few moments, realising the trap they were in, they fled. The danger we now faced was that the crossbowmen would join the battle. Robin's command from the gatehouse told me that he had seen the danger. He ordered his archers to switch targets. The height of the walls and the skill of our archers meant that before the crossbows could send bolts at the defenders they were slain. That was the end of the skirmish. It did not warrant the appellation of battle for it had lasted less than an hour and we were barely hurt. They fell back and we had a dozen nobles to hold for ransom. The captured men ensured that we were not attacked again. Instead, the Genoese blocked all the roads that led from Arcola. We could raid no more. It did not worry me for we had stripped the land of animals and grain. I knew that once the ransom was paid then the Genoese would redouble their efforts to take the town, castle and river crossing. In the end, it was unnecessary. The war between Venice and Genoa ended in June, two months before our contract expired. A Venetian emissary arrived to tell us that the war was over and Genoa had lost the prize that was Chioggia. Venice had won the war and this was the beginning of the decline of Genoa. We simply packed up and with laden horses headed back, this time along the coast, first to Pisa and then to Florence. No one hindered our passage and we did not need to draw swords again.

When we reached my home Donnina was delighted for we had almost doubled the Venetian fee thanks to the ransoms and what we had taken. The company was also happy for they had fought and won. They were all richer and men began to order better armour, buy stronger horses and hire more men to serve them. The ranks of the company were swollen and I could now look for another lucrative contract.

Chapter 6

When we reached home my life changed a little. Donnina would soon give birth to my third daughter, Anna. The fortune I had made ensured that my wife was more comfortable and there was no need for me to seek a new contract. My men were also less restless. The short campaign had seen them profit at the expense of Genoa and they too were happy.

Michael was the one who became more restless. Perhaps it was the birth of my third daughter that did it. He had met my sons and watched my daughters change from babies to toddlers and infants. His loins must have itched. Unlike me, he was allowed in the city of Florence. He was, indeed, much in demand. The rich merchants who thrived in the city often invited him to dine with them. I suppose it was in lieu of me. He was known to be like a son to me and could regale the old men with my exploits, not only of my wars with Florence but also those with Genoa, Milan, and Verona. It was inevitable that their daughters saw Michael as something of a white knight. He was a handsome young man; Donnina had told me that and there were few men who could match him for heroism and chivalry. He did not have to seek a bride, they sought him. Within six months after our return from Genoa, he was wed.

Maria Cialdini was the daughter of an immensely rich merchant. Carlos Cialdini traded spices from the East. An astute businessman, he used ships from many different nations to carry his goods and as a result, when one of them was embroiled in a war and could no longer fetch the spices, he had others who could. The result was that he had the greatest fortune in Florence. I know that did not influence Michael's choice. Quite simply he fell in love. When I had married for the first time, in England, it had not been out of love yet I had learned to love my first wife. Similarly, Donnina was an arranged bride but I had come to love her. Michael was different, he fell in love with the beautiful Maria and she returned that love. Unlike William Turner's wife, she did not resent the White Company. Maria never tried to turn him from a soldier to a businessman. She could have done so for her father bought them a palatial home in Florence. He had no need to draw a sword but Michael was loyal and, as he often told me, would have had no life at all except for me and the White Company. He promised to serve with the company until I was tired of it and retired. I could not see myself doing that.

One effect of his marriage was that I saw less of him. That was understandable. I no longer trained with my men every day. Michael had long since ceased to be my squire and Sebastian and Luigi fulfilled that function for me. I now needed men to join Gianluca and be my entourage. My Italian found the first man for me. Gianluca was a professional soldier and a blunt one at that. He had told me that my insistence on using my lance and sword as a signal was dangerous.

"My lord, you need to be able to command across a battlefield and not just with the men who can see you."

"But it works."

"Up to now it has, but what if you were to command the Florentine army?"

He was right and I was able to swallow my pride and agree, "What do you suggest?"

"Let me find you a trumpeter. I will find you a warrior who can fight and yet knows how to blow a trumpet and pass on your commands."

He was away for three weeks and when he returned it was with Zuzzo. I never knew his real name but Zuzzo suited him. Gianluca had found him in Bologna where he worked as a musician with a group of travelling actors. They travelled throughout Italy performing in cities and towns. He occasionally filled in as an actor, too, playing a Zanni. His ability with weapons also allowed him to act as muscle for the company. Zuzzo came to me when the rest of the band were arrested by a zealous Bishop who thought that the wearing of masks offended God. Zuzzo's natural skills enabled him to escape and find Gianluca. Zuzzo was unique. He was funny, incredibly skilled and as good a warrior as I had ever known. He was with me for many years and yet I never discovered his true story. Something had happened in his youth and it had changed him. He never married and yet was popular with women. He was the most unambitious man I ever knew and yet he was always the most popular in any gathering of men. Donnina and the girls adored him. He could entertain, pull faces, do funny voices and play a number of instruments. I never regretted hiring him.

We still had men who came from England. When William Coggleshall, my son-in-law, had returned to England he had shown his loyalty to me by spreading the word amongst the martially minded men of Essex and the east of England. We had a steady stream of men who came to seek employment.

John Edingham came from my village. He knew my brothers and had grown up hearing the exploits of John Hawkwood. William had seen the potential and had financed the young man to allow him to seek employment. He had to work his way on ships to reach me for William's support had just given him enough for a sword, helmet, brigandine, boots and a cloak. He had adventures on the way and that was no bad thing as it toughened him up. He had been sheltered in Essex but William had seen in him the kernel of skill that he knew I could develop.

He did not arrive alone. A Norfolk man, Robert de Saxlingham, came with him. The two of them arrived from Pisa, on foot looking weary and worn. John had a letter from William and directions to my home. That William sent him directly to me spoke volumes. The old soldiers who guarded my home and worked on the estate saw the two men and summoned Gianluca. I heard their stilted conversation for Gianluca's English was basic at best and I left the coolness of my hall to go into the summer sun.

"Gianluca, why do raised voices disturb my peace?"

I could see that the Italian was cross and he shook his head, "These Englishmen do not speak Italian, my lord, and I can barely understand them. One keeps waving a piece of parchment around as though it is something important."

I smiled, Gianluca liked me and he did not see either Michael or me as Englishmen. We were Italians with funny accents. "What are your names?" I held my hand out for the parchment. It was handed to me and I saw that it had journeyed as hard as their worn boots suggested. It was salt rimed and creased. I read it as they spoke.

"I am John Edingham, my lord, from Sible Hedingham."

I looked up when he said the name of the village where I had been born. His name suggested that his family had lived there for some years and simply dropped the aitch. "You are an Essex man?"

He smiled, "Aye, my lord, I began life as a billman and Sir Thomas Coggleshall saw some talent in me and had me trained with sword and spear."

Sir Thomas was another old friend. The sun was burning my increasingly thinning pate and I saw no threat from the two young men, "Come, we will go to the courtyard and enjoy some iced wine and the shade of my lemon trees." I smiled at Gianluca, "Thank you for your concern, Gianluca. Have beds prepared for these two with the other warriors." The other warriors were the old men and now Zuzzo.

Gianluca nodded, "Yes, my lord."

I could not resist adding, "And as the White Company is made up largely of Englishmen, Gianluca, perhaps you should improve your English, eh?"

He had the good grace to smile, and said, in English, "Yes, my lord."

The two men had the burned faces and hands of men whose skin was unused to the Italian sun. Their clothes might have once been whole but now they were holed. I knew that their boots, which were scuffed and scarred would be thin. They had travelled hard. I waved over a servant, "Fetch food, a jug of water and wine to the courtyard."

The fountain ensured that the lemon-shaded haven was the best place to escape the hot Florentine sun. I waved them to two seats while I continued to read the letter. The two of them looked around for somewhere to put their bags and I smiled, "Put them wherever you will."

The wine came and I waited until they had both emptied a beaker of water before trying the wine. They were English and I knew that they would never have tasted iced wine. Their faces told me that they approved. I put the letter down and said, "It says here, John Edingham. There is no mention of a second."

John Edingham said, "I am sorry, my lord, I should have introduced my friend. This is Robert de Saxlingham and we became close friends on the journey here. I ..." His voice trailed off. He did not know me and perhaps feared that I might be unhappy with the presumption.

I nodded to Robert de Saxlingham, "You come from Norfolk then?"

"Yes, my lord."

I tapped the letter, "I have here, John's story, yours is still to be told. While I eat these olives, ham and bread, regale me with your tale. John, eat. Do not stand on ceremony and if this platter is cleared then the girl will fetch another. I can see that you have enjoyed short rations."

He put a slice of the carved ham on a piece of bread and bit into it. I saw the pleasure on his face.

These men were starving and I could wait for the other story. "You, too, Robert de Saxlingham. I can wait." While they ate, I studied their weapons. John's sword was better than Robert's. Robert had a short sword with a broader blade. They both had rondel daggers. John's open-faced sallet helmet lay on top of his cloak and clothes. Robert just had an arming cap. John's brigandine was studded with metal while Robert's was a simple leather one.

Robert ate quickly and then began his story. "My father had a farm but, when the plague came, he took my mother and my brothers and sisters away from the pestilence. He went to the north where he laboured for another. I was born and my mother died giving me birth. My brothers and sisters left home and it was my father who brought me up. He had a falling out with the lord who was his master and we were forced to live by any means we could."

He looked up at me and John said "Tell him, Robert, for there should be no lies. I will stand by you. I owe you much."

There was a story here. I sipped my wine, "Nothing you can do or say will shock me, Robert. I am an old man now and nothing surprises me any longer. I swear I will not judge you for already your story tells me that you have endured a hard life."

"My father joined the outlaws who live in the forests south of Doncaster. It was how I learned to be a warrior. He was caught and hanged five years since. I managed to escape both the noose and the life. I made my way to Oxford and I became a soldier. I was given menial tasks to do and paid but a pittance. It was honest labour and after living in the wild, the roof over my head seemed almost like a luxury."

"And yet you are no longer in Oxford." I was intrigued by his story and wanted to hear more.

He smiled, "You are right, my lord. A new captain of the guard came. He thought that I was too pretty to be a soldier and, well, after disagreements with him about my terms of service, I left. I made my way east hoping to join a company. I heard that your son was raising a company close to London. That was where I met John."

John took up the story, "I was in London and I was staying there before heading down the road to Southampton. I was used to Sible Hedingham, my lord, where men are honest. I fell in with a crowd who thought to take my sword and helmet."

I nodded, "That is London for you. You would have been better to march fifty miles around it."

Robert took up the story, "I was heading for a house I had heard only charged a penny a night for a roof when I heard raised voices. I found John here and three men were around him. I did not stop to think but told them to hold. They did not. We fought and we were better. My life in the forest had made me hard and given me skills that these cut purses from London did not possess. We cut the three of them and they fled. We decided not to risk their return with confederates but headed over the bridge and we walked to Southampton."

"It was easier with two of us, my lord, as one could watch out for the other. Robert knew how to forage and we survived. We took passage on a ship that was heading to Bordeaux. From there we walked to Marseille. It was a hard journey for we spoke not the language but we survived. Some farmers paid us to help them in their fields and we ate. We took berths on a ship from Marseille. It went first to Spain and the Land of the Moors before Sardinia and then Pisa." He sighed, "And we are here."

I picked up the letter, "Sir William says that you wish to be a member of my company, John." He nodded, "And you, Robert?"

"Yes, my lord. I know that I have poor weapons and my clothes make me look like a beggar but within here," he tapped his chest, "beats the heart of an Englishman who is the son of a good man. I would serve you well, my lord."

I had long ago decided to hire them but Robert's words were the convincing argument. They were English and much as I liked my Italians, Englishmen, in my view, made the best soldiers. "Normally I hire lances." They both frowned and I explained the system of a man at arms and three others who served him. "In your case, you shall be hired to serve me directly. Gianluca is my bodyguard and Zuzzo is my trumpeter. You two shall be attired in my livery and armed like men at arms. You can ride?"

Their downcast looks told me that they did not have that skill.

"Then there is a caveat. You shall stay with me, be clothed and fed. You have one month to learn how to ride and how to speak Italian. Is that fair?"

They both grinned and nodded. John said, "Aye, my lord."

I saw that their platters and beakers were empty, "When you can prove that to me you shall be my bodyguards." I rose, "And now come and we will clean the wildlife from you."

This was Italy and the legacy of the Romans was the large number of baths. Donnina had a bathhouse built and I took them there. I waved over Ned of Shrewsbury, one of my old soldiers. "These men will need clothes. Go to the slop chest and fetch some."

He grinned, "Bath time, eh my lord, aye, and we shall light a fire to burn the garments that are alive." He turned to the two men, "Do not worry, your boots and brigandines will be saved but you shall not need your smocks or breeks. You are now the White Company and we have standards to uphold."

We had a man who looked after the bathhouse, "Antonio, we need to bathe these two. They are Englishmen."

He understood, "Do not worry, Sir John, soon they shall learn the benefits of Italy."

"When they are bathed and their hair and beards have been trimmed, have them dressed and bring them up to the hall where they can meet Lady Donnina."

My wife was playing with our daughters. We had a woman who looked after them but Sophia was closely supervised by Donnina. My wife ensured that they learned skills that would help them when they grew. Donnina had a plan and she would stick to it. She could see that I had words to say and she dismissed the children and Sophia, "Well, husband?"

I told her the stories that I had been told. She sat and I could see that she was thinking. When men saw my wife for the first time they thought her to be an empty-headed but beautiful young woman. She was beautiful but she had a mind as sharp as any, mine included. "This is good, John."

"I know it is but why do you see it as a good thing?"

"Your company, our company, is made up of Italians and Englishmen. Gianluca and Zuzzo are Italian and protect you. When you went to war and Michael was at your side then I knew that you were safe. He is now a leader and we both know that marriage changes a man. I cannot rely on Michael risking his life to save yours. You are no longer a young man. Let us be truthful, Giovanni Acuto may still have a sharp mind but his body is that of an old man. You need to be protected and it is right that you have these two young men with you. Four warriors will ensure that my husband comes back from each war and that his daughters will see their father when they are women grown. I look forward to seeing them."

When they arrived, I was more than surprised at the change that had been wrought by the bath, Antonio's use of shears and razor, not to mention the white clothes that they wore.

"Thank you, Antonio, if you would wait without, you can take them to their chambers when we have spoken to them."

Both were guileless young men and I saw their eyes widen when they saw the beauty that was my wife. I could almost read their thoughts as they wondered how such an old man as I had managed to win such a beauty. Donnina's smile told me that she had seen the look too. Donnina could speak English but it was heavily accented.

She held her hand out for the two men to kiss the back of it. Even though they had bathed I saw them look at their own hands as though they were too soiled to touch the porcelain-like hands of my wife. "Which one is John and which one is Robert?"

"I am John Edingham."

"And I am Robert de Saxlingham."

"Welcome to my home. I have looked into your eyes and seen honesty. That is good. What I cannot see yet, is the courage that you will have to show if you are to protect my husband. My husband is responsible not only for the prosperity of my family and me but also for many others. His life is the most important. I would expect you to give your own lives to save his. Could you do that?"

It was John who spoke, "I know that oathsworn warriors serve a lord and swear an oath to protect him. Robert and I would be happy to take such an oath but we would both prefer if we did not die protecting him. Better that we use our skills to ensure that he lives and we do too, eh, Lady Donnina?"

She laughed and put her two hands around John's, "A perfect answer. I like them, John." She smiled, "Now, learn Italian. As for riding, only a fool cannot sit on the back of a horse and you two have survived enough to show me that you are not fools."

I took them to the door and let them out.

Donnina nodded, "I will have surcoats made for them. I am sure that there is mail and plate for them in the armoury. We need them to be protected. The five of you should look almost identical when you go to war. From now on, my husband, wear a helmet with a face mask. Your face shows your age. If there are others on the battlefield that men take to be you then you are more likely to come home."

I smiled, "Thus far I have been successful."

"Or lucky and we cannot rely on luck. I am no soldier, my husband, but what I cannot understand is why men do not try to take you on the battlefield. Michael and Robin are all well and good but it is your ideas that win the battles. If I was an enemy then I would have men who sought you on the battlefield."

I kissed her, "Then I thank God that you are a woman, for if not then it would be you leading the White Company."

Chapter 7

The two men excelled themselves. They learned to ride in a week and thanks to Zuzzo, who took to them immediately, they could speak Italian, albeit haltingly in a fortnight. They understood more than they could speak and that was all that was needed. It was enough and although I had set the conditions, I had already decided that regardless of their skills in equitation and languages, I would hire them. Gianluca was a little distant from them but they got on so well with Zuzzo that the three of them appeared to be more like brothers and there was an understanding between them that transcended words. I knew that such things are important.

It was good that they came when they did for we did not have long to enjoy peace. That was the fault of the two popes. Pope Clement was known as the anti-pope. He lived in Avignon and as such was supported by the French and their king. I knew him as Robert de Geneva. He had been the cardinal who had ordered me to slaughter the inhabitants of Cesena. I had not and that not only made us mutual enemies but had resulted in a loss of pay for me and my company. When he was elected pope, it was a black day for me. The pope who was regarded as the legitimate pope, Urban, had supported Charles Durazzo and ordered him to take over Naples. The Queen, Joan, had foolishly supported and sheltered his rival, Pope Clement. Charles' Croatian army had easily taken Naples and the queen had been imprisoned in San Fele while Charles ruled Naples.

Such tribulations were common in Italy. Indeed, when I had heard of the overthrow I had been in Genoa and it had just been a topic for discussion while Robin, Michael and I ate in Arcola. It was after we had returned and while my bodyguards were training that we heard that Louis of Anjou, Queen Joan's adopted heir, had been ordered by Pope Clement to recover the kingdom. King Charles of France and Pope Clement had anointed him king of Naples. It seemed to me a little premature as Charles of Durazzo had control of the kingdom. We were still unaffected by the conflict for Naples was to the south and no threat to either Florence or to me. It was the execution of the queen by Charles that brought about our involvement. I say execution but the simple fact of the matter was that he ordered her to be strangled while in prison and he became king. Even then it did not directly affect me. It was the arrival of the papal envoy, Giacomo da Lucca, who signalled our involvement. He arrived at my home with some of the Florentine council, Michael's father-in-law included.

My wife knew how to entertain and a feast was seemingly seamlessly prepared. It was, of course, so that I could be told of the pope's proposal. As with all such negotiations, there were pleasantries to be exchanged first. My service to Venice was noted as well as my feud with Pope Clement. I knew that I was being prepared for a commission but I did not know exactly what it would be.

The envoy was a professional. Pope Urban had enough priests and bishops to show piety. Giacomo was more like a warrior diplomat than a priest. When the food was finished, he began.

"Pope Urban is well aware of your skills, Sir John, and we would like to hire your company to prevent the army of Louis of Anjou from wreaking havoc in Naples. This is, of course, with the support of Florence who are your employers."

I knew then that neither the papacy nor Naples would be paying for our services. It explained the heavy numbers who had arrived at my hall. I nodded, "It is rumoured that there are more than thirty thousand men with Louis of Anjou, Monseigneur. A thousand men, even the men of the White Company, would be hard-pressed to defeat such an army."

I said it without acrimony and he smiled as did the Florentines, "Of course, and we have other condottiere who can serve with you. Allied to the men that King Charles can provide you will have fourteen thousand men at your command."

I nodded for I had taken in that he had said I was to command. "Yet even that number may struggle to defeat the French in battle."

"It is not just the French, Sir John." He paused and glanced at Donnina, "Your father-in-law, Bernabò Visconti has supplied men."

Donnina's face was like stone and there was no reaction. I smiled, "What I know of Bernabò is that he will be far from the fighting and the men he hires will be lucky to be paid." I decided to be blunt, "Will we be paid?"

"You have your pension from Florence." Carlos Cialdini was clearly the spokesman of the council.

"The pension keeps me here to protect Florence, my lord. Naples is not Florence. War brings about costs, food, horses, and beds. All add to the expense."

They had clearly been prepared for the papal envoy said, "Of course, and there will be the sum of thirty thousand florins for such expenses."

Every word used by Giacomo was carefully chosen. None of them were wasted and he was telling me that the most I could extract from Rome would be the thirty thousand and that, unlike the Venetian contract, there would be no end date. We might be in the field for almost a year. My mind began to calculate how we might profit and, indeed, how I might conduct the campaign. I would use the mountains, archers and crossbowmen to thwart Louis' attempt to get to Naples. That might please the pope for I did not doubt that Bernabò Visconti and Pope Clement would be more than happy if Louis of Anjou sacked Rome. The pope did not want me just to defend Naples, he wanted me to stop the enemy from reaching Rome. The Tuscan hills would be our battleground. That meant I would not need to risk my horses. My men could fight on foot. My mounted archers would be my most potent force. The money we would take would come from ambush and the capture of nobles who could be ransomed.

I must have been silent for longer than I thought for Donnina said, "You are quiet, my love. Our guests await an answer."

"I am sorry, my lords, Monseigneur, but the task is not a trivial one. However, it is for the church and for Florence. Of course, we will heed your plea. If you would tell the other captains, Monseigneur, to muster their men and to meet me at Lucca then we can stop the French before they come close to us."

The relief on the Florentine faces was palpable. Giacomo looked as though he had never doubted that I would accept the commission.

The finer details were all sorted before our guests left. The monies would be taken to our bank in Pisa. I would arrange for my commission when I saw William. Left alone and while the servants cleared the room Donnina said, "I know you can do this, my husband, but I am curious as to how."

I smiled and as the last plate was cleared and the door closed, I said, "Simple, my love. We use ambush and avoid a battle. Let them think I am a coward, I care not. Fourteen thousand men seems a great number but if the French army and your father's mercenaries come in large numbers then it is not."

"You know that my father does not do this as an act of revenge."

I knew Bernabò well enough to agree with my wife, "I know that he will have the aim to gain power but do not delude yourself, my love. He will know that Pope Urban has hired me and this is a way to try to hurt us." She nodded. "And when he is gone then his nephew will do the same. I am a thorn in their side, a burr under their saddle, an itch they cannot reach and they will do all in their power to be rid of me for when they do then Pisa, Florence, and Padua will all be swallowed up by Milan."

She sighed but did so with a smile, "You are right, Husband, but I do not think that they will ever get the better of you." She stood, "And now there is more urgency for we need to make you and your bodyguards the same. You will be in danger and if we can make you all look alike then that can only help."

I summoned my leaders the next day. Michael, of course, had been prewarned. For Robin, it came as a diversion from his life of pleasure. My other leaders took their lead from my two senior lieutenants.

I had a map of the north of Italy before me. I tapped a place that was not on the map, "Here is Naples and it is more than five hundred miles from Milan. It will take Louis of Anjou and the Lord of Milan many weeks, months, even, to reach Naples. It is why I was hired for the pope believes that we can stop him here in Tuscany."

Robin snorted, "Aye, and our fight keeps him safe in Rome. He is a wily old bird."

I shrugged, "It suits us for we can fight here, in the land that we know. My plan is a simple one. We block every pass south and make them bleed as they try to progress to Rome and then Naples. We ambush their scouts and raid their baggage trains. We make them bleed so much that they will never reach Perugia, let alone Naples. I do not intend to wait for the other companies hired by Pope Urban for we can profit from this." I jabbed a finger at Lucca. "The road we used when we went to Genoa is a good one. The Luccans will not wish the French army to live off their land like so many hungry insects. We might even extract some money from them to stop the French."

Michael looked at the map, "And when they cannot come that way, they will head…?"

"To Prato and Florence." I smiled, "Your father-in-law will not want the French to stop his wagon trains. We may even have some Florentine nobles and crossbowmen to help us."

Michael gave me a sharp look, "How did you know that Florence has purchased five hundred crossbows?"

I tapped my nose, "Just because I do not enter Florence does not mean I know nothing of the goings on. The council is taking out insurance against us. I am more than happy to use crossbows for our ambushes."

There was much that Michael did not know. Even when he had lived with me, I had kept some of my activities secret. I did not tell him of the monthly messages I sent to the only king to whom I would bow a knee, the King of England. Nor did he know that Antonio went into Florence each day and drank, at my expense, in the inn that lay close to the main barracks. He was a feature there and was like the whitewash on the walls. Soldiers talked and he listened. That was how I knew the council's plans. I was not offended that they did not trust me. I had been their enemy for more years than I had served them. I was a hired sword and I think they knew that if someone offered me a greater pension than they did, I would take my company and serve another city-state. My business was war and I plied my trade well.

In the week or so before we left for the Luccan hills, I saw an unexpected side to Zuzzo. He was a trumpeter and I knew him to be a good musician, not to mention a great mimic and singer. When he was working with Gianluca, John and Robert I saw that he had skills as a swordsman. He had come with a sword, all soldiers, even archers carried one as well as a dagger. In most cases, the sword was a short one and just as likely to be used as a tool as a weapon. Zuzzo, however, had an unusual sword. It showed Arabic influences with a slightly curved end. It was not a scimitar but it was a distinctive-looking weapon. He could also use it well. I was not surprised when he easily disarmed my two new Englishmen but when he did so with Gianluca I was taken aback.

I stepped in, "Zuzzo, you have skills. How did you acquire them?"

Whenever he was questioned about his past my trumpeter would become vague and it was as though a gate came down across his eyes, "Before I worked with the travelling actors I had a life, my lord, and I learned to use a sword then. Often, I was used to protect the actors from thieves and brigands."

I waited for more but none was forthcoming. I changed my tack, "And the sword, whence came that?"

I could see from his smile that there was an attachment to the sword as well as a story, "The Holy Land. I served an emir who gave me the sword as a parting gift."

Had he been a crusader or, and from his story, this seemed more likely, a Turcapole, a Frank who served the Turks? I knew that it would be fruitless to try to draw more of his story from him. In any event, I was happy that he served me and that I could use his skills. Not only would he be able to protect me but he could train the two Englishmen. I saw that they were both brave and diligent. They worked hard but they were raw clay compared with the polished marble that was Zuzzo.

"I would have you spend all the time between now and when we leave making John and Robert as skilled as you."

He nodded and Gianluca said, "He is also a skilled horseman. Show him Zuzzo."

The horses of my men were tethered to a rail, their saddles waiting to be fitted. Zuzzo sheathed his sword and ran to his horse. He vaulted onto its bare back and in one deft motion untethered the animal and, using the tether as reins, galloped towards the gyrus where my horsemen trained. It was empty and the gate was closed. He did not falter but leapt the fence in one bound and hurtled around the ring. He got his horse up to speed and then stood on the animal's back. He rode around two or three times. The soldiers who were training applauded for they recognised the talent but when he rode towards the fence and leapt it the cheers were replaced by awed silence. He reined in next to me and leapt easily from the horse's back. He stroked the animal and tied it up.

As he tied it and with his back to me, he answered my unspoken question. "The company with which I travelled also had jugglers and clowns. I am a poor juggler and rarely make people smile but I am a good horseman. I learned such tricks and people paid to watch me."

Once more I wondered about his rich and colourful past life. I knew I would get no further information, but I was grateful that he had chosen to follow me. "John and Robert have even less skill with horses than with swords. When you are able, show them how to ride."

When I told Donnina of the incident she made the sign of the cross, "This is supernatural, my husband. Zuzzo and the others have come to you at a perfect time. You will need their protection."

I shook my head for I did not believe in such superstitions. That Fate might have sent them seemed to me not only blasphemous but also ridiculous. It was just happenstance.

She smiled, "Have you had bodyguards before?"

"Of course."

"And where are they now?"

She gave me a victorious smile when my silence gave her the answer. They were all dead. Few had lasted more than one campaign season. In battle, men came for me, the head of the snake as they saw it, and my bodyguards had died protecting me. She was right. Gianluca and Zuzzo were cut not from cloth but from beaten mail. If John and Robert became as skilled then I might have bodyguards who would last a little longer than their many predecessors.

We prepared to leave Florence just eight days later. We took with us all that we might need. Robin and his archers led laden sumpters. They had spare staves and arrows. Beneath their hats, they each carried half a dozen spare strings. They had their short swords and daggers. Although their arrows would wreak havoc on an enemy, the fact that many of the men who would come would be wearing plate armour meant that they would be as likely to kill with a bodkin blade as a bodkin arrow.

The lances had similar preparations. While the archers would be responsible for their own sumpters and war gear each man at arms had a squire and a foot soldier to worry about such matters. The foot soldiers were better than the militia but we still used them as both servants and camp guards. They cared not for they were well paid. I had long ago learned that parsimony, when it came to paying your men, was a fatal mistake. Bernabò Visconti and the pope had discovered that to their cost when they had reneged on payment. William Turner ensured that every man in the White Company was paid the agreed rate on the right date. If we were on campaign then they knew that their money would be safe in our bank.

I left Florence early and before dawn. I went with my bodyguards and ten chosen men at arms to ride, first to Pisa and thence to Lucca. Michael and Robin would bring the rest of the company. I was going to ease the passage of our company so that we would be waiting unseen in the hills above Lucca when the army of Louis of Anjou arrived.

Chapter 8

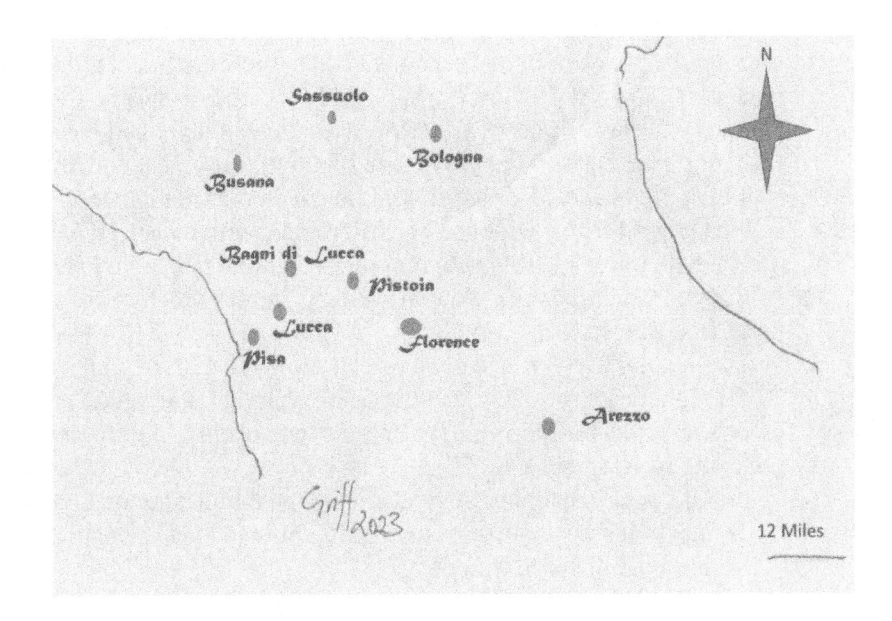

We reached Pisa just after dawn. The men who guarded Pisa's walls had served me and no matter what the Pisan council thought of me, they would always be loyal. I headed for William's palatial home. He was now a member of the council. My days of visiting the doge were long gone. William was my conduit to the council.

His wife did not like me. She thought our work was like trade and beneath her. I thought that was hypocritical. Her father made his money from being a merchant and he would not have amassed the fortune he had but for men like me. William had married her because of her father's money and her looks. She spent hours each day maintaining them. Using whatever she could to augment what nature had given her, she seemed to me like a marionette made by a puppeteer. We did not like each other and she assiduously avoided me and made certain that their children did not come into contact with Giovanni Acuto. I think that she feared they would be soiled by our contact. Gianluca and my men had never been to William Turner's and I had to show them where they would spend the day. I intended to leave for Lucca just as early the next day. I wished my movements to be hidden from French spies.

William had changed. He was still professional when it came to the company, after all, he had a vested interest in its continued success. The profits from the bank had financed his mercantile ventures. It was in his relationship with me that there had been a change and that was due, in no small part, to the constant carping of his wife Bianca. Her words had poisoned our relationship. Even when I had abandoned his sister and taken my sons from her, William and I still had a closeness that few men enjoyed. Now, however, it was awkward and I cursed the day that he had married Bianca.

"Sir John, have you spoken directly to King Charles?"

I sighed, we were alone in the small chamber where William conducted his business and we could speak openly. "William, has the money been paid?"

"Of course, Sir John, but it seems to me a little strange that the man you are supporting is still in Naples and yet the battles will be fought here in Tuscany."

I was blunt, "William, stick to your columns of figures and leave military strategy to me."

"Bianca thinks that this is dangerous for we are risking the wrath of both Milan and France."

"And your wife should stick to her needlework." My tone made my bookkeeper recoil. "Do you think that either Milan or France will ever be our friends? We have bloodied their noses each time we have met. Think of this as a coistrel that is half full. We make a friend of the most powerful kingdom in Southern Italy and we have the support of the legitimate pope. Remember Cesena? For I do."

"People still say that it was you who had the people murdered."

"And that is because of the lies spread by the anti-pope." My eyes narrowed, "And I hope that you do not spread them also."

He shifted uncomfortably, "Bianca says that there is no smoke without fire."

I had endured enough and I banged the table, "If I hear one more word about what that painted doll of yours thinks then I will sever our contract, empty my bank and build a new one in Florence."

I had shocked him but he still tried to summon up defiance, "This is Pisa and no longer your domain."

I laughed, "William, how soon you forget. I do not bother with Pisa for the council still lives in the past and dreams of forgotten glories." I leaned forward and said, softly, "If I chose, I could reduce Pisa to a pile of rubble. Now are you ready to become my bookkeeper again?"

I saw fear in his eyes as he recognised the truth of my words and he nodded, "I am sorry. Bianca can be very..."

"Annoying is the word you seek. Now, the company will be hard on my heels. When they come, they will need food, fodder and shelter. I also need the Pisan council to use Pisan light horsemen to scout the lands to the north and east of Pisa. We believe that Louis of Anjou will come through Lucca but if he does not then I need to know. Impress upon the council that it is in their interest to be vigilant. The French and their mercenaries could well choose to take Pisa. As a plum, it is past ripeness but it may well be a base they might wish to use."

I could see that he had not thought of that. He was no soldier. I knew that Louis of Anjou would know of my involvement. Pope Urban and King Charles had made no secret of the fact that Sir John Hawkwood and the White Company had taken the contract. Taking Pisa would allow them to put pressure on Florence.

He nodded, "All will be as you wish."

I spent the rest of the day detailing exactly what I wanted. He invited me, somewhat half-heartedly, to dine with him. I declined and, instead, ate with my men and the bank guards. Many were ex-soldiers and I preferred their company to the waspish Bianca.

We left before dawn and William came with us to facilitate our egress through the city gates. We headed for Lucca.

Lucca had overthrown Pisan domination but had no ruler of its own. Instead, it was an Imperial City. That effectively meant the emperor was only concerned with its affairs when he needed something. Marcello Gattilusio was the most important man in Lucca. His ancestor, Luchetto Gattilusio had been something of a hero and the family, although no longer as prominent, were still the ones to see when Luccan permission was sought. I knew Marcello well. As a young man, he had served in Ambrogio Visconti's company. He had not been a condottiere for long and, as he confided in me, had done so to gain martial experience and to see how the free companies worked. He was a clever man and an astute businessman.

I was known in Lucca and granted entry although I knew that Milanese spies would race to Milan to tell the Lord of Milan that I was there. I would not be there for long and, in any case, it was necessary, I needed Luccan help.

Marcello was a gracious host. I had last seen him when we had raided Genoa. That act alone had endeared me to him for Genoa was like an octopus and strangled free trade. "Sir John."

It was interesting that I was still addressed by my English title while, when I was spoken of outside my presence, I knew I was called Giovanni Acuto. Perhaps people feared offending me. I was quite flattered by the nickname.

"Sir John, it is good to see you. I wanted to thank you for curbing the growth of Genoa. I know you were well paid but the city of Lucca and I are grateful."

"As you say I was paid but I was glad to help a neighbour. It is important, in these parlous times, that neighbours help each other."

As I said, he was an astute man and he heard the message that lay beneath my words, "And what can this neighbour do for you, Sir John?"

"We can help each other. Louis of Anjou is heading south at the head of an army estimated to be between thirty and forty thousand strong. He intends to wrest Naples from King Charles' grasp."

He nodded as his servant poured us some wine, "It was not well done to have the queen strangled as he did."

I agreed but I could not say so. I was diplomatic. "Pope Urban supports the king and therefore condones the act. I have been hired to lead the Free Companies to stop the French and Milanese from doing so."

The mention of the Visconti piqued his interest, "Bernabò has his sticky fingers in this mess, too, then?"

"He does."

"And what do you intend?"

I used the same arguments that I had with Pisa, "Although Naples is his ultimate aim, I know the Visconti well. If he heads south then this would be a choice plum to pick on his way."

"The emperor might object."

"May I remind you that there is no emperor. When Charles died the empire was taken over by Wenceslaus IV of Bohemia, but he has yet to be elected emperor. He has enough problems in Bohemia and Swabia to worry over much about Lucca. The Hungarians also support Louis of Anjou and, whilst they are not involved, the last thing you need, my friend, is for the Hungarian companies to come through this land."

I had fought alongside Hungarians and Germans. Both were good soldiers but the Hungarians and Italians had a mutual dislike and a Hungarian company would not be welcomed in Lucca. The people there remembered the last time Hungarians and Germans had raided their countryside.

He shuddered, "As usual you have good intelligence and you are right. What do you require of us? We do not have a standing army, as you well know."

I nodded, "But you have men who know the passes and the mountains. I would not have your men fight for us, that is our task and we have been paid to do so but a hundred or so local men, who would be paid as scouts, would aid us."

"You intend to fight them here in Lucca?"

I shook my head, "No, but in the passes north of here. We stop them with ambush. I do not have enough men for a single battle that would determine the outcome of the war. What I can do is to make him bleed away his strength so that he has not enough men to take Naples."

He smiled, "Pope Urban and King Charles are very clever. They keep the war away from their lands knowing that you will fight here."

"It is the land that I know and will not affect your trade. I have spoken with the Pisan council and they know the danger of a French-backed Milan passing through this land. Louis of Anjou just wants Naples but the Visconti want northern Italy."

"And if they come through Bologna instead?"

"Then I will change my plans, but if they do come through Bologna then we shall know and be able to move behind them. We might not be able to block their progress but we could, most certainly, harry their lines of communication and raid their baggage train."

"You have thought this out well. I will arrange for the men you need. While you are more than welcome to my hospitality this night, I expect that you will want to be with your men when they arrive."

He was being careful. If we lost, he would open his gates to Louis of Anjou and broker a deal that would allow him to remain free.

"Of course, you know that I share all the hardships of campaign with my men."

"It is well known and does you great credit although it also allows you to keep greater control over your men. Captain Ambrogio learned much from you but not how to control mercenaries."

We headed for Bagni di Lucca, a town favoured by the Romans for its springs. It was a comfortable place to use as our base as it could be easily defended. It was upstream from the ancient Ponte della Maddalena. If the French came down the western side of the Serchio River then the bridge would be a place to stop them. I was still unsure as to which road they might take. Bagni di Lucca was close enough to Lucca as well as Pistoia for us to ambush them whichever one they took.

The warrior I spoke to in Bagni, Antonio Massimo, was the military leader of the town. He was an old warrior and as such had a sound sense of tactics. When I explained the threat, he concurred. Like Marcello he wondered why I was here and not further east.

"Call it arrogance, my lord. The enemy leaders will know I have been hired and Visconti would dearly love to hurt me. We have a bank in Pisa and I have a home in Florence. By coming this way he would try to defeat me and take all that is dear to me while intimidating both Florence and Pisa. If he could gain control of those cities by using mercenaries and his French allies then he might attain his aim of uniting northern Italy under his rule."

Bernabò Visconti was probably the most unpopular man in Italy. His nephew was a close second. Antonio shook his head, "That would never do for he is a venal and corrupt man." He laughed, "Why am I telling you this? You of all people have suffered at his hands. We will help you and accommodate your men. However, food…"

"Will be paid for. We will not take from the mouths of Luccan families. Whatever we need we will pay for but I hope that the French and Milanese will provide the bulk of our rations."

A day after our arrival the local light horsemen promised by Marcello arrived under the command of Alessandro da Vitiana. Although a noble he was young and, as I later learned, a keen hunter. He knew the forests well. I told him what I needed to know and he happily promised to scout for thirty miles north of the Lima which ran into the Serchio. It meant that even if Louis of Anjou headed for Bologna, we would have a warning.

My company arrived a day after my scouts had headed out. With them came an Italian company, the Company of the Star, of a thousand men under the captaincy of Astorre Manfredi. I had never fought alongside him but he was known to have fought against Visconti. His company achieved fame later on but when he joined my men his were in awe of mine. Our reputation outshone all others. He was happy to follow orders. The terms of my contract meant that I was in overall command but it was good that he accepted my command so easily. I had him send his men at arms south to guard the Ponte della Maddalena. His infantry and crossbows would guard Bagni di Lucca. I was now free to move my men wherever I wanted. I made Astorre my deputy in Bagni and told him to organise the other companies when they arrived.

I knew the area but a leader could never have too much knowledge and I went with Robin and my archers the next day to investigate the roads to the north of us. Alessandro da Vitiana had yet to report the presence of any French or Milanese and I wanted to find places where an ambush might hurt the potential raiders. We found one such place at Coreglia. There the slopes of the valley aided by the trees gave perfect cover for my archers and there was a good road to allow us to escape easily. The bridge over the river would slow down an advance and all that we really needed to do was to whittle down their numbers and wear down their morale. No matter how many or how few we killed, my plan would mean we would lose less than the enemy. While we were there, we explored the hinterland and discovered hunter's trails and fords that we could use but Louis of Anjou's army could not. When Alessandro and his men had found the French, they could show us even more ways to circumvent the defences they would put in place once we had forced them into making the first attack. We headed back to Bagni. I would use the thermal springs for the long days of riding were taking their toll on this old body of mine.

Before I indulged myself in the springs, I spoke with Astorre as well as Michael and Robin. We had to be of the same mind. I missed Giovanni at times like this. He and Dai had the ability to see things I had forgotten. By the time I had finished telling them of my plans the women provided by the town almost had the food ready.

"I will join you when I have bathed. We are not lords and nobles but soldiers. I will eat whatever you do not." I suffered the slow pace of feasts in my halls when you ate at the pace of the slowest eater. I liked food but I was no epicure. When the Florentine Council had dined with me and the papal envoy, some of the Florentines had picked at each course as though it was something to be eaten nibble by nibble.

Michael said, "There will be food for you, my lord."

The thermal baths had been there since Roman times and beyond. It was the whole reason for the existence of the town. Many Luccan nobles owned houses there just so that they could enjoy the baths and sleep in their own beds. We were using those empty houses for my senior officers. I knew that I was old but I did not look old or feel old except when I had been riding for long periods. The road to Pisa and Lucca had been long. The day spent finding the ambush sites had been a long one and my old wounds ached not to mention joints that often kept me awake at night. I spent an hour in the thermal baths and I felt as though I had shed years. A servant there oiled my body and trimmed my hair. I gave him silver for his troubles. If we used Bagni for any length of time I would use his services as much as I could.

There was plenty of food but I knew that the longer the campaign went on then the shorter would be the rations. We all knew it and by the time we had finished then every platter was empty. We were like animals preparing to sleep for the winter. We were storing up food in anticipation of days without any.

"The men are all well supplied?"

Michael nodded, "At the moment Bagni can cope but when the other companies come then it will be a different matter."

"Then as well as ambush we will need to get through their lines and raid their rear. Better that we take from our enemies and have them looking behind them for an attack as well as to their fore."

Astorre used a small and sharp chicken bone to scrape meat from between his teeth, "It seems to me, Sir John, that you and your archers will be the ones who bear the brunt of the fighting. For my part I am happy as we are paid no matter how much fighting we do, but your men," he looked at Robin and Michael, "are they happy?"

I smiled for I knew that Robin would answer for me, "Captain, with all due respect to your men, and I doubt not that they are skilled, the archers of the White Company are unique. We can ride as far as light horsemen and when we unleash our missiles then we can send almost eight times the number sent by your crossbows. If they come by the Coreglia road then your crossbows will augment our arrows but we will kill more. It is why the White Company was chosen by Pope Urban to lead this resistance to Louis of Anjou and Visconti. So to answer your question, aye, we are happy for if we do the job then it will be done well and we shall win. When we have suffered reverses then it has been because others let us down."

Astorre nodded.

I said, "And I will be with my archers too, Captain Astorre. I am not a leader who squats like a toad watching others die for him. I was an archer too and I can still handle a bow."

I saw Robin smile and shake his hand indicating that he was not sure I could.

I smiled too, "I will not, of course, but my men know that I could. How many mounted crossbowmen do you have?"

"We are a new company and not as well equipped as the White Company. We have just a hundred who are mounted."

"That will suffice and hopefully we will be able to supply horses that we capture."

Robin grinned, "And we will not overcharge you for them."

Shaking his head Michael said, "I have the twenty men at arms who will guard your chosen men already, Sir John."

"Good, then we wait for Alessandro to report."

It was late the next day when the scouts returned. They brought the news that I had been prescient and had chosen the right place to wait. Like a spider with a well-placed web, I had chosen the perfect place to wait for our enemy. They would come to us and be at Coreglia within the next few days.

Alessandro was a clever man and he knew that we needed to know how the enemy forces were made up. "The largest contingent, my lord, is led by Amadeus of Savoy. The Savoyards are used to fighting in the mountains." His words were a warning but I already knew that. "The vanguard is made up of Louis of Anjou's own men. They wear the livery of Anjou. The Milanese guard the baggage train. Your enemy has a good head on his shoulders. Each element of his army, the vanguard, the mainward and the rearguard are all self-contained forces. They can defend themselves from an attack."

I smiled, "Good, for Louis of Anjou is in for a shock. He has never faced the White Company before but soon he will learn why we are the best in Italy."

Chapter 9

Despite the order given by my wife, the five of us did not wear helmets as we waited in the trees for the enemy. For one thing, it was too hot and for another, the trees afforded us a disguise. Like the archers and the horsemen, we wore brown cloaks over our distinctive white surcoats. We did not wish to blazon our presence with a flash of white in the dappled sunlight. Alessandro's horsemen were still shadowing the French. Once the trap was sprung, they would use their own paths and trails to rejoin us. We were not mounted and our horses grazed where they could. Men watched them and they were hidden from view but, if disaster struck and we had to flee, they could be fetched and mounted before an enemy could get close to us. Robin had arranged the archers in tiers, rising through the trees. It meant that all of them had a clear view of the road and every bow could release an arrow to become a cloud of fletched death for the enemy. The crossbows were at the bottom for they used a flatter trajectory. They had made a rough barrier of logs that would give them some protection and allow them to use the logs to help them support their cumbersome crossbows, as well as giving them a shelter where they could load the weapons. It was mid-afternoon and hot. We had arrived at noon so that we would be in position well before the enemy appeared.

The Breton light horsemen who arrived first were not brightly coloured. Like us, they wore dull brown cloaks to make them harder to see. As they appeared, just half a mile from us, I nodded and the men at arms headed for their horses. They would take the Bretons. I heard the creak of bows as my archers strung them. I had been an archer and knew that each one of them would be choosing the first five arrows that they would loose. After that they would be a machine, pulling and releasing arrows as fast as they could. The Breton scouts were looking for the flash of metal in the sun. They were not scouring the trees for archers. They had travelled from France and Milan without hindrance. Once they were out of the mountains, they would expect to see our serried ranks and tell their leaders that the battle they sought was nigh. Here, they saw what they expected to see; trees that appeared to be empty. Had they been more vigilant then they might have noticed that the birds were silent but they did not. I heard their chatter as they rode towards the prospect of food and drink for they would be the first in the town and, as such, be able to find the best rooms and best provender. The Franco-Savoyard army had enjoyed a journey, thus far, free from enemies. That was about to change.

There was a short gap of a hundred paces and behind the Bretons marched the crossbows and the pikemen. I could see the first of the horsemen just behind them, their banners fluttering in the breeze. Louis of Anjou was showing skill. He was marching with a battle already to form. If he was attacked then the crossbows would be there to defend the pikes that would form a hedgehog before the horsemen. I knew that the sequence would be repeated throughout the column. He was not making the mistake of having each arm of his army concentrated together.

As the Bretons neared us, we all shifted slightly so that we each had the bole of a tree to hide us. The road was less than two hundred paces from the edge of the trees and we could hear the murmur of conversation, the sounds of creaking leather and the snorting of horses. If we had brought our horses close then the Bretons' horses might have reacted. As it was, they just passed by. The horsemen were reassured by the lack of reaction from their horses and as the horses moved along the road so we moved back into position. The rest of the army was marching with eyes fixed ahead for their scouts had passed and were unharmed. They would be sick already of seeing the rumps of the Breton horsemen. They would be looking up at Coreglia anticipating shade, shelter, and sustenance. Alessandro had told us that the French and Milanese were not paying for their supplies. They were taking them. Whilst not a chevauchée it was creating bad feeling in the villages and towns through which they passed. We had not warned Coreglia of the impending invasion and that was deliberate. We wanted the town to appear like the others further north, unsuspecting. I also took comfort from the fact that the enemy would not think that the men of Coreglia had colluded with us. If they thought that then a Cesena-type slaughter could follow.

The two Englishmen with me and Zuzzo were keenly interested in the ambush. This would be their first sight of the White Company in action. Zuzzo had travelled throughout Italy and he would have an idea about our attacks and the efficacy of our archers but the two Englishmen would never have seen archers raining death from the skies. They were craning their necks to see the effect.

The attack had to begin at the perfect moment and that mean an order had to be given. I could have done so but I had total faith in Robin and my master archer did not let me down. As the first of the crossbowmen reached the far left of our line Robin roared, "Loose!"

The mechanical cracks and snaps of the crossbows as they sent their bolts at their counterparts was as nothing compared with the almost musical sound of yew bows being released. To me, it was a thing of beauty. I watched as the arrows and bolts scythed into the crossbowmen. The Genoese mercenaries were knocked to the ground and the fore of the column was in disarray. From my left, I heard the clash of steel as my men at arms smashed into the Bretons. Louis of Anjou would need more scouts. French, Savoyard and Milanese horns sounded and the pikes were turned to face the threat. The pikemen wore brigandines; the leather might slow down a bolt or an arrow but it would not stop one and as the surviving crossbowmen fled towards the river, Robin's men shifted their missiles to the pikemen. The men with pikes were brave. Perhaps their position in the van had been a reward for courage. They lasted marginally longer than the crossbows and then they, too, fled. The horsemen who charged the trees were more fortunate. They wore plate and had shields. However, our cunningly placed ambush meant that they would not be able to get close to our archers and crossbows. The trees that were a barrier and the slope stopped them from using their greatest strength, a wall of horseflesh and metal to smash through light infantry. Robin and his men shifted their aim. They went for the horses that wore no armour and if both rider and horse were mailed then they sent bodkins and bolts to attempt to puncture the plate armour. Horses and men fell but not in large numbers.

When one of the Astorre's crossbowmen was lanced, I turned to Zuzzo, "Sound the retreat."

I had used trumpeters before but none were close to Zuzzo in terms of skill. The notes were clear and strident. We waited until the crossbowmen had left the log barrier before we headed to our horses. John and Robert were the youngest of the five of us and they ran ahead so that by the time we reached our horses they were holding them for us to mount. Astorre's crossbowmen were the last to arrive and to mount. My archers smiled for they enjoyed the victory. I waved my arm and we headed towards the road and Coreglia. We passed the Breton dead. My horsemen waited with the bounty of Breton horses and the liberated purses and weapons. They would be the only ones to have benefitted financially from the ambush. The dead Bretons would have small purses and poor weapons but they would provide a profit. If they wore good boots or had helmets then they would have been taken too. There was always a ready market for cheap boots.

It was after dark when we reached Bagni. Alessandro sent fresh scouts out to Coreglia. They would watch our enemy for he would only lick his wounds for so long and then advance again.

Astorre was keen to know about the ambush. I told him between mouthfuls. "We hurt them. The men in their vanguard will need to be replaced. They will need to have new scouts and next time we try this they will be warier. We may even have made them change their plans. We just need to be ready to react to whatever they do."

He nodded, "The Blue Company arrived while you were attacking." I nodded. "I put them in the hills to the east of Bagni. We now have a ring of steel around the town."

Michael frowned, "Blue Company?"

"They are from Gascony and they have some archers for there are Englishmen amongst them. They also have Castilians, Aragonese and Navarrese as well as Gascons. This is the first that I have heard of them working in Italy. The lure of King Charles' gold must be strong." Astorre added, "I spoke with their captain. It was the pope himself who asked for them. I think that was politically motivated. The Blue Company was upsetting the Castilians and their bishops. With no paymaster, they were acting like bandits. This gains the pope a Castilian ally and a company that should not upset his Italians."

Michael understood that all too well. The Hungarians and Germans were both feared and hated in Italy. It perhaps explained why we had smaller numbers than we might have hoped. I suspected that every Italian and English company was in the employ of King Charles and Pope Urban.

Our raid slowed down the French advance. The people of Coreglia suffered an enemy who took their food and used their homes as a barracks. It took Amadeus and Louis time to work out a strategy to move forward. It was the scouts who brought the news that they had decided to shift us from Bagni di Lucca. I knew that the Luccans would not wish this jewel in the mountains to become a battleground and I took the decision to meet the enemy north of Bagni. I brought in the other companies and sent the archers and crossbowmen with Robin to provide a flank attack. Some would be over the river at Salita and others on the steep wooded slopes. I led the rest of my foot soldiers and horsemen to meet Louis and Amadeus. We would fight on foot. I was confident that the narrow valley would restrict their ability to break us down with sheer numbers. I told the other captains my reasoning, "We simply hold them and let Robin and his men whittle down their will to advance. The order is to stand and fight. If we are able, we rotate our front ranks, much as the Romans did."

Astorre said, "That may be impossible. The men in the front ranks will be hard-pressed to hold an army that is more than six times our number."

"I will be in the front rank, Astorre, and I am more than willing to take the risk for I trust in all of you to do that for which you have been paid."

It was not bravado from me that placed me and my best men at arms in the fore, it was the knowledge that we had done this before and could do it. This time I went helmed as did my four men. They would stand behind me. John would hold my banner. Gianluca was not happy that he would not flank me but I had Michael, Sebastian and Luigi. I trusted them and, as I pointed out to the four of them, their weapons could help to protect me. I had three men with pole weapons and their sole duty was to guard my person. We left before dawn knowing that the Franco-Savoyard army would have to move much more slowly and with my archers and crossbowmen already in position they would be harassed as soon as they were sighted.

In the event, we reached the place I had chosen before we spied the enemy banners. They had learned their lesson and had plated and mounted men at arms in their vanguard. We had spears, pikes and poleaxes so we presented a steel barrier to bar their progress. The danger would be if they charged at us but even if they did then the narrow valley meant that they would only have a frontage of twenty men. They would be attacking a line of men thirty wide and twenty deep. Each horseman and lance would be faced by more than one pole weapon.

As they headed towards us, I knew that they would be intent upon revenge. We had hurt them with our ambush and stopped them from reaching their true target, Naples. They also had the chance to demolish the reputation of Sir John Hawkwood and the White Company. I knew it was a risk to stand in the front rank but I knew that I had good plate armour and that we had a position where we could not be outflanked. The arrows and bolts began to strike them. The distinctive ping as they hit metal was underscored by the screams from the horses as they were hit on their unprotected rumps. The men at arms who rode at us had shaffrons for their horses' heads but their trappers could not keep out a bodkin or a bolt. One horse tumbled to the ground and not only did it throw its rider from its back but it also disrupted the attack so that the solid line that had begun the charge now had holes in it.

I was not one for shouting encouragement to my men. I believed that the best form of inspiration was to be the first to strike a blow and the Savoyard horseman who rode at me afforded me just such an opportunity. I had a pike in my hands. My shield hung over my left arm. The man at arms pulled back his lance to strike at me. His weapon was longer than mine and would strike me first. His horse wore a mail hood. I swung my pike from left to right. It was a calculated blow for I was not only aiming at his horse's head but also bringing my shield around to my front. My swing would be completed before his lance struck and I was counting on killing his horse. The mail would protect the flesh from the blade but the pike had a heavy head and my blow would be the same as that administered to an animal in an abattoir. My arms were jarred as the head killed the warhorse. It began to fall immediately. Its momentum threatened to cause the beast to fall into our lines and the men around me jabbed with their spears, pikes and poleaxes. The lance of the man at arms did strike my shield but it slid harmlessly along it as the rider fought to keep his balance. His falling, accelerated by the spear that struck him, pulled his horse to the left, to fall as a barrier before his fellow men at arms and added to the confusion.

As I adjusted my pike, I reflected that an attack by dismounted men at arms would have been the better tactic. The now stationary column of horses and riders was an easy target for the archers and crossbowmen, not to mention the jabbing pole weapons wielded by men who knew how to use them. I was in a unique position. The dead horse was a barrier that prevented the other horses from closing with me. Sebastian's poleaxe ended the life of the wounded man at arms and I was able to judge our position almost dispassionately. The ragged attack had not struck our lines with any force. We had not been budged an inch and as horses were slain, I knew that the attack had been a failure. It was confirmed when a horn sounded and the survivors of the first attack began to drift back to the main army. The narrow valley was as much a part of our defence as the plate armour we wore.

As they fell back my experienced men darted forward with rondels in their hands. The badly wounded were stabbed while the three who were only slightly wounded were fetched to be held for ransom. Purses, rings, good weapons and better helmets were pillaged and before the survivors had filtered back through their own lines, my line was whole once more.

Michael raised his visor to speak to me. I raised my own. "What next, Sir John?" Michael had always been a good student and he was still learning how to be a leader. It was a good question.

I pointed my pike at our crossbowmen across the river, "They can do nothing about those men but they can try to rid themselves of the annoyance of the archers. They will send light infantry and their own crossbowmen into the trees." I grinned,

"Robin will enjoy that. Then they will dismount another column of men at arms and try a human, rather than an equine, battering ram. I think it will fail." I gestured at the five dead horses. Whilst not a solid barrier it would disrupt an attack and allow us to destroy the attackers piecemeal.

"What would you do, Sir John?" John Edingham was also a curious young man.

"Simple, I would fall back and then send light infantry into the trees to outflank us. It is clear that he outnumbers us and it is just the valley that holds him up. If this was a flat plain then he would have swamped us with superior numbers."

Zuzzo chuckled, "And that is why you met the enemy here in the mountains. Have you read of the Spartans, Sir John?"

I shook my head, "I rarely read."

"It was a story one of our company, a Greek, used to tell, how three hundred soldiers held up a mighty army of Persians at a pass called Thermopylae."

"What happened to them?"

"Oh, they were all killed but it allowed the other Greeks to destroy the Persian army. They are honoured still in Greece."

"And that is the difference, Zuzzo, I do not want to lose a single man. If the enemy outflanks us then I am not too proud to head back to Bagni and start again. We are mercenaries and not heroes. A dead mercenary cannot spend his pay, can he?"

He did not have the opportunity to answer for Amadeus or Louis, whoever led the enemy horde, did two things. Light horsemen, Bretons probably, and infantry headed into the trees to our right whilst pavesiers set up pavise so that the Genoese mercenaries could send crossbow bolts at my crossbows across the river.

I shouted, "The next attack will be by dismounted men at arms. Be ready to meet them."

The men at arms would be armed with pole weapons like us. I slipped my shield from my arm. It would be an encumbrance and I would only need it when my pike was damaged and I had to use my sword. The pike had been perfect for facing horsemen. Sebastian's poleaxe was now the best weapon. I would have to manage with my pike held firmly in two hands. The cries from our flanks told us when combat had begun. The cries were not of pain but orders as leaders on both sides adjusted their men for the new threat. I had confidence in Robin and my archers and knew that Astorre's crossbowmen could not be driven from the other side of the river. All that the Genoese crossbows, the mercenaries, could do was neutralize them. The situation had not changed. The enemy still had to drive us from our bottleneck.

This time we would be faced with equal numbers but they would not meet us as a solid body. The dead animals and men at arms would have to be crossed. If a man was not vigilant, he could slip on the bloody and slick ground and bring down another. His eyes would have to be on the land before him and to the fore. We would have no such constraint and my men were deadly killers. The battlefield was no place for kindness. It would be kill or be killed. I recognised the surcoats of some of the men heading for us. They were mercenaries. The enemy leader had mixed Savoyards, Frenchmen and mercenaries. I was not sure why but I would not have done so. My front rank was made up of the White Company. To my mind, a man fought better alongside men with whom he was familiar. If nothing else then the blows from the side would be more predictable.

As I had expected the horses and the dead made the line that approached us more ragged. The Hungarian who stood on the carcass of the warhorse held a pole axe and, using the extra height, swung it at my head. The pike had a wickedly sharp head and whilst his torso was out of range his legs were not and, ducking my own head below the swing of the pole axe I swung my pike in a wide arc. I still had archer strength and my shoulders and arms could generate a great deal of power. He wore poleyns on each knee and had greaves but the pike's head smashed through both to hack into his flesh and shatter his left knee. No man can stand on one leg. Already overbalanced, he fell forward and Robert's spear ended the Hungarian's life as he tumbled to my feet.

Our two lines were engaged but those following the first line of warriors saw the fate of some of their fellows and wisely chose different approaches. The horse's body was now seen not as an advantage but as a road to sudden death. They came at me around the horse and that meant passing Michael, Sebastian and Luigi, not to mention Gianluca who had insinuated himself next to me. The first five men all fell but eventually enough numbers arrived to mean that each of us had an opponent. My pike had been used just twice and would still be sharp. The man at arms who managed to face me had a long war axe and shield. He looked like an old-fashioned Frankish warrior. His weapon was a deadly one and if he struck then the head would damage my plate and the weight would crush the bones beneath. I used the tip of the pike to poke at him. The ploy worked for he had to bring up his shield to block the blow and could not swing his axe. I used the blade of the pike to swipe sideways as I withdrew my weapon. It caught the side of his right arm where there was no plate. Slicing through the mail it scored a line along his flesh. It would barely slow him but I knew that he would be warier. When he swung his axe at me, I only had one recourse, I had to block it with my pike but as I did so he punched at my head with his shield. Even though I tried to bring up the shaft of the pike I knew that I was doomed to failure. The blow connected and I reeled. He tried to seize his opportunity but the distinctive blade of Zuzzo's sword darted out like a serpent's tongue and the surprised Frank was stabbed in the throat. He gurgled his life away at my feet. I would thank Zuzzo later.

I realised one disadvantage of my position in the front rank. I could not see the ebb and flow of battle. However, when the attack weakened and the horns sounded from the enemy side, I knew that we had won this segment of the battle. We had lost men and as the wounded were taken back, I shouted, "Astorre, relieve us!"

"Star Company move forward."

My men were already taking from the dead so all we had to do was to filter back through the ranks of men with fresh weapons and arms that were not weary from wielding weapons. "Thank you, Zuzzo."

He shrugged, "I am not a man who likes to be inactive. I was happy to use my skill. You should have let us be the barrier before you."

I wondered if he was right.

"John, fetch Caesar."

I wanted the height my horse's back would afford. My men were drinking from ale skins. Fighting gave a man a raging thirst. Robert handed me a skin and I let the ale soothe my throat.

"We held them, Sir John."

"That we did, Michael, and the question now is what will they do next?"

I mounted Caesar and had a clear view of the battle. We had slain three men for every one we had lost and many more of the enemy were wounded. The archers had won the battle of the woods and I saw light horsemen heading back to their own lines. When arrows began to fall on the backs of the Genoese crossbows, then I knew the other flank attack had failed.

"White Company, mount your horses."

I had no intention of making a foolish attack on a superior enemy but I was gambling that Amadeus and Louis of Anjou would see us mounted and wonder what we intended. I was bluffing but hoping that they would buy the bluff. By the time we were mounted and with lances in our hands the Genoese had all fallen back and the enemy had a wall of pikes ready to repel us. Pikemen are an excellent deterrent to a mounted charge but are vulnerable to arrows. When Robin's archers sent arrows to slam into men who had no shields to protect them, then it precipitated horns that sounded a retreat. Amadeus and Louis retreated their army back up the valley. We had won this battle but I was planning to win the war.

Chapter 10

Even while the road was cleared and men began to hack the carcasses of the dead horses for meat, I was holding a conference with Astorre, Robin, Michael and my other leaders. "What would you do, Astorre, if you were Amadeus and Louis?"

"If I had lost as many men as they have I would choose a different route to get to Naples."

There were nods of agreement.

"And that means backtracking north until they can find a road that takes them east."

"East?" One of the Italian captains asked.

"West means that they would have to use the narrow coastal road. It is as dangerous as this one and we have taught them to avoid narrow roads with tree-lined places from which to ambush them. They will use the land around Pistoia which is flatter and it means he can threaten Florence. They have to march almost thirty miles north to Busana to find a road that heads east. They will then have almost as far to march until they find the road south. That gives us two or three days to get into position. We have the advantage that we can use the road east from Bagni and get ahead of them."

Robin shook his head, "They will be expecting an ambush and will be ready. The land to the west affords them the opportunity to use more men."

I smiled, "You are right but they will not expect an attack on their rear. I intend to take the mounted element of the White Company and get behind them. Astorre and the rest of you, along with my foot, will be where they expect to see you, before them. Take the other companies and use the road east from Bagni. Straddle the road to Florence. When they arrive you keep falling back until we have attacked their baggage train. Without supplies, their army cannot last long in the mountains."

Astorre said, shaking his head, "I can see your logic, Sir John, but this presumes they will do as you predict."

I turned to Alessandro, "I think you have fulfilled every requirement I had of you. I ask for one more task before I release you. Follow this army with some of your men and let me know where they go. If they continue north from Busana then the invasion is over but if they head east then we know they are doing that which I have said."

He smiled, "My men and I are more than happy to play this game of cat and mouse with our enemy." He patted the purse on his belt. "We have yet to lose a man and we have taken many of their scouts. There is profit in this for us and besides I do not like foreigners passing through our land."

"We are foreigners, Alessandro."

"You were born abroad and have strange names but you and your men have shown that this is your home. We have adopted you. We will do as you ask and find you."

That done it was a simple matter of organising my horsemen. There would be just five hundred of us. Some men had been wounded and others killed. We would not need large numbers to do what I intended. My aim was to make them rue this invasion and find another way to get to Naples.

Once at Bagni, I told the nobles there of our victory. I did not confide in them. My plan was my own but I told them that my men would head east to stop an attack on Florence. They understood that. Antonio Massimo said, "And we will be watchful, just in case you are wrong and the enemy soldiers come back down this road. You and your men have shown us what can be done. We will not allow an enemy to ravage our land, especially not one funded by the anti-pope and the Visconti."

It was my plan but as we rode from the thermal spa, I could not help but reflect that I had given myself the harder task. There would be no inns or castles along our route and we would have to pay for our food. The sumpters we took could only carry so much food and we would, perforce, be on short rations. While we waited for news of our enemy, we would have to leave the road and live like brigands in the forests. We might have weeks to wait. I consoled myself with the fact that we were being paid and the reputation of the White Company was being enhanced.

It took a whole day to reach Fiumalbo but we did have shelter when we reached it. There was a small monastery on the slopes of Monte Cimone to the east of the village that owed its loyalty to the city of Modena. St Francis was a small monastery for it had not been endowed by a great lord. Men like Visconti chose larger monasteries and priories. The Land of Saint Benedict around Monte Cassino had been made so rich by Byzantine Emperors that it was able to build a ring of castles to protect its land. The Franciscans of St Francis had no such benefactor. They lived simple lives eking out an existence on the slopes of the mountain. They tended to the spiritual needs of the village and contemplated God. They were the truest monks I ever met. Their church was unadorned with gold but they had pure faith and I felt more at peace when I was there than in any other place. Although they had no accommodation for us they welcomed us. I would not take their charity for I saw that they were poor and I insisted upon paying for the food we enjoyed. They gratefully took my coins but assured me that they would not be used to beautify their monastery but to make the lives of the villagers better. Our coins were well spent.

We erected tents and built hovels while our horses grazed on the slopes of Monte Cimone. I spoke to Michael and Robin, "This seems as good a place as any to wait for our enemy. We have shelter, of a sort, and we will be fed."

Robin pointed to the other side of the road, to the west. There, trees rose like a palisade on the rising slopes. "Whenever Alessandro appears we can take shelter there." He looked at the monks toiling in the fields, "I would not place these holy men in danger though, Sir John. I would have their lives continue in peace."

"And I have no intention of doing so. We hide, like children playing a game until our prey has passed and then we emerge and follow them. I saw many places on the road south."

Michael said, "Where the road forks to Bagni is a place I think the enemy will camp."

Michael had grown so much on this campaign. He knew, as I did, that when the enemy broke camp the baggage train could be half a day behind the vanguard. The army we sought was so large and the roads so narrow that it could be spread out over six miles or more.

"I will take some men tomorrow and seek trails in the trees." Robin grinned, "And if we happen to find some game then it might fall into the monks' pot."

I knew that would endear us to the monks. They trapped rabbits and squirrels but nothing larger and they would benefit as much as we did from the meat.

It was late in the afternoon of the next day when the two riders sent by Alessandro rode in. I had just emerged from the cool darkness of the monastery's church, Chiesa del Santi Donnino e Francisco, when I spied them heading from the village. I felt at peace after my hour in the church. The older I became the more I reflected on my mortality. I had been excommunicated but Pope Urban had removed that. Would I still be allowed into heaven? I knew that while I had never been the best of men, I had been far from the worst.

The men reined in, "Sir, John, we bring word from Lord Alessandro. The enemy is heading to Busana and Sassuolo. They will be heading down this road."

"But how did you get here so quickly?"

They grinned and one said, "This is the main road, it is true but there are two other roads if one knows the land," He pointed to the southwest, "Bagni is less than ten miles in that direction and there is a road that is but twelve miles. It is a little precarious in places but we know the land."

"Then when you have rested here this night, I would have you ride to San Marcello Pistoiese and tell Captain Astorre your news."

"We will."

"And how long do you think we have before the vanguard will pass through here?"

"You have five days before you can expect them. This road is an easier one than the one through Bagni but it is still narrow. The Savoyard snake will be constricted as it slithers down the road." The men of Lucca did not like the Savoyards. Amadeus and the Savoyards not to mention their allies, the Genoese, had often raided Luccan land. Their involvement in our campaign was of choice and not finance.

Robin arrived while they were unsaddling their horses and they had managed to hunt four deer. The monks were more than

Condottiere

grateful. It was not just the meat that they would use but every part of the animal. Even the hooves would be used to make glue. While we ate that night the two men told us how the retreating army's progress was marked by the graves of the wounded who died along the way.

"Your companies have hurt them, Sir John, but they are still a powerful army."

I heard the doubt in his voice, "You do not think we can defeat them?"

"This is not the road to Bagni, Sir John, and your army is to the south."

"But until Pistoia, they have to shift us from every narrow part of the road. They will be watching for ambushes and by the time they are in a position to bring their greater numbers to bear we will have worn them down. You may be right, we cannot defeat them but we can make them bleed and tear the heart from them."

I spoke to the prior the next day as the two Luccans rode south, "We will be leaving tomorrow." I handed him the purse of silver, "This is a donation to your monastery."

"You are a good man, Giovanni Acuto, for you have paid us already. You and your men will be in our prayers." He made the sign of the cross. "I will not ask where you go nor will our eyes follow you. When your enemies come, I will be able to speak the truth that the White Company stayed awhile with us and paid us for food before leaving."

"We will be leaving before dawn."

"And we shall be at prayers. All will be well. You should return when there is peace, my lord, for I see that the monastery and the church, not to mention the mountain, have a calming effect on you. Your face looks more at peace."

"Perhaps you are right. The mountain and the monastery make me closer to God."

"And that is why our founders chose this site. It may not be the one that attracts the gold but we Franciscans are not worried about such worldly matters. The coins you have given us will be put to good use and pay for that which we need but cannot grow."

Condottiere

We heard the monks at prayer as we left the monastery before the sun had risen. We passed through the village and headed up the road. We had told the villagers that we were leaving and that if any enemy came they should tell them where we had gone. It would not help the French for by the time the sun had risen we would be following the mountain trail that Robin had found. His hunting expedition had been rewarding, not only for the meat but also for the knowledge that he had gained. He had found a clearing where a storm had ripped down some mighty trees. It was a natural fortress and we used it as our camp. There was grazing but we needed some of the squires to move the animals around each day to ensure that they were all well fed. We then established a watching post some two miles north of the village. A dozen men camped at the outpost. We had a rota so that the men were changed three times a day. We needed alert men. They were a mixture of archers, men at arms and squires.

We waited.

The Luccans had been remarkably accurate in their estimate. The scouts appeared down the road just when they had been predicted. The outpost sent word and I went with Robin and Michael to witness the passing of the column. By the time we arrived, the vanguard was marching down the road and I could see that they had learned their lesson. The horsemen in the centre were flanked by a mixture of spearmen and crossbowmen. Their eyes flitted and flicked to the trees seeking danger. My outpost was too well hidden to be seen. We wore brown cloaks and no plate. We said nothing as they passed. My men had made a mark on a stick, a tally, so that we would know their numbers. I would assess the danger when they had all passed down the road. The column of two men and horses abreast, flanked by their foot, meant that the column took hours to pass us. When I saw a gap appear, my spirits rose. They had large numbers but the baggage train was more than a little tardy. It was understandable for the road rose and fell, twisted and turned. The draught animals had wagons laden with missiles, weapons, armour, food and the parts for their siege engines. They had not needed them against us but when they reached Neapolitan territory then they would. There were guards marching alongside the wagons. They were spearmen wearing padded jacks and helmets. They carried spears and small shields hung over their backs. It all boded well. It took the wagons of their baggage train an hour to pass us.

As soon as they had passed, we packed up the outpost and headed back to the camp. There we could talk.

"It is better than I hoped. They are so worried about being ambushed that they are not looking behind them. We trail them and wait until they are south of the monastery. I would not have the monks harmed for collusion."

Robin nodded, "There is a place five miles south of the village and a trail heads across the mountains. We found it when we were hunting. It will take us to the Bagni road and we can rejoin Astorre and the others. It is narrow but we can easily manage it. Our enemies will not."

We left before dawn and headed not down the road but through the trees. We were shadowing a large animal and we had to remain hidden. The huge beast was slow to rise as it left Fiumalbo. We had a good vantage point in the trees overlooking the village and saw that the carters, wagon drivers and guards did not even hitch up their wagons until the rearguard had departed. Louis or Amadeus had made a serious misjudgement. Most armies had their rearguard behind the baggage train but our action at Bagni had made them so nervous that they had isolated their wagons.

We were in Robin's hands and he led us south as we shadowed the baggage. Each time we came to an incline, however slight, then the wagons slowed and the guards had to haul on ropes. That resulted in the gap between the rearguard and baggage widening. It was just past noon when we reached the place we would ambush. The archers had strung their bows and were heading towards the road when the wagons stopped. There was a farmhouse just a hundred paces from the road and there would be water there. Whoever the poor farmer and his family were, they were going to be impoverished even more. The wagon drivers and their guards were going to rest and eat. It was perfect. We donned helmets and held our lances. The squires guarded the sumpters and held the horses of Robin and his men. It would be they who would initiate the attack with a storm of arrows. My men at arms and I would be the ones who charged them. We would have to work quickly for the rearguard were just a couple of miles ahead and when they heard the cries and the clash of arms, they would send men to investigate. We had plans in place for that eventuality.

We walked our horses to the edge of the trees. I daresay we might have been visible but the guards were too concerned with food and slaughtering the animals that they had taken from the farm. When the first arrows fell, men looked at the arrows sticking from the dead men as though they had appeared by magic. It took a second flight and more deaths for the alarm to be sounded and by then our lances were wreaking a harvest. It was all too easy and the ones who could, simply fled. As soon as the ones who had survived had vacated the wagons, Robin and his men mounted their horses and headed up the road. The squires joined us as we unhitched the horses and took from the wagons any treasure. Hams and cheeses were slung onto the backs of the draught horses. Weapons were also taken and we found two chests. They were both filled with coins. The four men who had guarded that particular wagon had fought harder than any. We took the treasure.

"Bring fire and burn the wagons."

We might have taken more but time was pressing and the draught horses were laden. The squires took the captured animals and our booty towards the trail to Bagni. When the fires were burning well, we headed down the road. I had left four animals as compensation for the farmer. He had lost animals and the four horses might make up a little. He would probably salvage something from the enemy dead. We had left their weapons and helmets.

As I led my men down the road, I hefted my shield. My four bodyguards were all close to me. Michael and his bodyguards were at the rear. The enemy rearguard had sent horsemen to investigate the clamour and Robin's archers had ambushed them already. As we turned the bend in the road and emerged, I saw that they were clearly disrupted. With lances lowered, we slammed into the disordered men at arms. Their shields were held to protect them from arrows and they had no spears. Each of us managed to skewer a man at arms. We ploughed down the column of eighty men and when I reined in, the horsemen had been destroyed as a fighting force. There were still men and horses who were alive and unwounded but they had fled back down the road. Our enemies would need to send a larger force and that would delay them once more.

"Zuzzo, sound retreat!"

My men grabbed the reins of loose war horses and, as my archers mounted and joined us, they too took the enemy horses. We could not spare the time or take the risk and strip the bodies of plate. That treasure would have to wait. We could have taken the wounded to ransom as we had after the skirmish at Coreglia but caution was still our watchword. We had profited well from the encounter. The two chests alone felt heavy enough to equal the pay we had already received.

Robin, Michael, and I rode at the rear of our men as they headed down the perilously narrow track through the trees. When Robin had mentioned it to Alessandro's riders, he had been assured that it came out on the Bagni road. We had to trust to our allies. They had not let us down yet.

"Will that be enough, Sir John?" Michael wanted to go home. His wife was with child and he wanted to be there when his son or daughter was born.

I shrugged, "They have lost irreplaceable supplies and I hope so but Louis has been promised a crown by the pope and he will want to make an attempt, at least, to claim it. If we can bloody his nose again then he may have to scurry back to the French king and ask for men."

"And will the French king supply them?"

"The anti-pope lives in Avignon and has the support of the French king. If Louis of Anjou was King of Naples, he would be a powerful ally for the French king. I can see a time when French troops rather than mercenaries will follow Louis south."

Robin nodded, "And Visconti would benefit for with the French and Naples as his allies he could gobble up the land between them."

"Even the papal states?" Michael was still learning and Robin and I were the best of teachers.

"Especially the papal states, for then Clement could move to Rome and Urban would be the one in exile." I had already thought this through. It was the main reason for accepting the contract. The last thing I wanted was for the land between Paris and Sicily to be controlled by the French and Pope Clement.

We reached the road in the late afternoon and headed east to join Astorre.

Although the companies were quartered in San Marcello Pistoiese, the defences were at Mammiano, the village two miles to the west of the larger town. The rest of our men having passed through the barriers, we were cheered by the guards. They had seen the horses, loot and booty that had passed along and knew that we had enjoyed a victory. Now we had to complete the journey and win the war.

The mistake the two leaders made was that they delayed in making a decision or, perhaps, it had taken them that time to recover their baggage and move it closer to their army. They took three days to reach our position by which time I had fortified it and made it impregnable by all but a direct attack. They should have raced down the road and attacked before we were ready. They did not. What they did do, and this was reported to us by Alessandro before he returned to Lucca, was to send five thousand of their men, mainly Savoyards, to Abruzzo where the duke there seemed to be considering joining the alliance. If he joined the Savoyards and the French then Naples might be assaulted from the east. I sent Luigi and Sebastian to give the information to King Charles. He was north of Rome with his army. He was a cautious king and he knew that he could find protection in Rome and keep the fighting far from his rich land. I knew that the bulk of the enemy still lay to the north of us, if we followed Amadeus then all our work thus far might be undone. Besides, as I told my leaders when we dined one night in the hall we had been given, King Charles had not had to lift a finger yet to defend his crown. His men could easily deal with five thousand men.

The enemy made a camp and waited. We had bloodied them three times and they were wary. I would have loved to be a fly on the walls in their debates. They would know it was me who had thwarted them and their plans. What would they do next? How would they outwit Giovanni Acuto? We needed to do nothing but simply wait. We had the Franco-Savoyard supplies and the Neapolitans were still sending us food. Naples was a very productive country. When Michael's men returned it was with the king's thanks for the warning and more wagon loads of food. Soon we would also need the second instalment of our pay but I was confident that would come. If we were not paid then we would simply melt away like a valley fog and Louis would have a free hand in Naples.

Robin and I frequently rode to spy out the men camped with Louis of Anjou. They were seen as invaders and had no cooperation from locals. Worse, the locals stole from the French and Italians who began to desert. As the weather worsened so dysentery and then the pestilence struck their camp. It was now winter and while not as cold as England, it could be as wet. Some of our men fell ill and a couple died but we knew that Louis of Anjou was having to bury ten to twenty men each day. When the news came that Amadeus of Savoy had died in Molise of illness not war, then the Savoyards simply deserted the army and Louis was left with an ever-dwindling force. He was forced to make an ignominious retreat back to France.

Our work was done and we were paid off. Astorre felt guilty that, his crossbowmen apart, he had little to do with the victory. I told him not to worry. We had profited greatly from the short war and with two chests of coins in our possession our extra efforts had been worthwhile.

It was as we headed back to Florence that I told them the intelligence I had gathered when I had spoken to the envoy from King Charles who rode to tell us that the contract was no longer needed.

"Louis, it seems, ransacked the French treasury when he was regent for his nephew, King Charles of France. The reason such a large army came south to claim the inheritance was because he funded it from his fraudulent activities. He and Bernabò are cut from the same cloth it seems."

"And what now?"

"He may well return again but if he does, he will not have Amadeus and his Savoyards with him and he will not try to come the same way. My guess would be through Bologna and Cesena. However, Michael, you need not worry. It is April now and by the time he reaches France, it will be summer. I would not expect any attempt before next year. Your child may well be toddling by the time we have to return to the field."

"King Charles will want us again?"

"And why would he not? We chased away an army three times our size and not an inch of Neapolitan land was lost."

Chapter 11

Donnina and William were delighted with the turn of events. Things could not have gone better for us. We had gained a herd of eighty horses as well as the weapons, armour and treasure we had taken. We arrived home in time to enjoy the summer sun and peace. Donnina was already spending my money and had plans for an extension to our home. So long as I had my quiet spaces, I was happy. I loved my girls but I liked having a place to escape to. William was investing the company profits in mercantile ventures. Our pot could only grow.

The first morning back my four men appeared, waiting for orders. I smiled, "You all did very well on the campaign and I have no need of your services for a day or so. Go into Florence and spend some of the coins you have earned."

They all seemed reluctant to obey me. Gianluca said, "But what if danger comes whilst we are away? We are your bodyguards and need to protect you."

"I promise that I will not leave the confines of the estate and besides, there are men here who were serving me as warriors when your mothers were still wiping your noses. Go. Enjoy your money and return back here in three days."

They did as I asked. I knew that what I needed was for my body to be rested and for me to recover. I was no longer a young man. I was never sure of my age but I had to be more than sixty years old and, these days, I felt it. The campaign had been short but sleeping rough and the miles we had ridden had taken it out of me. I had not been wounded but my body had suffered. I intended to use my baths and have Antonio arrange for a masseuse. Donnina might have arranged that but her head was filled with rooms, stones and marble and beautifying our already splendid home. She and the architect would be busy for days. When that was out of her head, I might get some attention but I needed to be healed now.

Antonio filled the bath for me and poured in the aromatics that would ease my muscles. He shook his head as he and the other servant undressed me, "You have lost weight, my lord. Did you not eat on the campaign?"

"We ate well but we also gobbled up the miles and wielding a sword takes it out of a man."

As I was helped into the steaming bath he said, "You are the captain of the White Company, my lord, you should not have to draw a sword. It is not as though you have anything to prove."

He was right. The only person I was trying to impress was me. It went back to the butts when I was a young archer. I was always trying to beat the other youths but even when I did, I was never satisfied. I wanted to beat myself. I was my own biggest critic. As the water soaked away the ingrained sweat and dirt from my body, I realised that whilst such over-achievement was understandable at the training ground, in battle it could be a fatal flaw. Perhaps, I should do as I had once done when fighting for Pisa, stand in a wagon and watch the battle. I would be better placed to see the right moment to launch a counterattack or reinforce a weak section of the line. Coreglia had been unique. The narrow road and terrain meant that it was a toe to toe battle. Had we been on a plain then it might have been different. Now that I had such an accomplished trumpeter as Zuzzo then I had far more control over my army. There might be a time when I needed to mount Caesar and ride but I doubted that I would need to stand and trade blows with an enemy. My body was not the body it had once been. When Robin had dared me to draw a bow, I had felt how much strength had left my body since Poitiers.

The masseuse was a man, a Greek, and he was good. He had powerful hands but he used them the way Zuzzo used his sword, with delicate touches. I actually fell asleep as he ministered to me. When I woke, I was covered in a towel and Antonio was standing over me and smiling. "That must have done you good, my lord, you slept like your daughter Anna, peacefully."

"Has the masseuse gone?"

"He has and I paid him. Will you want him again?"

"Make it a weekly event while I am at home."

"And will you venture forth once more this year, my lord?"

I shook my head, "I have no plans and unless Florence is attacked and calls me to fight, I cannot see myself stirring until next year. We profited well from this last war, Antonio."

"And we all benefit. Lady Donnina pays us well when you are successful. You have a happy estate, my lord."

His words reassured me, I knew the value of keeping people happy. We had retained more men in the company than most other bands of mercenaries and that was because they were paid well. Even so, I knew that some would leave to find other contracts. The pension I paid them to retain their services was generous but not as generous as serving in another company and using their skills to fight.

By the end of the week, I felt like a new man. My buttocks had recovered from the pummelling of the saddle and the muscular aches from wielding weapons had gone. We had not eaten badly on the road but Donnina knew my tastes and the weight I had lost soon returned. My four men also looked refreshed when they returned to serve me a few days later. All had spent some of the money that they had been paid. In Zuzzo's case it was clothes while the other three had bought better weapons and, in John and Robert's case, breastplates. I knew that the two of them would not have much money left for the breastplates were of the finest quality, but it showed their commitment to their trade. I had been the same and never spared spending that which would keep me safe on the battlefield. They came to my hall each morning and I was able to send them to practise their skills. Zuzzo was determined to make the two Englishmen as skilled as he was. I had still to find out how he had turned out the way he had, Gianluca and the other two had simple stories but Zuzzo's range of skills and the fact that he had travelled so wildly made me curious about him.

While a trickle of men left us so we had volunteers who came, mainly from England, to join the White Company. John and Robert had told me that we were legendary. When warriors gathered in ale houses and taverns, they spoke of the White Company who had yet to be defeated. That was not quite true but it explained the numbers who arrived. The archers were sent directly to Robin. I knew what to look for in an archer but Robin led them. The lances I interviewed. To be honest if they were

German or Hungarian, I often sent them to von Landau or another condottiero, but if they were Italian or English then I spoke with them and, generally, hired them.

John Coe was special. He and his squire arrived with just one horse between them. Peter, the squire, carried a frame on his back and was like a pack animal. The two looked a little like John and Robert had. Their clothes were dirty. Peter's buskins were almost worn through and they had the gaunt look of men who had not eaten well for some time. As I had done with others, I had the horse unsaddled and fed grain and watered. Peter's load was taken from him and John and Robert took him to the hall where they would be given food. Zuzzo and Gianluca hovered nearby until we were sure that this was not a papal assassin sent to kill me. When I was satisfied that I was in no danger, I nodded to Gianluca and Zuzzo who left. I sat with John Coe. Zuzzo fetched water for him to wash the dirt of the road from his hands and face while Carlo fetched food. Apart from saying their names and asking to be hired, John had said nothing. I waited until he had eaten and drunk before I interrogated him.

"So, John Coe, what is your story? I can see that you have no spurs and are not yet a knight but you have a squire. From his words and his manner I can tell that Peter is born of a good family. What brings you to Florence to seek work with the White Company?"

He smiled, "You are too modest, Sir John. You have a fine reputation. The king speaks well of you and as your recent battles with the Savoyards have shown you have lost none of your skills despite your advancing years."

I frowned, "While I do not wish honeyed words nor do I wish to be insulted, John Coe."

He gave me a smile, "And I merely speak the truth, Sir John. Your white-flecked beard bears testament to your experience. However, I apologize if I have insulted you. Peter and I are wellborn but both of us are the youngest sons of impoverished knights in England. I tried to make a life at the tourney but I was never quite good enough. There are fewer such opportunities. My father did well but that was in the time of the Black Prince. We made enough at one tourney in Calais and decided to make our fortune as swords for hire." He shook his head, "We made a mistake and joined a band of Flemish condottiere. Jean of Ypres was not an honourable man. He led us into Germany, took a contract and, when we won, he left with our gold. We were abandoned in Swabia. I can speak French but not German and we struggled. We lost Peter's horse in the winter and we were forced to labour for a Swabian farmer." He shook his head, "It taught me German but I learned to hate the Swabians. We left as soon as spring came and hearing of your success hoped that you might have a place for us in your company."

I nodded, "Normally I hire lances. A man at arms such as yourself, a squire and a foot soldier."

"Peter is as good a warrior as me. If you hire us then we will be as three such men for, as I understand it, a squire just tends to a horse. Peter can do that and use a weapon."

I smiled for I liked the way John Coe defended a position. I had decided to hire him but I wanted to push him. "And yet Peter has neither horse nor weapon."

"When next you go to war, my lord, that shall be remedied."

I laughed, "You have much to learn yet you have the right sort of attitude." I waved over the hovering Zuzzo, "Take our new lance to John and Robert. Have them find clothes and then have the two bathed and shaved. Two more Englishmen can only make us stronger."

He dropped to one knee and kissed the back of my hand, "I swear that neither of us shall let you down, my lord."

I waved him away. I need not have feared for John and Robert were quite protective of our new recruits. My two English bodyguards had been given old breastplates and now that they had bought their own, they gave the old ones to Peter and his master. All my bodyguards had a good collection of weapons and the two were well supplied. John Coe's horse was little better than a sumpter and it was Zuzzo who took it upon himself to give them two good horses we had taken in the last campaign. It was a little presumptuous but Zuzzo had saved my life at Coreglia and I owed him. The two men settled in and lived, not with the rest of the company, but at Casa Donnina. Robert and John became their mentors and teachers. Soon the two could speak Italian and when we went to war would be inculcated into the ways of the White Company.

It was September when we had our next visitor and it was another pair of Englishmen. The summer had been a hot one but there had been enough rain so that the crops that we grew on the estate were good ones and the harvest promised to be one of the best. I had begun to train again with my men and it was when I did so that I realised how good the four of them were. That was down to Zuzzo who had managed to improve even Gianluca who was already most skilful.

It was almost noon and we were getting ready to rest and take wine when two men rode through my gates. I recognised one as Geoffrey Chaucer, the English diplomat. The other was unknown to me. Chaucer worked for King Richard of England and I had served the man I still viewed as my king as faithfully as I could. I had never met him but I had followed his father the Black Prince and despite the bad feelings his father had felt towards me when I had left English service, I bore his son no malice. I wondered if the English king needed my help once more. I did what I could as both a spy and a diplomat. I found out information and sent it to the king and I made sure that he had allies in Italy. I still sent messages to my son, daughter-in-law and my manors in England. We had paths we could use and we used them. If Chaucer was here then this was something different.

Gianluca's hand went to his sword when he saw the two men approach and I restrained him, "One of these, at least, is a friend. I do not think that the poet, Chaucer wishes me harm." Gianluca nodded, "John, tell Lady Donnina that we have two guests and they will probably need rooms."

"Yes, my lord."

Chaucer had grown older. It had been almost ten years since I had last seen him at the wedding of Lionel, Duke of Clarence. He was no warrior but a diplomat and a poet. He dismounted and I embraced him for we were old friends. "Geoffrey, what brings you to this firepit in high summer and without servants?"

"We have servants but they are accommodated in a Florentine inn. I did not wish to impose upon your good lady. As for the timing of my visit," he lowered his voice, "I come at the bidding of King Richard. This is Thomas Wyndham who serves the Duke of Lancaster, John of Gaunt. The king wished me to make an introduction, nothing more. When I am done here then I can return to England. I will first travel to the tomb of Francesco Petrarch in Arquà."

Everyone knew of the great poet, Petrarch and I nodded, "That is close to Padua, my old comrade in arms, Giovanni d'Azzo Ubaldini lives there. I will write a letter of introduction. It will save you spending your own coins for rooms."

"You are too kind."

I was aware that the two Englishmen were sweating and Thomas Wyndham looked as though he wanted to speak about more important matters than his friend's visit to a tomb.

"Let us withdraw into my house. Robert, see to the horses. Zuzzo, bring the bags."

By the time we reached the house, Donnina had been apprised of the identity of our visitors and she was prepared. She curtsied, "My lords, it is good to see you again, Master Chaucer."

The old poet was flattered, "You remember me?"

"Of course, for you were amongst the most important men at the wedding of my sister to the Duke of Clarence. I am honoured that you visit us but I beg you to forgive the chaotic nature of our home. We are having some rebuilding work. Zuzzo, take the gentlemen's bags to the guest rooms in the east wing." As he nodded, she smiled, "It is cooler there. I can see that you are not accustomed to the sun as my husband is. And now, if you will excuse me, I will see to the preparations of food and leave you to speak to Sir John."

When she had gone Geoffrey said, "She is a force of nature, Sir John. You are a lucky man."

I nodded, "I know and now if you will accompany me to the courtyard, we can enjoy some iced wine and you can tell me what King Richard wishes of me."

Once in the cool courtyard where the fountain's tinkle masked our words from any who might eavesdrop, we sat on the cushioned seats. Refreshments had already been prepared for me and the servants merely trebled the quantity. I was ready for it after an hour of hard exercise with swords. When the servants had gone, we ate and I studied the man who served John of Gaunt. He was a handsome young man with dark hair. He had eyes that my wife would call wild eyes and he had a nervous energy about him. He ate as though it was merely fuel and quaffed the wine so quickly that I knew he had not tasted it. He was desperate for the business of the day to begin and I decided to toy with him.

"You will like Padua, Geoffrey, and now that she and Venice have won the war with Genoa then prosperity has returned."

He nodded, "In truth, Sir John, I am anxious to return home. I began, a couple of years ago, a work which will be my legacy. It is a series of stories about pilgrims."

I smiled and shook my head, "You should speak to my trumpeter, Zuzzo, he is the one who reads and likes poetry. I do not understand it. I am a simple knight."

"You are in it."

"Sir John Hawkwood?" My eyes narrowed.

He realised his mistake and shook his head, "No, my lord, but every writer takes inspiration from the people he meets and you impressed me. I used you as the model for the knight in my story."

I smiled, "Then that is good but I fear it will be a dull story if I am the inspiration."

Thomas Wyndham had endured enough of what he clearly thought were banalities, "My lord, we have travelled many miles to speak to you and I would know if you can be of service. I would tell you what is required of you and then we can complete my quest."

I turned and gave him the kind of stare I used to give my archers when I commanded a company of archers.

He quailed, "I am sorry and I know that you are being hospitable but if you cannot help us then I will have to try to complete my task alone."

Geoffrey smiled, "Sir John, you must excuse Thomas. This is his first appointed task for the duke and he is keen to complete his mission."

I nodded and deliberately turned away from the ambitious young man. It would do him no harm to have to wait. "So, Geoffrey, what does England require of me?"

"King Richard is grateful for the service you did by defeating Louis of Anjou. He seeks an alliance with King Charles. You are the key to such an agreement."

"That I can understand but Thomas here," I did not look at him, "serves the Duke of Lancaster. You could have brought the message and then gone to Padua. Why does the Duke of Lancaster need my help?"

The poet sighed, "The duke would reclaim his Castilian lands. To that end, he needs the support of the pope and you have done service for the pope too. It seemed right that you should combine the two. I hope you are not offended."

"By the request? No, but by the rude manner in which it was demanded."

The young man bowed his head, "Forgive me, Sir John, I am your guest and I know how to behave. Perhaps it was the heat for I am unused to such a sun."

It was an olive branch and I smiled and took it, "Of course, I will help the duke and the king. I am still an Englishman and whilst I have not been home since Poitiers it does not take away my loyalty." They both looked relieved, "Be aware, however, that my agreement to help you does not guarantee success. I have never met the King of Naples and having been successful on his behalf does not mean he will listen to me."

Chaucer had been a diplomat and he smiled, "His enemy is Louis of Anjou and by association King Charles of France whose country financed the invasion. They share a mutual enemy. The pope is another matter." He was warning his young companion that John of Gaunt's request might end in failure. Castile was closer to Rome than to England. The pope was a political animal and it would not be right or wrong that helped him to make his decision, it would be the enlargement of his power.

I leaned forward, "Let me be clear about this, Geoffrey. You shall not be with us in either Rome or Naples?" He nodded, "Then this young man will be the one who delivers King Charles' answer back to England."

Geoffrey was a clever man and he picked up on the implied question. To whom did Thomas owe loyalty? The king or the king's uncle? "Do not worry, Sir John, Thomas here may be the duke's man but he knows that his future prosperity lies with King Richard."

The petulance returned, "You talk of me as though I am not here."

"Then give your thoughts voice and join in the conversation. Trust me, young man, you are about to embark on a perilous road. There is the physical one through an Italy where the next ambush is just around the corner and the one that the poet here might write about in his stories, the road to success. Choose the wrong master, especially when it is a king or a prince, and any mistake could result in the loss of a head."

"Yet you have survived in what must be the most perilous of professions."

"And there is a simple answer to that, I am the best but when I was your age I was still learning. I was making mistakes in a smaller pool than the one in which you are about to dip your toes. Are you ready for this? I can attempt to make an alliance with King Charles and speak to Pope Urban. You and your servants could simply head back to England when I return with the agreement."

He shook his head, "My lord, I am touched by your concern but I have set my foot on this path. I am no storyteller like Master Chaucer and I am no warrior like you. If I am to have success then it must be as a trusted servant to the king."

"My concern is self-centred, Thomas Wyndham. I would rather not ride through Italy with a wet behind-the-ears youth. If I went with just my men then I would have an easier and safer passage."

An uncomfortable silence descended but I did not regret my bluntness. Chaucer was the diplomat and he eased the situation, "Sir John, you will not have to do this altruistically, King Richard has sent this purse for you." He handed me a purse. I opened it. It was filled with the new Venetian ducats. They had only been minted a year ago. My eyebrows were raised and he said, "The Doge wished for a trade agreement with England," he shrugged, "he does not use our waters much but he wanted the king's assurance that our pirates would be contained. They were a gift, a secret gift. King Richard sent some of them to you for here they are a more common form of currency."

"They may be but these are the first I have seen. I would have served my king without payment but I never refuse gold. And you, Thomas, it is good that you are loyal to the duke but he is an old man. What happens when he dies? King Richard is the man to follow, as I have."

"I know but I will do this one thing for the duke. As for my safety, Sir John, fear not, I have a sword and whilst I am not a warrior I know how to fight. It may not be the clean fighting seen in tourneys but I am guessing that the men we fight will use any means that they can to overcome us."

I smiled, "I may have misjudged you, Thomas." A servant appeared and caught my eye, "Come, food is ready and you will meet my wife. A word of caution, Thomas, my wife is the cleverest person I know. Do not patronise her nor try to keep anything from her. I do not."

"Yes, Sir John and if she is from the loins of Bernabò Visconti then I can understand your words."

There were just the four of us in the small dining room we used for lunches. Two of my daughters would normally eat with us but my wife knew that matters of high politics might be discussed and she would need all of her attention on the matter at hand.

"I enjoy reading, Master Chaucer, will your new work be in English or Italian?"

"English, my lady, for it is a tale of England and the people who inhabit that isle."

"A shame for I cannot read English. If you would send a copy to my husband though, he could read it to me?"

My heart sank for whilst I could read, I did not enjoy the process but I smiled and said, "Only if it is convenient."

Master Chaucer beamed, "The story is written in episodes, my lady and Sir John is mentioned, as a character, you understand, I will send that one to him when I have finished the process."

"The process? Do you not just write and then it is done?"

"No, my lady. I re-read and make changes. I ask advice from other writers and when I am satisfied with it then it is ready for the wider world to read my humble offering."

"And I look forward to seeing how my husband is portrayed."

"Why, as a most chivalrous knight, of course."

She turned her attention to Thomas. Geoffrey had been the first course of her conversational meal. He had been the one to amuse the taste buds but Thomas was the meat on the bone. "And you, Thomas, you serve two masters, a difficult trick is it not?"

He was about to swallow and her words, allied with her hawk-like eyes almost made him choke, "Have wine, Thomas, before you answer my wife." I was giving him the chance to compose himself.

He did so and said, "I owe the Duke of Lancaster much, my lady. My father died in his service and my mother relied upon the generosity of the duke to bring me and my sisters up. He had me educated so that I could read and write and brought up as a gentleman. I would not be here today but for him." The young man was clearly trying to show us that he was well connected. "The duke is the king's uncle."

She was enjoying herself, "Thomas, you seem like an earnest young man. I am a Visconti and I have seen people who tried to serve my father and my uncle or my father and my cousin. Most of those who did so are now dead. Had they chosen one or the other then they might have had a chance of survival." My wife kept up to date on all the politics of every kingdom. She had seen how her father kept abreast of world events, "There are men in England who oppose the king and I do not just mean those foolish peasants who thought that they had rights, I mean lords who seek the crown. All it takes from the duke is one misplaced word or a conversation with an enemy and he could fall foul of the king."

Her words had an effect and I saw him reflect on his position. "I am young, my lady, and I have much to learn. Perhaps I was meant to come here and continue my education."

She laughed, "How my father would laugh at such words. He thought me an empty-headed pretty face."

I put my hand on hers and bringing it to my lips kissed its back, "And how wrong he was."

She then spent the rest of the meal impressing both of our visitors with her knowledge of the papal and Neapolitan courts. Every visitor of note who passed through Florence was invited to dine in my home and my wife made them pay for her hospitality with titbits of information. Her reasons were, of course, financial. They helped the White Company and me. When she married me, she became my partner.

In the afternoon I walked my woods with the two men. It was cool there and the hunter in me enjoyed the quiet. We clarified our quest and made the arrangements. Geoffrey would leave the next day with my letter to Giovanni and I would take my men as an escort and travel first to Rome and thence to Naples. My buttocks would be sore once more.

When we returned to my home, I excused myself. I had a letter to write and I needed to speak to my men. I think the two Englishmen were happy to have the time to talk about the words that had been spoken. Thomas Wyndham was about to have a lesson in life without Geoffrey Chaucer as his guide. It was like paddling in the edge of the sea and then walking to a quay and jumping into the deepest part. It would be a shock to his system.

I wrote the letter in Italian. I was not sure if Geoffrey could read Italian but I knew that Giovanni would struggle to read English. That done I sent for my four men and we met by the lemon trees and the fountain. The four were comfortable with me. Coreglia and Fiumalbo had bonded us. Men who fight together and risk their lives for one another are not bound by normal conventions. I was still their lord but I was also a sword brother and that meant an easy air between us when we spoke.

"We ride tomorrow, first to Rome and then to Naples. We will not need plate or lances for we do not go to war. This is a diplomatic venture." They looked at me in anticipation. They knew there would be more. "We are to escort a young Englishman and his servants."

I sipped my wine to allow them to ask me questions. They did not disappoint. "Can they speak Italian, my lord?"

"No Gianluca, not to any great extent."

"Can they fight?"

I looked at Zuzzo. Although he had been a performer, he was the most martially minded of my men, Gianluca included. "The young man says he can handle a sword, as for the servants…" I shrugged, "we shall see."

Gianluca was the captain of my guards and he said, firmly, "Then we will have to assume they will not. Zuzzo, and I will ride at the rear and John and Robert can be the scouts."

The three named nodded as Gianluca gave them their orders. They liked the simplicity and clarity of the instructions. They each knew that their position had with it a different responsibility. The two Englishmen would need to be ready to react quickly to any danger ahead and to be able to sniff out such danger. The ones at the rear would take charge if we were ambushed. By implication, I would be relegated to watching Thomas Wyndham. The servants would have to fend for themselves.

Zuzzo said, "You know that until we get south of Montepulciano, we will be in lands that bear no love for Sir John Hawkwood?"

"I do and for that reason, I will not ride Caesar and we will travel in clothes without marks. Plain clothes and simple weapons."

Gianluca sighed, "We have a journey of three hundred miles or more. Even beyond Montepulciano, we will be in danger."

"We will pay for our accommodation." The Venetian ducats, or a couple of them, at least, would be put to good use. I also had plans to milk a little more money from our two former employers. I would serve King Richard but I would also try to fatten the purse of the White Company.

"When do we leave?"

"I want you, Zuzzo, when we have finished here, to ride with Master Wyndham and fetch the servants hither. They can sleep in the stable so that we may leave early tomorrow."

Gianluca grinned. He always looked like a wolf when he did so even if he did not mean to. "And we can gauge the mettle of the men."

"That never hurts. Is all well?"

The four nodded. There were things I had not said like: choose a good sumpter, pack food, ale and wine, ensure we have vinegar and honey, and secrete weapons where they would not be seen. Had I done so then they might have been insulted.

Chapter 12

Despite Zuzzo's warning, I knew that the first day, at least, would be safe for we were in Florentine land. It allowed Gianluca and my trumpeter to get to know Ned and Edgar, the two servants. I guessed that someone other than Thomas Wyndham had chosen them, possibly the duke himself. Both came from the north, the land around Burscough in the heart of the duke's domain. They had been soldiers and had served in Castile with the duke. They were almost as old as Geoffrey Chaucer and I could see why they had given up the bills that they had used when they had served the duke. Both were widowers and had little for them in England. Ned's daughters had married and Edgar's sons had died in battle. They were both happy to serve the duke even as servants. My men got on with them. Thanks to John and Robert when the men had arrived, conversation had been easy and my men had managed to teach the two men some Italian. As we headed south, I heard Zuzzo teaching them more. Zuzzo's travels had made him multilingual and whilst his English was imperfect, it allowed him to teach the two men the words they would need should danger come. For their part, Ned and Edgar enjoyed learning a new skill. I tried the same with Thomas Wyndham but with less success. I did not have Zuzzo's patience.

We reached the Holy City without incident but that term was a misnomer. It was far from holy. I had not yet been on a crusade but I doubted that Jerusalem would live up to that appellation either. Rome was about power and control. Popes were elected and were not kings but, in many ways, they wielded far more power than any king could hope for. They had the power of excommunication. They could deny even a king's passage into heaven. The pope answered to God and yet received revenue from every Christian kingdom in the land. Indulgences were sold and that was highly profitable. As we headed for the gate in the Leonine Wall which represented the rather unprepossessing entrance to St Peter's Basilica, I reflected that I had suffered from a pope's ire and been excommunicated. Although it had been rescinded, for a short time I had been a young man thus excluded from God's grace. I wondered if I might view such an act more seriously now that I was older and nearing death.

Zuzzo had been to Rome before and he identified features of the heart of Christendom. He pointed to the wall which was clearly not Roman, "The wall was built after the Saracens raided the church and took all the treasures away. It is not as sturdy as the Roman ones but it would hold an enemy up. What say you, Sir John?"

I reined in to give thought to my answer, "It is impressive but it would need to be continuously manned to be of any defence to the church. I doubt that the pope has such an army."

Zuzzo grinned, "Aye, you are right and that is why they have converted what used to be Emperor Hadrian's mausoleum into the Castel Sant'Angelo. It is a fortress and if the Leonine wall fell then it would be a refuge for the pope. The Aurelian wall that surrounds the city on the western side is a stronger defence for it has lasted many years."

We urged our horses on. The gates were manned and although we were scrutinised as we passed through the gate, we were not hindered. The rider who galloped and passed us as we headed south told me that our arrival would be reported to the pope.

From a distance, the church looked impressive. Thomas Wyndham said so, "I thought the abbey of Edward the Confessor was the most splendid church on earth but this one dwarfs it."

Zuzzo shook his head, "I am afraid, Master Wyndham, that appearances can be deceptive. The walls were badly made and at one point they are leaning alarmingly. It holds up to four thousand when the pope speaks but I would not be one of them for fear that the sheer numbers might make the walls fall."

Zuzzo might have been right but from a distance, it looked magnificent. The obelisk erected by Emperor Caligula, covered in the hieroglyphics used by the Egyptians drew our eye, as did the ancient Fontana della Pigna in the courtyard where we dismounted. Leaving our horses with my men Thomas and I prepared to enter the church. I did not expect to see the pope but we had to announce our presence and seek an audience. We passed the new statue of St Peter cast by the artist Arnolfo di

Cambio. I knew why it had been made so large and was placed where it was. Popes wanted the visitors to Rome to be in awe of the line that went back to the time of Christ. They were seeking reverence through association.

This time, as we dismounted and headed across the courtyard, we were stopped. A pair of papal guards walked up to us and asked, "What is the purpose of your visit, Sir John?"

I had been right and they had been forewarned.

"We are here to seek an audience with Pope Urban."

"Come with us."

We were led, not to the basilica but to a smaller building standing in the courtyard. It was unadorned with frescoes and statues. To me, it looked like a more functional building and I was proved correct when we entered a room with clerks and clerics. A couple of cardinals were there but also Giacomo di Lucca, the papal envoy who had been our conduit to the pope. When he approached us and seemed unsurprised by our presence, I saw that we had been victims to a game played by the papacy. We had been identified and the guards could have brought us directly to Giacomo but they wanted us to feel small. It might have worked with Thomas who had almost hidden behind me when we had been led from the courtyard.

"Sir John, a most unexpected pleasure." He smiled but it was not with his eyes. A visit from a condottiero was always viewed with suspicion. "What brings you to Rome?"

I could play games too, "We seek an audience with Pope Urban." Neither my face nor my manner gave anything away.

"His Holiness is a busy man. You may have to wait."

I waved a hand as I smiled with my lips but not my eyes, "I have never been to Rome and this seems like a good time to do so. We will stay in the city and await the pope's pleasure."

I could see that I had discomfited the cleric. He had no idea who Thomas Wyndham was, not even his name and men like Giacomo di Lucca liked to be in total control.

Giacomo pointed south, "There is an inn close to the Piazza Navona, the *'Red Grapes'*. Mention my name and you will not be robbed. We shall send for you."

"Thank you." We bowed and I turned to leave. Thomas was still staring at the men who were scribing away like so many tonsured ants. "Come, we will have the opportunity for a closer look when we return."

The heat from the sun hit us as we left the cool shade of the office. I knew, as we mounted our horses, that we would be followed. This was Rome and there were more spies and servants of the papacy than ordinary folk. I did not mind. Knowing we would be followed stopped me from getting a crick in my neck seeking them.

I said nothing to my men as we crossed the bridge by the Castel Sant'Angelo. "Zuzzo, we seek the Piazza Navona."

He snorted, "The Stadium of Domitian was becoming a ruin and so they renamed it. Why do we go there, Sir John?"

"We have been told to wait there at the *'Red Grapes'* and we will be summoned."

"I know not the place. We shall see."

Zuzzo was a sceptical and careful man. He had been one of my better appointments.

In the event, the inn was clean and looked safe. There were stables and our animals would be looked after. I guessed, after speaking with Carlos, the innkeeper, that it was owned by the pope and used as a place where guests could be kept safe but not close to the basilica. I relaxed a little but, as we unpacked in the three rooms we had been allocated, I cautioned my men, "Say nothing of our quest." I tapped my head, "Keep those thoughts to yourself. Until we are summoned, we will visit the sights of antiquity. Zuzzo shall be our guide."

He nodded, "Keep your daggers to hand and your purses well-guarded. This inn seems safe enough but the city is another matter."

We dined in the inn and found the food palatable. Being tired we retired early. Ned slept behind the door of our chamber. It was his choice but it marked him as a careful man. The protection would be needed not for me but for the naïve young Englishman.

No one came for us by the time we had enjoyed a hearty breakfast and so I decided to visit the ancient ruins. New buildings had sprung up around the ancient forum and when we reached the Campidoglio, formerly known as the Capitoline Hill, we found a lively market. Despite the array of goods on offer, it was as well that all had heeded Zuzzo's advice. The cutpurse who tried to take John Edingham's purse found himself pinioned by my two Englishmen.

Zuzzo's stiletto was at his throat, "My friend, find another pitch for if we see you again then it will be more than your belt we cut." His hand dropped like a flash of lightning and the razor-sharp edge sliced through the man's belt. It fell with a clatter to the cobbles.

Gianluca put his foot on the man's dagger which had fallen from its scabbard, "And we will retain this little toy as a memento."

The man reached down and grabbed his belt. He waited until he was twenty paces away before he gave us the sign of the fork. He was cursing us.

Zuzzo laughed and tossed the knife to John, "An extra knife is always welcome."

The other thieves, and there were many of them, in the market had seen the incident and we were not bothered again. Word would spread amongst the robbers of Rome that there was a band of men who were not to be touched. By the time we reached the inn, late in the afternoon after an expensive and not particularly tasty meal, we found that a messenger had been and we were to present ourselves at St Peter's the next day at sext. Either the pope was a late riser or he wished to consult with his advisers before meeting with us. I did not mind. The meal we ate in the inn seemed all the tastier having been overcharged for poor food at the Campidoglio.

As we ate, in the almost deserted dining room, we spoke of the day's events. Thomas seemed particularly disturbed by the incident, "If I had been by myself, I should have been robbed."

Ned shook his head, "Master Thomas, we are your guardians and you would never be alone. We are beholden to our two countrymen for they are younger and have quicker reactions than we two old warhorses but you would be safe. Edgar and I know foreigners, they are not to be trusted." He suddenly realised what he had said and turned to Gianluca and Zuzzo, "Present company excepted. No offence was meant."

Zuzzo laughed, "We have the same opinion of Englishmen," he paused dramatically, "present company excepted."

The invitation to meet the pope had been quite specific, Thomas and me. We decided that Gianluca would take my men and see if there were any men worth hiring in Rome. We all doubted the likelihood but my four men needed occupation and, in their wanderings, they might pick up valuable intelligence. It was worth a try. Edgar and Ned would wait for us outside St Peter's. They had already proved to me that they were both good men.

Even I made an effort to dress well for the audience. I might have a more practical view of the pontiff but that did not mean I did not recognise his position. With groomed hair, my best hose and tunic, we rode across the bridge to await the pope's pleasure. Ned and Edgar had found a small bar, a cart with an awning, and they would wait there in the shade of the wall and the awning. They could view the gate and observe all those who entered. Once more we sought intelligence. The slightest nugget could prove useful.

As we strode across the courtyard I said, "We may have to wait. I know we are on time but that does not mean we will have an audience at sext. Popes, like dukes and kings, sometimes like to play games. You speak little Italian and I will do the speaking." He suddenly stopped and stared at me. I shook my head, "If you cannot trust me then we should depart now and head for Naples. I will say what is needed and I will translate for you."

He saw that he had little other choice and nodded, "I would that we succeed."

"To that end, I am not confident. I cannot see what Pope Urban has to gain for agreeing to your master's suit but we can only try." The reality was that I knew the pope would do nothing. John of Gaunt now had no power. When his nephew had been a minor then he had power. I also knew, from some archers we had hired who had served in Castile with the duke previously, that he had little chance of winning over the Castilians' support for his claim to the crown. The pope would smile sympathetically and nod in the right places but the only way his support could be gained would be with a chest of gold that we did not have.

Giacomo met us with a smile, "Come and I will take you to the antechamber. The Holy Father has many supplicants and we may have to wait but we can talk while we do so."

I knew then that we would have to wait and that the pope's man would seek to extract information. It would be like a battle but one of words and I was confident that I would be able to handle it.

We were alone in the antechamber and I waited for him to speak to me. Alarmingly he spoke in English and to Thomas. Giacomo was clever and had recognised an innocent abroad. I could guard my words but Thomas could not.

"So, Thomas, how long have you served the duke?"

I saw Thomas grin. He was flattered. He would not have to sit there like a piece of furniture, "Since childhood really, my lord."

"I am not a lord, Thomas, call me Giacomo."

Once more Thomas was flattered and I found myself admiring the papal envoy more and more. He was using an old trick and it was working. He was feigning friendship by the use of his Christian name. It was Thomas' naïvety that saved him for he just rambled on about being a young man in the duke's household. It was as though he had forgotten our mission to Naples. I felt relieved.

"And I hope, when we return from Naples, that I will be rewarded."

It was his last sentence that sank us. I had been ready to intervene had he begun to talk of a time after Rome but he just jumped to it. Giacomo's eyes widened in triumph. He glanced at me and rose, "I will see if the pope is ready yet."

I knew he would be. The delay and the interrogation had been for a purpose. When we were alone I shook my head.

"What did I do wrong, Sir John?"

"You told him that we were going to Naples."

"But he and the king are allies. The information cannot hurt us."

"Neither the pope nor his envoy needed to know, that is the point. You have much to learn, my young friend. From now on choose every word as you would a morsel from the platter of someone you know is trying to poison you."

We were kept waiting just long enough for Giacomo to tell the pope what Thomas had said. The smiling envoy opened the door, "I pray you to enter, his Holiness will see you now."

The room was empty save for a tonsured clerk with a wax tablet. The pope was on a throne and next to him was a table with a jug of wine. There were no chairs and we would stand. The room was plainly decorated and that surprised me. I realised, after the meeting, that it was deliberate. We were not important enough to impress. Thomas was a minor Englishman and I was a sword for hire who could be bought and sold like a whore.

He held out his hand, richly bejewelled with rings and we kissed it. There was a stronger smell of perfume than in a gathering of ladies in William Turner's home. Was he trying to hide some ailment? I was a suspicious-minded man.

"So, Sir John, what brings you here? Your service to me is complete although as we hear that Louis of Anjou is with his nephew King Charles of France raising another army, it might well be that we need your swords and lances next year."

"I am here as an Englishman, Pope Urban. I am not a condottiero today but an English knight. The Duke of Lancaster asks for your help to recover his Castilian lands. They are his by right and he is denied them." I bowed my head and spread my arms, "It is a simple request, Pope Urban." I translated for Thomas. It served two purposes. It told the pope that Thomas did not speak Italian and it allowed the pope to weigh my words.

"Not as simple as you might think, Sir John. The Castilian king, John of Trastámara, is popular with the Castilians and Leonese whom he rules. In addition, as you might know, I excommunicated the last king, Peter the Cruel and he was the duke's father-in-law. You can see the difficulty I have with this."

I translated and Thomas said, "But Queen Constance is not her father and the Duke of Lancaster is a good man."

I did not even get the chance to translate before the pope answered. He could speak English. "Your fervour and passion do you great credit, Master Thomas. Let me think about this and give it due examination. When you return from Naples, I will have an answer for you."

Thomas had learned enough Italian to answer the pope himself, "Thank you, Holy Father."

"And now, if you would wait without, I need to have words with Sir John." He smiled, "I wish to thank him for his services to the church."

I knew it was something else but Thomas did not and he left us. Once alone the pope reverted to Italian. I think he was more comfortable in that language.

"This visit to Naples, Sir John, what is its purpose?"

I could see no reason to lie for the diplomatic mission could not possibly hurt the pope. "King Richard wishes an alliance with Naples. As you know, your Holiness, England has a legitimate claim to parts of France which are denied us. You know the phrase, '*my enemy's enemy is my friend*' well, King Richard wishes to build an alliance of like-minded nations. I know that France is also a thorn in the side of the legitimate papacy."

He smiled, "The Bible tells us that we must hope that sinners repent and come back to the flock. I am the shepherd of the church and King Charles of France is young. Young men make mistakes. As I recall, you made mistakes when you were young. If King Charles sends an army to Italy, then I will oppose him but, thus far, it is only words that are being gathered."

The silence felt awkward to me but I could not fill it. I had to wait while the pope chose his words, "King Charles of Naples, I have heard, conspires with my enemies." He shrugged, "I have many and not all are open in their opposition to me. I have heard that some of my cardinals also conspire to overthrow me and bring in the imposter to replace me."

"Surely King Charles would not support Pope Clement, your Holiness, Queen Joanna gave the imposter a home in Naples."

"That surprised me too, Sir John, and that is why, when you visit Naples, I would have you keep your ears open for any news that might concern me. I will give your young friend his answer when you return." He nodded to Giacomo who approached me and held out a purse. "This is for your inconvenience and silence. You now work for the church."

It was clearly a command. If I did not agree then it could have dire consequences not only for me but the White Company. I nodded, "Of course, Pope Urban." I put the purse on my belt and, after the pope had blessed me, I left with Giacomo.

As we neared the door he said, in my ear, "A wise decision, Sir John, and one that will bring both work and gold to the White Company."

Thomas waited until we were outside before he spoke, quietly to me, "Well, Sir John?"

"You have, it seems, dropped me in the murky waters of Italian politics." I smiled, "I know not why I complain for I chose this snake pit as my home. Come, we should pack and head for Naples. Mayhap that part of our quest may be simpler."

I did not think it would be. If King Charles was plotting against the pope, then any alliance between England and Naples could jeopardise the young English king. I would have to walk as though I was creeping through an enemy camp. I was now Pope Urban's spy.

Chapter 13

The journey south would be through unknown land to me. We headed for the coast road. It was more twisting and turning than the alternate route, however, the sea breeze was cooling. The Englishmen were suffering in the sun as they were unused to the heat and the breeze made life more bearable for them. The purse I had from the pope was papal coinage and that seemed to smooth our way as we headed south. We stayed at monasteries when we could and better quality inns when we could not. Thomas had seen the virtue in learning a new language and after Rome, he was a more diligent pupil and took advice from all of us, but he was a slow learner. Even Ned and Edgar were more proficient in speaking Italian than the Englishman. If he was going to be of service to the Duke of Lancaster, he would need to be far more adventurous in learning new skills.

It was late afternoon when we reached the kingdom. Naples showed its Norman influence. King Charles was not Norman but the men who had wrested the land from the Moors and the Lombards had been and the Hautevilles had ensured that the southern part of Italy was Norman.

My name was known and when we entered the city I was greeted with smiles. The men who stood a watch on the gates and the walls knew that it was my company's efforts around Bagni di Lucca that had saved Neapolitan land from war. The disappointing news was that King Charles was in Capri where he kept a summer home that was cooler than the melting pot of Naples. A messenger was sent to the commander of the garrison and we waited in the cool of the gatehouse. I was not offended by being made to wait. The lowly guard on the gate could not decide where I should stay.

"Captain Giovanni, I hoped I would get to see you."

I recognised the voice but the man who had served in the White Company before Cesena was now wearing the fine clothes of a nobleman. "Alberico da Barbiano? A captain now?"

He nodded and we clasped arms as old comrades do, "After I left you, I headed south and gathered men of Italian blood who were like me. Men who had been condottiere. I formed the Company of St George and the King of Naples employed me. Had you not been so successful in the north then we might have fought alongside one another. Sergeant Giuseppe says that you wish to meet the king?"

I nodded, "I come here not as the Captain of the White Company but as an Englishman serving King Richard."

"Then you shall have rooms in the palace and I will send word to King Charles. It will give me the chance to speak to you while we dine." He looked like an eager puppy reunited with his master, "This is a most happy meeting. The Fates have, indeed, been kind."

He led us through the crowded streets of the prosperous and busy city. I could see why the jewel that was Naples was so desirable that Louis of Anjou would bring forty thousand men to take it. I knew, as we headed for the palace that he would return.

"Will it take long for a message to reach the king?"

Alberico shook his head, "A ship will reach Capri by this evening and we will have an answer by the morning." He stopped, "The king may choose not to see you, Sir John."

I wanted to know the reason but I did not want it to be discussed in public, "We will talk later," I lowered my voice, "when we are alone."

"Of course."

It was clear that Alberico commanded in the absence of the king and that made sense. His company would be the best soldiers in Naples. Even the king's bodyguards would be inferior in skills to Alberico's Italians. There might be Neapolitan nobles who were better mounted and equipped but Alberico's lances would win any tourney just as mine would. We were given good rooms. Thomas and I were given our own and our men shared two rooms and each had a bed. Our horses were well stabled and the ostler, knowing that we were friends of Alberico's, promised them the best of care. Thus far it was a better reception than the one we had received in Rome.

My room and that of Thomas were adjacent to one another and I said, as Alberico hovered nearby, "I will fetch you when it is time to dine, Thomas, until then rest for your service to King Richard resumes on the morrow."

"Thank you, Sir John. I can see why the king trusts you for you have eased my passage and I do not know how I would have survived without your help."

"It is nothing." When he closed his door Alberico followed me into the chamber where my bags had been deposited by the servant.

He shook his head as I sat on the only chair in the chamber, "He is truly an innocent abroad, Sir John. Has he begun to shave?"

I laughed as the Italian poured us each a glass of iced wine, "I suppose we must all have looked that young once." I took the glass which was of good quality and raised it, "To old friends."

"To old friends." He drank and asked, "How are Giovanni, Dai and Robin?"

"Giovanni now commands the men of Padua. Dai has returned to England and Robin," I chuckled, "Robin never changes. He is what he is and I am grateful that he commands my archers."

"I have a good company but, being all Italian, what I miss are your archers. It is why the White Company is so successful."

I nodded, "We have little time alone, Alberico. Let us save the mutual compliments until we are in a public place where we cannot speak our secrets. Why might the king not see me? Is it me or King Richard?"

He shook his head, "He has nothing but praise for you and I know not his feelings in the matter of England but he went to Capri to meet people." He shook his head, "I know not who they are but when he took only his bodyguards and went by sea I wondered. King Charles is a complicated man and a ruthless one. He had Queen Joanna strangled you know?" I nodded. "Aye well, the likes of you and I serve to win countries and land so that men like King Charles can rule them. I say this so you do not take offence if he says that he cannot meet with you."

I nodded, somewhat relieved that I was not the cause, "Or we may be left to cool our heels here until the king returns."

Alberico brightened, "And that would be no bad thing for I could enjoy your company a little longer."

"Aye, I was sorry when you left me."

"Many of us left after Cardinal Robert de Genève ordered the massacre. We knew you had nothing to do with it but so long as you served him then other atrocities would follow."

"And now we fight against him. Strange is it not?"

"It is and now I will let you refresh yourself and I will ensure that food and drink are prepared for you and your men."

As I washed myself I thought about the way that Fate works. I had genuinely been sorry when Alberico left the company as was Giovanni. We had been grooming him to become a leader of lances. Pope Clement in his former guise as Robert de Genève had much to answer for. It would be no hardship to cool our heels in Naples but I had been away long enough already. I wanted to be in my Florentine home. I found myself missing Donnina. She had become the friend and confidante that I had always needed. Until she came into my life I did not know how much. Even Robin and Giovanni could never be as close as she. Dai, Sir Andrew and the others who had left my company showed me that all those who served with me had a limited life but Donnina would be part of me and my life until death and that was a comfort.

Alberico was a soldier and he recognised that my four bodyguards and Thomas' servants were all soldiers and they dined with us. They were not on the high table where Alberico had invited senior churchmen and nobles, but they were present and I saw the gratitude on their faces. In Ned and Edgar's case it was something that would never have happened had they travelled alone with Thomas.

The Bishop of Naples said Grace and as he was seated next to Thomas, began a conversation. It was almost amusing to watch the young Englishman try to understand the bishop and then reply with the handful of phrases he had learned. I felt sorry for the young man and I translated for him.

When the bishop was satisfied with Thomas' answers to his questions he said to me, "And how is it that you and Captain Alberico are such friends for it is clear that you are and yet, as rival captains, I would have expected enmity."

I looked at Alberico who waved an arm and said, "You are my mentor, Sir John, give the bishop his answer."

"Firstly, Bishop, Alberico served with me and there are bonds formed when men do that but secondly, we condottiero do not bear grudges. I have fought alongside men like von Landau but if I had to, I would fight against him. We are professional soldiers and we behave professionally. The day a condottiero takes things personally is the time to retire."

The answer seemed to satisfy the bishop who said, "If you do not mind me saying so, Sir John, those grey hairs upon your head suggest that you might have sheathed your sword for good many years since."

"I can still wield a sword but, more importantly, these grey hairs are the evidence of my experience. I am a condottiero and I command much as Captain Alberico does. The difference is that he is younger and has a longer career ahead of him. I might have seen more than sixty summers but that does not mean I am in my dotage."

I think the bishop thought he might have offended me for he blustered, "I am sorry, Sir John, I meant no offence."

"And none was taken. As Captain Alberico well knows, a condottiero who does not keep his mind constantly active as well as his body risks losing on that most important of places, the battlefield."

Alberico said, "And from the reports I have heard, at the Battle of Coreglia, it was Sir John and those four men you see eating yonder, Bishop, who bore the brunt of the fighting."

I shrugged as the bishop looked towards my four bodyguards, "It was more of a skirmish than a battle for the passes in the mountains mean that only a handful of men can fight at any one time."

"And will Louis of Anjou come again?"

Every eye was on me and the conversation on the table ceased as the bishop posed his question.

I nodded, "Having seen your rich city and knowing that Louis of Anjou either risks wresting the crown of France from his nephew's head or marching south to take Naples, I would suggest that he will come again but this time will not risk the mountains. That may have been the arrogance of Visconti who thought he ruled the passes but the next time will be different. When the enemy army comes again, it will head down the east coast. There his numbers will allow him to bully places into submission or, more likely, even as we dine here, he will be making diplomatic overtures to princes and lords to facilitate his army's movement. King Charles has enemies does he not?"

I had spoken the truth and my words made men think and heads turned to digest, along with the fine food, the meat of my words.

Alberico chuckled, "You are still Giovanni Acuto and I can see that there are years yet ahead of you to show us, youngsters, what it is to be a condottiero."

The rest of the meal was taken up with my old comrade and me reminiscing about the old days. It was what old soldiers do and I enjoyed that evening more than any for some time. It confirmed, in my mind, that the White Company's loss had been a great one. Alberico was a good soldier and a loyal friend.

The next morning, as we breakfasted in the Great Hall with the air still stinking of stale wine, a messenger arrived and reported to Alberico. This time our men and servants were seated with us. The clerics and the nobility were in their own homes. The messenger's words were whispered in Alberico's ear. After Alberico spoke to the messenger he was dismissed. The Captain of the Company of St George had a wry smile on his face, "The king will, it seems, see you but not here and not in Capri."

His eyes locked with mine. I knew what that meant. The king had visitors in Capri that he wished to be hidden from us.

"He asks that you travel to Sorrento. He has a fortress there, guarding the harbour and he will sail from Capri to meet with you."

"Sorrento?"

"A thirty-mile ride along the coast. It is too late to leave today as it would mean going there when the sun was at its hottest. We can leave in the early morning before the sun gets too hot. I will bring twenty of my men to escort you."

"Is it not safe?"

He smiled, "Sir John, King Charles will wish to speak to me and he will want me there with you. Besides, my horse needs the exercise."

He left to organise his men and I spoke with the others, "Keep your eyes and ears open. King Charles is playing games. I know that Captain Alberico is as much in the dark as we are but there may be others who are privy to information that they may let slip." I was, of course, addressing my four men. The Italian of Ned and Edgar would not be up to the gathering of such intelligence.

"What does this mean for our quest, Sir John?" Thomas was curious only. He had seen that I knew what I was doing and that he could trust me.

"If nothing else it tells us that King Charles is not opposed to an alliance. If he was then there would be no meeting." What I did not say was that I also had knowledge that I could pass on to the pope. I had no idea who these men were that the king was meeting on Capri but if he was hiding their identity even from his own captain, then it was something.

The next day we rose before dawn so that we could travel in the relative cool of the morning. We passed the brooding and smoking mountain that was Vesuvius. Alberico was philosophical about the volcano. "The last eruption was more than two hundred and fifty years ago."

"But Captain, I see smoke."

He turned to Robert who had spoken, "It always smokes, and it means nothing. See, men now farm the rich soil from the last eruption. The people who live close by know the volcano better than we do. It may erupt again, but not, I think, in my lifetime."

As we headed down the coast, he pointed out the island of Ischia and then the island of Capri. He told us of Emperor Tiberius who had slaves thrown from his palace at the top. It was done, so Alberico said, so that he could study the effect of the drop. It seemed to me rather cruel. Enough slaves would have died of natural causes for him to use their bodies. I think he had been a wicked man. Once again, I thought about the effect of power. Some men could clearly handle it and others could not. Which kind was King Charles?

We stopped close by the town that had been wiped out in the most famous eruption. It had happened in the same century that Christ had died and some thought that it was God's vengeance for the death of his son. I did not for our local priest had explained to me when I was a boy, that Christ had to die to give men the chance of salvation. The older I was the more relevant that became as I contemplated my own mortality. A village had grown up close to the road and the volcanic earth was clearly fertile as they sold their produce to passers-by. We enjoyed a refreshing repast in the shade of an orange grove. The sharp oranges and lemons did not suit the Englishmen but I found them delicious.

We reached Sorrento in the early afternoon. The presence of Captain Alberico ensured a quick passage into the fort that overlooked the harbour and a messenger was sent to tell King Charles that we had arrived. I knew that he would not arrive until the next day at the earliest. It would give me time to improve the linguistic skills of Thomas Wyndham. The problems he had suffered when speaking to the bishop meant that he had made desperate efforts to improve since then. I helped him by translating many of Alberico's words. He was still woefully unprepared and so I spent the last hours of the day coaching him. It was not in my nature to fail and having come so far it seemed silly not to do all in my power to make the mission a success.

The fort was a place of defence and so when we dined it was in a more functional hall than the Great Hall at the palace. Even so, the food was better than might have been expected and the wine, of course, was superb. Thomas and I had to share a room although we each had our own bed. As we prepared for sleep, I said, "Tomorrow, Thomas, weigh every word before you speak. I will speak the most but you are the envoy. King Richard has entrusted you. Do not let him down. I will do all in my power to ensure that we are successful but you will be the one who returns to England. I know you serve the king's uncle but it is King Richard who is your liege lord. Remember that."

"I will and I want you to know, Sir John, that I am grateful. When I think how I first spoke to you," he shuddered as though a chill had descended upon the room.

"Forget the past and think of the present for that will shape your future." There was hope for Thomas Wyndham who was maturing and learning well. By the time he would leave Italy, I knew that he would be better placed to survive in the treacherous world of service to the Plantagenets.

On Alberico's advice, we rose early, before dawn. He had told me that the king liked to take people by surprise. He did not give the reason but I knew it. It was a way of catching men with their guard down when they were unprepared. In such situations, men often made errors of judgement. I knew that I would not but it was as well to be prepared and Thomas would need guidance. As we ate in the hall I went through the phrases and words he would need to use. King Charles was not Italian and Thomas' poor Italian might not be a hindrance. I wanted him word perfect.

"But Sir John, you will be the one who speaks for me, will you not? You have an easy manner about you and as I saw with Pope Urban you are not as I am, terrified of these great men."

I smiled, "I always remember that they are just men and if you are like Alberico and me and have faced all types of men on a battlefield, then you are more confident in your own abilities. Is that not right, Alberico?"

"I am still learning but you are right, Sir John." Thanks to his time with the White Company Alberico was quite comfortable when speaking English. "Even so, Master Thomas, make no mistake, King Charles is a very clever man."

Our early breakfast proved to be a sound move, for as the sun rose over the hills to the east the galley flying the royal standard pulled into the harbour below us. "Do we go to meet him, Alberico?"

He smiled and waved a hand at the breakfast, "Better to let him think that we are just finishing our food."

I had already instructed our men to be discreet and to report anything to us that they thought was important.

The king was not a big man hence the nickname, given to him by his detractors, Charles the Short. He did, however, have energy and it burned in his eyes. He was not yet forty but he was not only King of Naples and Sicily but also the titular King of Jerusalem. As Alberico had told me, the king also had aspirations to be King of Hungary to which he had a viable claim. I fully understood why King Richard would want him as an ally. The question was, did King Charles have the same view?

We rose and bowed when he swept into the room. Alberico said, "King Charles, we did not expect you until later."

I saw a smile ooze across the king's face, "It was cooler and I thought to join you at breakfast. We will sit and eat with you. I find that men are more honest when they are eating."

We sat and Alberico said, while the king's servants served him food and wine, "May I introduce, King Charles, Sir John Hawkwood and Master Thomas Wyndham."

I decided to take the initiative and I bowed and said, "I had the honour to lead the men who stopped Louis of Anjou and Amadeus of Savoy from attacking Naples, and I am here to say that the White Company is ready to do the same, should you need us, if Louis returns. Master Wyndham comes from King Richard of England and I am here today more as an intermediary and translator rather than a condottiero."

The smile the king then gave me was, to me, a genuine one, "And can I, on behalf of my people thank you, Sir John. What you did with a handful of men was nothing short of a miracle. Do you think the princeling from France will risk war again?"

I chose my words carefully for although I would gain little from an Anglo-Neapolitan alliance, I was a loyal Englishman and I would serve my king, "I believe that the French will back Louis. He ruled France as regent before his nephew was crowned and, in my experience, the French seek an empire to rival that of the emperor. I believe they still yearn for the days of Charlemagne when the Franks were pre-eminent."

The king turned to Thomas and suddenly said, "And from what I was told your king wishes an alliance. What do you say?"

I was glad that we had risen early and I had been able to prepare the young Englishman. He looked nervous but his words were well spoken and he had heeded my advice, "King Charles, my king seeks an alliance with Naples for both trade and mutual defence. England has never had any Italian aspirations and we share a common foe in France."

The king nodded and ate some bread and ham. It gave him thinking time and made the rest of us wait. When he had swallowed, drunk some wine and wiped his mouth, his head whipped around and he said to me, "I hear that you visited with Pope Urban before you came here."

If this had been a combat with sharpened swords then the king had just made a dart at my head while he thought me preoccupied. I nodded, "For two purposes, King Charles. I went to offer my services to the pope, should he need them, against

Pope Clement and Master Thomas had a message for the pope from his master the Duke of Lancaster."

That King Charles was well informed became clear when he smiled, "Ah, yes, Castile." He turned his attention back to Thomas, "That is closer to Italy than to England, Master Thomas, does the duke have ambitions here in Italy too?"

I had not prepared him for this but Thomas had gained confidence from his initial words and he shook his head, "The duke merely wishes what is his by right of marriage, the crown of Castile. If anything, King Charles, if he was able to reclaim his kingdom then he could also put pressure on France from the south."

I smiled. Thomas had picked up more words than I had thought and he must have been preparing such a speech for although he did not pronounce all the words correctly, he managed to convey the meaning perfectly and the king clearly approved. He nodded and wiped his hands.

Alberico asked, "Will you need your rooms here, King Charles?"

The king stood, "This is a functional fort, Captain Alberico, and my palace on Capri is where I will return. Master Thomas, you may return to England and tell King Richard that I agree in principle but I would have the treaty drawn up by men who are neither soldiers nor messenger boys. He can use Sir John here as the conduit to me." He turned to me, having insulted Thomas, and said, "I would retain the services of your company, Sir John, for I agree with you. I will arrange for the payment to be sent to William Turner in Pisa." He cocked an eye, "That is where your company banks, is it not?"

He was well informed, "It is and I thank you."

"Captain Alberico will let you know who the other companies hired to defend me, are." He nodded to Thomas Wyndham, "And you have a future, young Master Wyndham. I wish you well."

With that, he swept from the room and we were left alone. No one said anything for a while. I drank some more wine until Zuzzo returned, "The king's ship has left the harbour. All the men he brought went with him."

"Thank you, Zuzzo." He left us and the three of us were alone, Alberico having dismissed the servants when the king left.

Alberico turned to me, "Interesting, eh, Sir John? My king clearly has spies in Rome and they must report to him regularly."

I shook my head, "We left Rome the day after our meeting with the pope and we rode hard to get here. His spies must have left the same day we met the king. That concerns me." I wondered if it was a coincidence or something more sinister. I realised that Thomas looked downcast. Despite the king's last words the insult of *'messenger boy'* must have rankled. I said, "You did better than well, Thomas. The king was using words as a weapon when he called you a messenger boy. Ignore it. You have done what King Richard wished. There will be a treaty and had you not come there would not be. We will return to Rome and see if the other part of your quest has been successful."

"Thank you for your kind words, Sir John, but I can see that when I came here to Italy I was not as prepared as I might have been. I will return to England a better man."

"Do you stay another night in Sorrento, Sir John?"

"No, Alberico. We will head back to Naples if that suits. I would leave for Rome as soon as we can. I am anxious to return home and King Richard will wish to have Thomas' news."

We left within the hour.

Chapter 14

The ride back was hotter and more uncomfortable thanks to the time of day. The horses were weary and we stank of sweat. When we reached Naples, it was clear that we would not be able to leave the city as quickly as we had wished. My decision to leave Sorrento so soon was not the best I had made.

Alberico was philosophical about it, "You have an extra day here, Sir John, and I would use the time to talk to you about my company. I know there are ways we could make it a better one and what better way than speaking to the master of the condottiere."

"You flatter me but anything I can do I will."

While the two of us sat and talked my men went with Thomas to buy supplies for the journey home. We needed grain for the animals as well as food for us. As Naples enjoyed good trade with the Moors, then my men knew they could purchase items in Naples that they could sell for a profit in Florence. A day in Naples' markets would be time well spent.

We left Naples in the early morning. It was so early that Captain Alberico had to come to the gates to facilitate our egress. He had introduced me to the man who would be the messenger from the king. It was always better to have actually met the man and I would know him again. Once on the road, we adopted our familiar formation. With Robert and John at the rear, Ned and Edgar behind Thomas and me, Zuzzo and Gianluca rode a little way ahead of us.

Zuzzo had chosen the route south and he did so as we headed back to the Holy City. Zuzzo was a careful man and, where we could, he varied the route. On the way south we had not anticipated any problems but to be sure when we came to a fork in the road then, normally, Zuzzo would choose our path. There was only one part where there was no choice. We had to pass along a section of road between San Marco and Cicerone. After that, we could take the coastal road through Gaeta. That was a longer road but, as it was by the sea, was cooler. Before that, we could head into the mountains to take advantage of the cooler air.

The eight miles or so between San Marco and Cicerone left us no choice but to use the road that was bordered by the sea and the mountains.

We had left the inn ten miles south of San Marco before dawn. It had been a mansio from Roman times and, as such, a secure place with protection for both our horses and us. We stopped at San Marco to water our horses and then headed along the coast road. The Romans had built the road and planted trees for shade. Few people lived on that particular section and the vegetation was lusher than in other places. It was there that we were ambushed.

If we had not used Zuzzo then it might have ended in disaster but as he and Gianluca were riding twenty paces up the road from Thomas and me, his sharp senses and quick reactions came to our aid. Zuzzo shouted, "Trap!"

I saw him draw his sword as did Gianluca. My sword was already in my hand and I was spurring my horse when I saw the half dozen or so men ride from the trees towards our two scouts. A movement from the corner of my eye told me that more men were coming for Thomas and me. We had discussed what to do in case of an attack but, as with all such plans, the reality could be different. Knowing that there was no danger from our left as the sea lay there, John and Robert spurred their horses towards the men closest to us. Ned and Edgar let go of the reins of the sumpters, drew their swords and followed me. Thomas was the one, predictably, who almost froze. He had never been in action before and the rest of us had.

As I headed into the trees, I held my sword behind me. I saw that there were five men before us. Had Thomas done as ordered we would have outnumbered them. As it was this would be a battle of even numbers for us although Zuzzo and Gianluca would need our help to defeat the six men that they fought. The man who came at me wore a mail brigandine. That told me he was a soldier and not a bandit. Even as I swung my sword to hack at his leg, I took in that his clothes were good quality. I was wearing leather gloves and as he swung his sword at me, I dropped my reins and grabbed his descending wrist. My sword sliced through his breeches and into flesh. I never carried a dull sword and the blood that spurted told me that he was out of the battle.

I grabbed my reins and wheeled to my left. I had to trust that the other four would deal with their attackers. John and Robert were of the White Company and Ned and Edgar were old soldiers. The clash of steel from my left were the reassuring sounds that Zuzzo and Gianluca were still battling. I headed through the trees and saw that Gianluca had a wound. I could see the blood. Two of their attackers were down but both were fighting at two-to-one odds. Zuzzo had a sword in each hand. It was Gianluca who was in danger. I had no compunction in attacking the back of one of those trying to kill the leader of my bodyguards. I rammed my sword into the back of the warrior who was raising his sword to strike at the blind side of Gianluca and had the assassin's blow connected then Gianluca would have died. I liked a sharpened tip to my blade and it slid into the leather jack and then the flesh of the man. I must have struck his backbone for I felt the blade grate on something hard. His arms dropped to his side as he fell dead. Standing in my stirrups I brought my sword down as the other attacker, sensing my presence, turned. My sword struck and split his skull as Gianluca's weapon drove up into the man's side. The two fighting Zuzzo turned to flee but Zuzzo was having none of it and he slashed his curved right-hand sword around to hack into the side of one of them. The would-be killer fell from his horse. His other hand brought his sword to slash down the spine of the last man who tried to escape.

I turned and looked at the others, they were all whole, even Thomas. I shouted, "Fetch the horses and the healing kit. Gianluca is hurt. Collect the horses."

Gianluca shook his head, "It is nothing, Sir John, my arm is cut that is all."

"And you are bleeding heavily. We will tend to you."

Edgar galloped up leading a sumpter and as I helped Gianluca from his saddle he was already dismounting and had the vinegar, honey and catgut ready. Edgar was an old soldier and knew what to do. He said, "One is alive there, Sir John. Leave Gianluca to me."

I nodded for we had to know whence came these killers and if we were likely to encounter more.

Zuzzo had already sheathed his swords and dismounted. He was kneeling next to the man he had slashed in the side. Zuzzo had moved the weapons from the man who was clearly dying. I could see his ribs and his vital organs and the pooling blood told its own story. Zuzzo was already questioning him as I knelt.

"Who sent you?"

The man had his eyes closed. He was holding his crucifix and mumbling prayers.

"You tried to murder us and you will not be allowed into heaven."

He opened his eyes and smiled. A tendril of blood trickled down his cheek. "I have absolution for I serve God and my sins are already forgiven. As for you, you are doomed and…" He expired.

I took his purse to examine it. I was not robbing the dead but trying to get an identity. I poured the coins into my hand and showed them to Zuzzo. There was more copper than silver and no gold. "This man was not paid well to kill us."

I shouted, without turning, "Fetch me the purses of the dead."

Zuzzo made the sign of the cross, "The man truly believed he would go to heaven. I think these men were sent by the church."

I stood and nodded, "I agree, but which church? Was it Pope Urban? Pope Clement or someone else?"

When the purses were all brought, we discovered that none of them had been paid well. By the time Gianluca's arm had been stitched the stray horses had been gathered.

"What do we do with the bodies, Sir John?"

"They died trying to kill us. We owe them nothing. Take their weapons and cover them with their cloaks. The ones who escaped might well seek to fetch others and finish off their work. From now on we ride as though we were behind enemy lines. Robert, you ride with Zuzzo. John, watch Gianluca."

"I need no watcher, Sir John."

"And I say you do. Ned and Edgar, are you happy to lead the four strays with the sumpters?"

"Yes, Sir John."

Leaving the six dead men we headed up the road. We had almost ninety miles to cover and we had a wounded man with us. I was wrapt in my thoughts as I tried to work out who had sent the men. It was clear to me that the church in one form or another was behind the attack. I did not think it was Pope Urban but when I met with him again then I would know one way or another. Either of the other two options seemed likely. Pope Clement and I did not like each other and he was a clear favourite. I was not protected by my company and if he wanted Louis of Anjou to be successful then he needed me to be out of the way.

"I am sorry, Sir John. I let you and the others down."

I turned, "Thomas, I knew that you were an innocent abroad when we came. I am just happy that you survived. King Richard would be less than pleased if I had his envoy killed in my care."

He shook his head, "I do not think that the king would care one way or another. You have the means to let him know of the arrangements."

He was right and I nodded, "I am still glad that you are alive and unhurt."

"Thank you but the rest of you were placed in great danger because of me."

I shook my head, "We did not even think about you, Thomas. The rest of us are soldiers and we know how to fight. When you do fight you do your best to hurt as many of the enemy as you can. We were lucky that only Gianluca was hurt."

"But how did you manage to overcome so many of them?"

"Zuzzo is a skilled swordsman with quick hands and he held up the larger group. I fought a man who went for the kill and failed. I made a wound that I knew would incapacitate and it did. You chose good men. You should reward them for they fought as well as any in the White Company."

"But if we are attacked again?"

"Then draw your sword and be aggressive. Attack before you are attacked and use your young reactions to save you. You will get better."

He nodded and after a few moments said, "If I survive."

I smiled, "Exactly! Let us be optimistic and hope that I can put you on a ship at Pisa and you can return to the peace of England."

We found a doctor in the first large town we reached. We paid him to look at the wound and for a silver coin he confirmed that Edgar had done a good job. He offered a salve to speed up the healing but we declined. The coin had come from the body of the man who had wounded Gianluca and we did not begrudge its spending.

We viewed every traveller we passed with suspicion and our hands were on the hilts of our swords for the whole journey. When we ate, we huddled together with one man watching our animals. It was when we ate that we discussed the paymaster of the killers. Zuzzo had a mind which worked logically and he also had a good memory for faces.

"When we were in Sorrento, I saw one of those we fought. There was nothing remarkable about the man and as he was entering a church at the time, I thought nothing of it."

"Then why do you remember him?"

Zuzzo rubbed his chin, "A good question, Sir John." I could see him running through the incident in his mind. His face broke into a smile, "His sword. I notice such things and I saw that it was the sword of a soldier and not a noble trying to impress the ladies. I suppose I wondered if he was from some other company."

Gianluca nodded, "And they had served in some company." He looked at me, "Captain Alberico's company are Italian and these were Italian."

I shook my head, "I am not saying that I trust every man in the Company of St George but Captain Alberico is a sword brother." I drank some wine and thought about Gianluca's words, "If they came from Pope Clement then they would be more likely to be French." They all nodded. "Then it seems increasingly likely that they came from another master."

Zuzzo said, "The visitors that the king did not wish us to see, perhaps they worried that we might know their identity."

"Suppose they were not sent by the church." Thomas was trying to be helpful.

Zuzzo shook his head, "The words the dying man spoke to Sir John were those of one who had been assured by the church that he had absolution for his sins. A priest of some kind sent them."

I thought of the pope's words, "But we know not who."

I was relieved and terrified at the same time when we reached Rome and St Peter's. I was relieved because our journey was almost at an end and terrified for we knew that churchmen were behind the attack and yet were in a place filled with priests. Whom could we trust? We went directly to the basilica for I wished to seek an audience and leave for Florence as soon as possible.

Giacomo greeted us and I was taken into his office. Much to his chagrin, Thomas was left outside. "Word has come that you were attacked on the road, Sir John, and I see from your man's wound that it is true."

My eyes narrowed, "How did you know?"

He smiled, "It is my job to know what is going on and my watchers were keeping an eye on you both south and north."

"Then they did not do a good job. We were attacked."

He sighed, "My watchers are in the main towns and you were attacked on a quiet stretch of road. It was well planned. What do you know?"

I was blunt, "Did Pope Urban send them?"

He laughed, "If he did then you would have been arrested as soon as you entered St Peter's." It was as though he suddenly realised what I had said, "Why would you think that?"

I decided that what he had said made sense and I told him of the attack and of the dying man's words. I also told him what we had deduced.

"I cannot fault your logic. I agree that Pope Clement, while he is capable of such things, would have used Frenchmen and, as far as I know, even if he did know you had left Florence for Rome, would be so far behind you that his men could not have attacked you. Tell me about your visit to King Charles."

I was intrigued by the questions and I answered them honestly.

When I had finished, he said, "Then I think that the king's visitors were the ones responsible and I have an idea who they are." He stood, "It will be safer for you and your men to stay here this night. Pope Urban needs to be informed about all that has occurred."

"I am anxious to return home."

"Stay the night where you can be protected and you can leave on the morrow."

"We are prisoners then."

"If you wish to view it thus then, yes, but I give my word that you will be safe."

We were taken to a wing of the building that had rooms. They were functional and we all shared one large one but that suited us. I guessed that they had been, at one time, a barracks. Sant'Angelo appeared to fill that role now. We were fed but there was a guard on the door. When asked he assured us that it was for our own protection but that did not change the fact that we were not allowed to leave. Our horses, we were told, were being looked after and we could just enjoy the papal hospitality.

Gianluca's arm was healing well and he said, "We could make an escape attempt this night if you wished, Sir John."

"Giacomo assured me that we were safe and I believe him. Besides he is right, if we were in any danger then we would be in a cell in Sant'Angelo by now and not here. Let us bide our time."

Thomas shook his head, "I have brought this upon us all."

I laughed, "If anyone brought this upon us it was the king and his uncle. Do not be so despondent. We have not failed and our purses are a little heavier than when we left. We have four horses and saddles to sell as well as swords and daggers. Learn to see the coistrel as half full."

In the event, it was the next day when we were summoned to the pope. Thomas was allowed to accompany me and the pope gave him his verdict on the request from the Duke of Lancaster. "You have made a good case, Thomas Wyndham, but so have the royal family of Castile, who dispute the Duke of Lancaster's claim. I am afraid that I cannot support either party. I am not Solomon the Great. You may tell the duke that I will not oppose him if he attains the throne and when he is crowned, he shall have my support, but until then I shall be an interested observer."

I could tell that Thomas was disappointed but our talk the previous night must have had an effect for he took it with good grace and did not object when he was dismissed.

Condottiere

The three of us left alone, Giacomo came to the meat of the matter. "Sir John, while the attack on you was unfortunate, it has delivered us vital news. I now know why you were attacked. Your news of visitors to Capri coincided with the absence of five cardinals from Rome. The five men returned last night and they are being questioned even as we speak. I have no doubt that there was some conspiracy that involved the King of Naples."

The pope smiled, "We are in your debt, Sir John." He nodded to Giacomo who handed me a large purse. I was not crass enough to count it. "This is payment for services rendered and a papal escort of twenty lances will take you back to Florence."

I wanted to know more, "And King Charles?"

Giacomo smiled and said, "Not your concern. If you wish to be paid by him again then Pope Urban will not see it as a threat so long as you are not hired against the church, do you understand?"

"I do and if Louis of Anjou and the French come again…"

"Then you may be hired by His Holiness for we would rather that papal lands were not ravaged by our enemies."

The cynic in me realised that while he might no longer support King Charles, he would want any fighting to be well north of his lands.

We left that day with our escort. Whether it was purely for our safety or to ensure that we did leave Rome completely I am not sure, but their presence ensured that we had good accommodation in religious houses and we had stabling as we headed north. We paid for neither. Five days after leaving Rome we reached Florence.

We learned, much later, that the cardinals had revealed under torture, that King Charles had been plotting against the pope. It meant that the king was excommunicated and the papal alliance with Naples ended. It did not affect our ability to seek employers. If anything the whole incident had proved to the world that I was an honest man. I took Thomas and his men to Pisa to take a ship home. He went back to England a better man. I was sorry to see Ned and Edgar go. They had been good men. My work for King Richard was not yet done but as it would take some time for Thomas to return to England and for King Richard

Condottiere

to send a message back to me, I could concentrate on my business, The White Company.

Chapter 15

With winter upon us we began to train even harder, for word had come that King Charles of France had given Louis of Anjou an army and a commander who was competent. Enguerrand de Courcy was a professional French soldier and was at least as good as Amadeus of Savoy. Word came from the pope that my company was hired to ensure that the French did not come through Florence. The contract was not a rich one but it paid our wages and gave the White Company some profit. King Charles of Naples did not offer to hire us.

The purses had pleased my wife who knew how to extract the greatest profit from every florin I earned. We lived well and I ate and dressed like a prince but Donnina always ensured that we invested wisely. The girls and their nurse dined with us but the three of them were whisked away as soon as they had finished. Now that I was older, I ate more slowly. When I had first left Essex I had always eaten as though the meal I was devouring was the last food left on earth. It meant we were still eating when they were hugged, kissed and sent to their beds.

Left alone Donnina was able to dissect the events of the Neapolitan and Roman trips. "I did not know this Alberico, can you trust him?"

Her mistrust was understandable for he was tied to King Charles, "As I told my men, I trust him as I trust Michael or any of my men. Besides, he had more than enough opportunities to kill us. The road from Naples to Sorrento and back is steep and the sea hides bodies well. Now as for King Charles…he is untrustworthy and the clandestine meeting should have alerted me to danger. I wonder now if the meeting was to allow his cardinal conspirators to head up the road to Rome and organise our ambush."

She delicately nibbled on the fowl's leg and when she had finished wiped her mouth and said, "You say the ship landed before dawn and you were breakfasting?" I nodded, "Then that is when they performed the trick. At least the pope is now our friend and in our debt. His commission is not as rich a one as before but it pays the men and makes us a profit."

"I am not sure about the debt part but you are right. Still, we need another employer for next year or we may lose men again and the company I have now is the best I have ever led."

She smiled, "Good." She reached over to take a fig and cut herself a morsel of goat's cheese to eat with it. "Even though Dai and Tom have left?"

"I still have Robin and Michael has grown into his saddle. I am content and the four men we hired to guard me make me feel like I have an extra layer of armour."

The Christmas celebrations were now over and, as we entered January, we had a new year before us. I had met and celebrated with both Michael and Robin during the Christmas period. With Michael it involved Donnina and I visiting him in his home and enjoying a quiet but celebratory feast. Robin invited both soldiers he liked and women he hired, making it more of a Bacchanalian orgy. Needless to say, Donnina was not invited to that feast but she was a wise woman and knew what had gone on. She was philosophical about such things.

William Turner came to see me in February to tell me that the first of the payments from Pope Urban had been sent but that there were no other commissions on the horizon. It was he who gave Donnina and me some news that was not entirely unexpected but distressing for Donnina.

"Your father, Lady Donnina, has been arrested by his nephew and his titles taken from him."

If you did not know my wife then you would have thought the news had no interest for her but I knew her well now and I caught the tic in her left eye and the slight catch in her voice as she said, "Was a reason given?"

William shrugged, "The Lord of Milan said that his uncle's corruption could be borne no longer and the people were sick of his misuse of Milanese money."

She snorted, "What is that saying you have, John? A kettle and a pot?" I nodded. "My cousin is a bigger thief than my father. It is just that he is better at hiding it." She drank half a goblet of wine, another sign that she was upset within, "But, if you dine with the devil then one day you pay the price and my father has enjoyed many such meals." She smiled, now in control, "And how is your family?"

In public that was the extent of her tears but that night, as she lay in my arms, she wept, "He ignored me while I was growing up, he gave me away as soon as he could and he abandoned us but he is still my father and his blood courses through my veins. I would not have him incarcerated."

I kissed her forehead, "I could visit with Galeazzo if you wished. I might be able to arrange something."

She squeezed me, "That is good of you but my father cut us off and I would not have you make an enemy of Galeazzo."

I laughed, "It is a little late for that, my love."

"Oh, I know that he supported Louis of Anjou, he probably still does, but that is just business. Like my father, he seeks a kingdom and he will support any pretender who can gain him a little more land. I believe that is why the last army came the way it did. Louis of Anjou and Amadeus of Savoy might have seen it as a passage to Naples but had you not defeated him then Lucca, Pistoia and even Pisa might have been added to Milanese lands. No, my love, we stay out of Milanese affairs. It may well be that my cousin hires you or offers to, at any rate. If he does then we must be wary for he is treacherous."

"That is why we are paid a stipend by Florence. It guarantees that none of their enemies can hire my company. It is still feared by Florence."

I know not when the seed was planted but in March Donnina told me that she was with child. The news of her father had upset her but the growth of a new Hawkwood in her womb made her content. She was still desperate to bear me a boy. My other sons were now far away, one in a monastery and the other... I knew not. I did know that I was a grandfather for Sir William had written to me and given me the news. I doubted that I would ever see my grandchildren for I could not see a time when I might return to England.

It was in summer that the French came again. This time there were just mercenaries and Frenchmen under the command of Enguerrand de Courcy. Louis was not even with them. He was in Apulia at Bisceglie with just his bodyguard. It showed me that the French Commander knew his business. Louis could wait in the south of Italy where he would be well placed to join his army when they had won him his kingdom, but he would not be able to interfere as he had when Amadeus had led his forces. It was not only the pope who reacted but the council of Florence. We were ordered to guard the eastern border of Florence for de Courcy was not coming over the mountains but down the east coast of Italy. Once more it was an army of forty thousand and there was nothing in Italy to stand in its way.

My company looked and felt remarkably inadequate to resist such an army. We would have no passes to defend and no other companies to join us. Alberico was heading from Naples, leading their army along with King Charles, but we would not be joining them. We had one task, stop the French from turning west and threatening Rome and Florence.

Robin, Michael and I met at my home and pored over a map. Michael shook his head, "Sir John, this is impossible. We have less than a thousand men, how can we stop such a huge army?"

Alberico had already sent a man to tell us that he and the Neapolitan army was gathered North of Caserta. That was just a few miles from Naples itself and on the eastern side of Vesuvius. They were two hundred miles away and, clearly, King Charles was hoping that the French army would not reach him intact. He could save his florins and hope that the cities that lay between his kingdom and the invaders would whittle down the enemy and make it easier for his army to defeat. When I had heard the news, I wondered why he did not simply head to Bisceglie or send killers there. The death of Louis of Anjou would end the threat.

I jabbed my finger at a place not far from Florence. "Pelago. It is just twelve miles from Florence but it is a narrow pass. If this de Courcy wishes to threaten Florence then he has to come along that road or head further south and then backtrack north and west. If Florence is his objective, then we can hold him as we did with Amadeus of Savoy."

Robin nodded, "Aye, my archers will harvest a fine crop of Frenchmen there."

"And if he continues to head south then what?" Michael's marriage had begun to change my acolyte.

I beamed, "We will have done our job and we can head home and count our coppers."

Whilst seeming a simple plan it was far from that but it was a plan and Michael took it to the council who approved my strategy. We left Florence and were at the small town within the day. We camped on the eastern side and my archers made hovels under cover of the trees. The men at arms dismounted and the horses were put to graze for if we fought, it would be on foot. I sent scouts out to the main road south, the one that led to Arezzo. We three stayed in the home of the lord of Pelago. He took his family to their home in Florence. The middle-aged merchant had no intention of risking his family's lives when there were mercenaries willing to do so. It meant we had beds and as the servants had been left behind, we dined well.

"Will Arezzo join the French or oppose them?"

Michael's question was a good one. The town had built a good wall some sixty years earlier and whilst a small state was, nonetheless, independent. "It could go either way. If Galeazzo had men with this French army then the city would oppose them. The Milanese would love to own the jewel that is Arezzo. I do not know if there are Milanese with the French and I know not the mind of this de Courcy." I nodded towards Robin, "He is French and fought against the English. He will know about our archers. Amadeus was taken by surprise."

"It is one thing to expect a shower of arrows and quite another to have any means of stopping them."

He was right. We had no chance of defeating such a huge army but we could bloody their nose and make them choose another route. It was not glorious but, then again, the White Company was not in the business of glory hunting. Sir Andrew de Belmonte had always been disappointed by that attitude. He had been a true romantic.

The scouts brought news, a week after we arrived, that a French column was heading along the road to Pelago. Hob and Edward were two of my most experienced scouts and they were calm as they reported to us,

"There are two thousand men, my lord. They are all mounted. There are two hundred Bretons and the rest are a mixture of men at arms and Lombard light horsemen."

Robin asked, "Crossbows?"

The look that Edward gave suggested that the archer thought the question an insult but his voice was calm as he said, "Just horsemen, my lord, as we said."

Robin nodded, "Just checking."

"Did you recognise the leader?"

"No, Sir John. He is a knight for he had spurs."

"And how long before they reach here?"

"The main body is at Stia. They will have to stop to camp. Their plated men slow them down."

Hob rubbed his chin, "Consuma is just six miles away. It is the biggest place on their route and they cannot travel beyond it. They will camp there."

"We could raid their camp, Sir John."

I shook my head, "We ambush them here. If they are six miles away then they will be here by Terces. That gives us plenty of time to prepare. We move out at Laudes. Inform the men."

I had no objection to raiding a camp but we could hurt them more this way. We had a plan and we would stick to it. I could see no reason to risk mounting men and alerting the enemy to our presence. Better to give them a painful surprise. I had worked out that this venture, with just two thousand men, was a probe. The French wanted to know if they could come through Florentine land. Their leader had sent a sizeable force. He would learn they were not enough.

Our men were all ready for action. My bodyguards had already had excitement on the road from Naples but now that Gianluca was fully healed they were ready to protect me. However, as we headed up the road to the ambush Gianluca said, "Sir John, there is no need for you to risk your life and to put us into danger. We are paid to do so and do it happily but this ambush is the work for archers and unless you intend to string a bow, better that we watch and you command. Zuzzo cannot use his horn to give orders if you are dead."

There was a time when I would have torn into him with a tongue known for its savagery but he was right. We had no choice when we were ambushed but now I did. "We will watch and we will remain hidden, however, my little guardian angels, as they have no crossbows, you do not object to them seeing me so that they know who it is that they fight?"

Zuzzo nodded, "So long as when they close with us, with murderous intent in their hearts, you allow me to lead your horse from the battle."

I snorted, "No man has ever led my horse."

Zuzzo was not discomfited by my words, "There is a first time for everything, Sir John."

It was then that I knew I was getting old for I accepted his words.

The men were in position before the sun began to rise. Scouts were waiting along the road and they would race back to warn us when the column approached. The dismounted men at arms were further down the road behind a barrier of carts. The ambush would be sprung before the enemy saw the carts. The barrier was there to prevent a disaster should the ambush fail. I did not think that it would. The glint of sunlight off metal in the distance told me, before the scouts returned, that the enemy were on their way. My archers had seen the glint and they each strung their bows. Their arrows would have already been selected. I moved my horse a little further back into the undergrowth. It was not fear that made me do so but the need to be totally hidden. My plate was covered by a cloak but it would not do for the condottiero to be the one who spoiled the ambush. The scouts ran first to Robin and then to me.

"The same as before, Sir John, and they have dismounted two dozen men who are slipping through the woods."

I nodded. This knight was cautious but Robin's men could easily take care of the dismounted Bretons. We were all so still that we could hear the jingling of metal as they approached and the gentle clip-clop of the horses' hooves. I kept my hands on my reins; I was not tempted to draw a sword. We were at the western end of the twin lines of archers. I saw the horsemen as they appeared four hundred paces from us. They could not see them but the archers were on both sides of them. The lack of shouts and screams from the dismounted Bretons told me that Robin's men had killed them silently. I could almost visualise the deaths. Two archers would have approached each of the scouts from behind. One would have held the man's arms while the other would have silenced a scream and simply slit his throat. The body would have been lowered to the ground and when all the dead had been accounted for the archers would have picked up their bows and resumed their positions. Purses and weapons would be taken after the ambush. My company was made up of professionals.

When the four men at the front of the column were so close that I could almost see the colour of their eyes, I heard the creaking of bows. The Bretons heard it too. There was no way to avoid the noise made by so many yew bows but even though they knew what was coming, it was too late. Some of the archers were within thirty paces and at that range even plate armour is of little use. The Bretons had leather and the war arrows tore through them. Such was the skill of my archers that not a horse was hurt nor did any arrows miss their target to threaten the men on the other side of the ambush. The screams of men filled the air. There was a collective hiss as swords were drawn but it was too late for the front half of the column. We did not have enough archers to cover the mile-long column but in the front half, the first thousand were either thrown from their saddles or they turned to flee down the road to the safety of the other men. A few of them charged the woods but as there were just a handful who had been lucky enough to avoid death, they soon joined their comrades. The horn from the rear, their leader had been slain already, signalled their ignominious retreat. I had no idea what de Courcy intended, a chevauchée, a scouting expedition or a flanking move but whatever it was it had failed.

The archers waited a short while and then emerged from the woods to collect purses and horses and to give a warrior's death to any who were hovering close to death. When I heard the four horses trotting east, I knew that Robin had sent his scouts to trail the survivors.

It was noon by the time the horses had been taken back to our camp, the dead had been stripped of weapons and purses and the piles of French and Breton dead placed on funeral pyres. We had dismounted and were enjoying some of the food we had liberated from the riders. By late afternoon our scouts returned.

"They have rejoined the main army and are camped at Prato Vecchio."

"Then, Captain Robin, take your men back to the camp. The men at arms can camp by the barricade. Let us see what they do next."

It took six days to discover that they had headed south and were attacking Arezzo. De Courcy was clearly a practical man and his priority was not to defeat a single company but to win the crown of Naples for his king.

It took less than two weeks for them to take Arezzo and when it fell and the French settled there, we headed for home. What we had done had been little but it had been enough. If King Charles needed me to bolster Alberico's army then he would have to pay me. We reached home having been away for a short time. The men were all richer for we had taken many horses, lifted purses and stripped so much plate that my company had earned as much in a single battle as some companies earned in a year. I knew that some men, like von Landau and Sterz, regarded the taking of mail as profit for the company. I did not. What men took on the battlefield as a result of their endeavours was theirs. I suppose that, and the fact that they were all paid promptly and regularly, kept them loyal and ready to fight.

Donnina was pleased to see me home, "It is good that it all went well. Our coffers are swollen and none were hurt. You are a good general, husband, my father chose well."

Chapter 16

The council came to see me a few days after my return. They had disturbing news. Siena, it seemed, had taken advantage of our absence and raided the Florentine land adjacent to their own. It was a foolish thing to do for Florence was a far more powerful state than little Siena. While I listened to the council complain about the ravages, I wondered if there was a conspiracy. Siena had supported the former Queen of Naples, Joan. Could Siena be a secret ally of Louis of Anjou? I knew the council would not think of such things but I was a condottiero and I did.

Michael's father-in-law was the spokesman and when he had finished, I said, "So, Carlos, what is it you wish of me and the company?" I leaned forward, "The retainer makes us available but we need further payment if we are to draw our swords. Do we march on Siena at the head of a Florentine army?" If he thought that being Michael's father-in-law gave him special favour he was wrong.

The six men who had come on behalf of the council became quite agitated and Carlos shook his head, "We do not want a war and we certainly do not wish to take our men from their labours to fight. Of course, we shall pay you. Five thousand florins will be paid to you. What we want you to do is punish the Sienese for their treacherous attack. Raid their lands for a month. It is their busy time too. The five thousand florins are for a month of war. What is it that Michael called it? Ah yes, a chevauchée."

I nodded, "Then I know precisely what to do. I pray that you do not announce our intention over your food. Keep it a secret until I have unleashed my men." I saw the disappointment on some of their faces. None were brave men but by speaking of our actions, before the event, it made them feel like warriors and their self-importance would swell. "If word leaks out before we are on the borders and they are waiting for us then our fee doubles." My words might not stop them from gossiping but the thought of spending twice as much would. I stood. As far as I was concerned the meeting was over.

They realised that and standing, gave me a bow and left. I sent John to fetch Robin and was not surprised when, before I could send Robert for him, Michael arrived. By the time Robin joined us we had the maps out and I was making notes on a wax tablet.

Robin shook his head, "Getting there and remaining unseen will be tricky, Sir John."

"I know and that is why I want three columns. We divide the company equally and the three of us each lead one section. I am counting on the fact that when we are spotted, they will expect us to act as a single company. We will not. If the council wishes us to punish them then we will do so. We raid for just one month, no more. We take what we can and each of us chooses our targets." I used our goblets to mark out the areas in which we would operate. "I will raid to the north of Siena, Michael to the east, around Vescona and Robin to the west, around Ampugano. It keeps us all within half a day's ride away from one another. I do not expect it but if we have to, we can rejoin and fight any army sent from Siena."

Robin nodded, "A good plan for they will not wish to risk losing crops and animals further south by mustering the levy." He smiled, "We get to keep what we take?"

"Of course."

Donnina was happy at both the thought of profit and that it would be just a month that I would be away. Siena was so close that I could be home within hours. Robin and Michael divided the men equitably. It meant I had a hundred good archers, a hundred lances and twenty men to guard and lead the horses laden with plate. Altogether I would have almost three hundred men under my command. The ones who were not happy were my bodyguards, for they knew that I would be putting myself in danger. Gianluca seemed to think that I was getting too old for war. My grey hairs, balding pate and growing girth made him think so.

"Gianluca, I am still a warrior. Before you joined me, I practised with my archers and could still hit the mark." I patted my stomach, "Do not let this evidence of good living fool you. I still have skill but you need not fear. I am here to lead and lead I shall. Your job will be to protect me and to gather the treasure that I take."

We left before dawn using three different routes and headed through the dark along familiar roads. The border was a flexible one but we saw the evidence of the Sienese raids when dawn broke and we saw the burnt-out Florentine farms. When we reached the first village that was untouched, we knew we had reached Siena. We skirted that first village and pressed on until we were just eight miles from Siena. The council had heeded my warning and there were no patrols and the gates of the estates were not barred. I had Hob and Edward with me as leaders of my archers and I used Hob to select a good target. The estate he found was clearly owned by a noble for a standard fluttered from the house. It was a defensible estate and there was a gated wall and a small tower but this was summer and the earliest crops were being gathered. Young animals in the fields needed tending and the grapes and olives had to be closely watched for pests. They were not prepared for the human pests who were about to descend upon them. While my archers raided the fields, I led my lances through the gates and towards the house. That we took them completely by surprise was an understatement. The lord, his steward, and men I took to be his personal retinue were in the courtyard talking about I know not what when we thundered, swords drawn to surround them.

"If you do not oppose us then you shall live."

The lord, I later learned he was Rodolpho di Roderuccio, realised that he could do nothing and he looked up and said, "You are Giovanni Acuto?"

"I am."

He shook his head, "I told the Dodici that it was a mistake to raid Florence. It was like poking a sleeping dog and you, Sir John, have sharp teeth. What do you wish of us?"

"You have a home in Siena?"

"Of course."

"Then take your family there. You may take a wagon and two horses to draw it." I did not want to have men watching him and his family and my apparently generous act was a way to give myself a comfortable base from which to operate.

I saw him open his mouth as though to ask something else and then he realised the futility. He nodded. By the time my archers returned with the animals they had taken, it was almost dark. We had secured the gates and now had a defensible temporary home to use. I set the watch and then ate in the large hall at the heart of the house.

I briefed my leaders. "Tomorrow, we leave ten archers and ten lances to guard our new home. We take the animals north and while I raid that first village we passed, the animals we took can be taken to Casa Donnina. I will arrange for their distribution when we are done here."

My men had already discovered the treasure hidden by Lord di Roderuccio and that would be taken back too along with the fine tapestries we had stripped from his walls and the spices from the kitchen. Being given a free hand by our council made me feel like a brigand but as Lord di Roderuccio had said, the Dodici had set the avalanche in motion when they raided Florentine land.

The village close to the border was not expecting an attack, especially from the south and we took it as quickly as we had the estate. When we had taken all, we headed north to Florentine land. As soon as we were out of sight of the village the bulk of my men joined me to head back south, using the side roads and trees to do so unobserved while the animals and treasure were taken back to my hall.

That night my leaders asked me what we would do on the morrow. I smiled, "We wait for the Sienese will come to us."

Edward was an exceptional archer but had limited knowledge of such raids, "How do you know, Sir John?"

"Simple. Lord di Roderuccio will have told the Dodici that I have taken his land. He will demand that they get it back for him as they were the cause of its loss. I expect men to come tomorrow to retake it. We will wait for them and defend these walls."

I spoke confidently but knew that if they did not come it would do no harm to keep the villages close by guessing. The men I had sent to escort the animals back to my home would be back within a day and then we could raid once more.

We kept a good watch and the sentries reported the Sienese at Terces. We manned the wall as the three hundred or so men approached. They had some nobles, crossbowmen and the local levy. They were led by a dozen knights I took to be the Dodici. They saw the walls manned and halted. I smiled as I saw the hasty conference gathered by the Dodici. They had the crossbowmen line up and they dismounted their horsemen. They were all plated.

Hob said, "Bodkins for the knights, war arrows for the crossbows."

We were on the gate which had a small roof and was crenulated. The rest of the wall was stone with a fighting platform. I had alternated archers and lances. We would be able to repel an attack in whatever form it came.

Zuzzo shook his head, "They are fools, Sir John. They cannot take defended walls. We would have struggled and we are the White Company."

"It is pride, Zuzzo. I would have swallowed my pride and walked away had we been forced to risk losing men to take this place."

I nodded to Edward, the captain of my archers who gave the order to nock. I bellowed, "If you advance, I will give the order for my archers to unleash an arrow storm, my lord, and men will die."

The Dodici were willing to sacrifice men's lives to prove that they had been right to raid Florence and risk the wrath of condottiere. They remained stubbornly silent.

I sighed, "Release."

Edward commanded, "Draw!" A heartbeat after the yew bows creaked to full draw he said, "Release."

He did not release his own arrow with his archers. Instead, he aimed at one of the Dodici. They had positioned themselves behind the crossbows and the dismounted knights thinking that they were safe. Even for my archer, it was at extreme range but I knew that he had weighed it all in his head. He had the height of the gatehouse and what breeze there was came from behind him. Even if he did not hit the noble, he would give him a scare. As crossbowmen and dismounted men at arms were felled, I followed the trajectory of Edward's single arrow. His archers were not watching. They were drawing and releasing as fast as they could. The arrow rose and then descended. The Dodici were blissfully unaware of the fletched missile plunging towards them. It was a bodkin and when it slammed into the shoulder of one of the nobles the effect was out of all proportion to the injury. To a man, they turned their horses and headed down the road. The noble's squire led the wounded man's horse. The arrows were still falling but when the levy saw their leaders leaving it did not take long for them to join them and by the time the demoralised men at arms realised that they had been abandoned and they, too, fled, the action was over. A mere handful of the crossbowmen, professionals like us, survived. The rest lay dead. Like the dead men at arms, they had been sacrificed for pride.

My company did not cheer for they knew that this had been unnecessary. It secured our position and meant we could raid with impunity but we had a bad taste in our mouths.

"Clear the bodies and make a pyre to burn them."

This time there were one or two men who were lightly wounded. My men tended to their hurts and then sent them back to Siena. The dead were all piled together on a pyre of crossbows and wood. Their plate and weapons were gathered but while we might have been able to sell crossbows, my archers hated the weapon they called the devil's machine.

By the end of the week, we had raided the land for ten miles around us and when the Dodici returned it was not for war but to buy us off. The wounded noble was not with them. They came under a flag of truce and with a wagon. It was reparations for their raid and two thousand florins to ensure that the White Company raided them no more. I agreed and sent riders to recall Robin and Michael. When they acknowledged my orders, we headed back to Florentine land. We had a wagon with loot and my archers flanked the column in case of any reprisal from the locals. There was none and that did not surprise me. The failed attack had shown them the inadequacy of their army. If they wished to fight against condottiere then they needed to hire their own company. I knew that there were none in Italy that could rival my company.

We waited at the border and Robin and Michael, also with wagons and loot, joined us so that we could make a triumphal procession through the land that had been raided. Many of my detractors call me mercenary, cunning and corrupt. Some of those criticisms may have been true but as we passed through the devasted borderlands I used the reparations given to me by the Dodici to make the lives of those robbed a little better. Had I been all that people said of me I would have kept it.

We reached my home close to dark. Our loot was placed in my barns and my men were told to return on the morrow for its distribution. Michael and Robin stayed in my home so that we could speak of the raid. That was our way. We tried to learn from our successes and, when we had them, our failures.

"The Sienese are badly led, Sir John."

"I know, Michael. When I spoke to Lord di Roderuccio, I realised that. The council is self-serving. When the town was ruled by the bishop it was well managed but now that it is an imperial city it has lost direction."

"Do you think that King Charles of Naples had anything to do with the raids?"

I looked at Robin who was a clever and thoughtful man, "I cannot see what he has to gain from the attacks."

Robin shrugged, "His mother was Hungarian and he is heir to the Hungarian throne. The emperor is Hungarian. Siena is imperial." He tapped his finger in a line as he made each point. "I cannot see the reason either but these points all conjoin do they not?"

"Perhaps and as King Charles' enemies were not stopped by us then the Neapolitan ruler might feel he has no need of us."

"And you were responsible, albeit indirectly, for his excommunication and the exposing of the conspiracy." Michael had joined up his own thoughts in a single and compelling line.

I decided that they were both right, "It matters not for the French are not coming hither and we are all richer as a result. You, Michael, may go back to your family and Robin back to your debauchery. I have a new child who will soon be born and life is good."

Life was indeed good and when my son was born, healthy and also named John, then my life was, indeed perfect. We also heard, not long after my son was born, that Louis of Anjou had died, apparently of illness, in Bisceglie. The war was over and the army of de Courcy squatted in Arezzo.

I was somewhat surprised when the council of Florence came, with Michael, to visit me.

"Sir John, you have heard of the death of the pretender?"

"I have."

"We are led to believe that Enguerrand de Courcy wishes to return to France."

I spread my arms, "He can go and does not need my permission."

Michael's father-in-law smiled, "He wishes to go back a rich man. He is willing to sell Arezzo to us. We would have you escort the wagons with the gold to Arezzo. Michael here has agreed to act as a seneschal of Arezzo until we can meet with the council of Arezzo. He will need some of your company as a garrison. They will, of course, be paid."

I looked at Michael, a little hurt that he had not mentioned this to me. He saw the look and said, quietly, "I was asked to do this, Sir John, this morning. If you do not wish me to take it on then I will not. I am of the White Company."

I saw no deception in his eyes and I smiled, "Of course, I wish you to take it on for the White Company is to be paid and our coffers will be filled."

We left two days later. I did not need all my men. Michael and Robin chose the two hundred men he would command and we added fifty lances as an escort. Robin remained in Florence to command the rest of our men and to recruit more. Our profits meant we could afford more men. I could not see a war in the future but I had learned that in northern Italy the next war was just a knife in the back away. Mantua, Verona, Padua, Bologna, Ferrara and the rest each wished to have larger lands. Florence, Venice, Genoa and Milan were the powerful states and the smaller ones all wished to emulate them. Pisa, Lucca and Siena were all now backwaters. They were the smaller fish waiting to be gobbled up and when they were it would be by men such as the ones I led. That was life in Italy.

Chapter 17

We enjoyed a peaceful and prosperous year following the death of Louis of Anjou. Michael only spent six months in Arezzo but it did him good. He commanded without me looking over his shoulder and the lessons I had given him seemed to have been good ones for the people of Arezzo saw him not as an oppressor but a kind man who ruled fairly and was a good arbiter in civil disputes. His familia grew and when our men returned some had wives from the time in Arezzo.

It was a good year but marred by the murder of Bernabò Visconti on the orders of his nephew. He was strangled in his cell. It was a sad end for a man who had manipulated the lands around Milan for almost as long as I had been a condottiero. Donnina wept and, as she lay in my arms I said, "Would you have me wreak vengeance on your cousin?" I was not afraid of Galeazzo Visconti for he was no warrior and any company he sent against me would be like boys against men.

She kissed me, "It is good of you to ask but no, we are in the business of hiring out our swords. If we seek to use them for ourselves then we would be making a mistake. No, my cousin will be punished for murder, if not in this life, then the next. I am more concerned with the effect it has on us."

I shook my head in the dark, "Milan seeks to use its tentacles to strangle the lands close by. Verona, Padua and Mantua are the ones in the greatest danger. Perhaps, when the ripples from your father's death have died down, I will travel to Padua. The council there hired Giovanni and, who knows, they may wish to hire the White Company. If your cousin tries to attack the lands of Padua then we may profit from it."

"Is that likely?"

My spies in Florence brought me news and gossip. The Paduans, under Francesco il Vecchio Carrara had taken Treviso. I knew that he had relied heavily on the skills of my former comrade but it had made his neighbours suspicious. I had heard a rumour that Venice, Verona and Friuli were speaking to one another and an alliance against Padua was being formed.

"There is a chance. I will give it a month and then ride with a handful of men to Padua." My thoughts were to see if there was a chance of a contract in the north. Florence had no problems with a Padua that sought to protect itself from its rivals to the north.

I did, as was needed, speak with Michael and Robin. Michael's experience had changed him a little. He was now a leading citizen in Florence and did not suffer from the antipathy that I enjoyed, he was allowed to live in the city and his time in Arezzo had made him a popular man. It did him no harm that he was also seen as a warrior but a more acceptable one than Giovanni Acuto. When the two of them visited with me I could tell that there was something on his mind.

"Come, Michael, we have endured war and hunger together, there is nothing that you can say to me that will upset me. I never see my firstborns and you are like a son to me. Speak."

"I have been approached to take command of the Florentine army."

Before I could speak Robin snorted, "Pretty little boys with swords and old men with rusted helmets do not constitute an army, Michael."

He smiled at the apt description, "I know and that is why I was chosen. They wish to learn from the White Company."

I still had all my faculties and I saw the hand of Michael's father-in-law behind all of this. I said, quietly, "And those men you led at Arezzo, the ones who are now married, would be the heart of the new army."

Even Robin was taken aback, "Even my archers?"

Michael smiled, "Aye, Robin, for some are as old as you are and I know that one day, perhaps soon, you will string your bow no longer."

The guilty look on Robin's face told me that Michael had hit the mark. I would deal with that later on.

"I am not sure how I feel about losing some of my company."

Michael sighed, "The last employment for the company was Arezzo and before that Siena. It is a long time between wars. Do you have another contract, Sir John?" I shook my head. "Then I can tell you that many of the company are thinking of joining other companies. The Company of St George would readily hire those who had served in the White Company. Our old comrade in arms, Alberico, would snap up any lances and bows that sought a new employer. This is inevitable, Sir John." He tried to make it easier but failed when he said, "You are getting old, Sir John. Is it not time to hang up your sword as you did the bow?"

I was about to become angry and then realised that Michael was not trying to insult me. He was being like a concerned son. "I know you mean well, Michael, but I am still a soldier and I will carry on as long as God allows. I wish you well and you are right. We can always hire men who wish to fight for the White Company."

The news from Michael both pleased and depressed me. There was no conflict and I was not being overlooked. I knew that I could never be the leader of the Florentines. I had hurt them too much in the past. It was the scale of the change I did not like. The men who would be staying with Michael as the heart of the Florentine army would be those men who had served me the longest. They were not friends but I knew them and their skills. Was Michael right?

I took the opportunity when time allowed to speak privately to Robin. I invited him to ride with me on a piece of land I kept for hunting. I had my gamekeepers guard it jealously and the only ones who hunted there were invited by me and they were few and far between. It made for the guarantee of good hunting. We took a couple of men and our bows. We did not discuss our futures until we had made our kills. We were both too good at what we did for that. We had a purpose. We stalked and whilst we did not move as easily, on foot, as we once had, we were skilful and brought down four deer. The boars we started were ignored. They were not the beasts to be hunted with arrows. For those a hunter needed boar spears and beaters. I noted where we had seen them and stored that knowledge for another day. Nobles enjoyed hunting wild boar and it was a lure I could keep when I needed to gain a favour. I was not too proud to stoop to such acts.

While the men we had brought began a fire and then gutted the deer I spoke to Robin. We knew each other too well for Robin not to know that I had brought him hunting with an ulterior motive. One of the men poured wine into our coistrels and we toasted one another.

"Well, Sir John, I am here and I enjoyed the hunting. If you brought me hence to demonstrate that you are still a skilled archer then you have done so, but I think that there is something else in the invitation."

The fire spat as the blood from the heart, liver and kidneys of the deer began to drop and sizzle on the burning wood. Soon the smell of cooking meat would make me hungry. I downed my wine and held out my arm for another, "It was the talk with Michael that set me thinking."

"You are happy to let him go then? Even though he is like a son to you."

"It is because he is like a son that I will let him go. I have trained him and, even though I do say so myself, I have done a good job of it. No, it is you, old friend, and your future that is in my head. I saw your face when Michael spoke of getting too old. I saw your thoughts behind the mask that you wear. I would know your intentions."

He too emptied his cup and it was refilled. The smell from the cooking offal was tempting me and clearly Robin too, "I am still the finest of archers."

"Of course."

"Having said that I am not as strong as I once was."

I laughed, "You have spread your seed so often that it is no surprise to me that some of your power has gone."

He smiled, "Aye, there will be sons of mine spread through England, France and Italy. It is a shame that they will never know that they have the blood of an archer coursing through their veins." I waited for more as the men we had brought turned the sizzling meat on the sword used as an improvised skewer. "I will do as you have done, Sir John, I will continue to lead the archers but I will do so as a commander. I have younger men I can bring on. Do not worry that Michael has taken your older archers. They are experienced, that is true but they do not have the hunger that we do."

"The food is almost ready, my lord."

I nodded and continued to study Robin. It was clear to me that he had not finished, "Marrying Lady Donnina did not make you less of a warrior. You made a good choice in that one for despite her youth she has wisdom beyond her years. I have no wife to slow me down but those who go with young Michael think of their wives at home. If Michael is merely to protect Florence, then they will do well but we need young men who want the spoils of war and the coins that come from winning."

The men brought us the sliced heart, liver and kidneys on two wooden platters and we ate the slightly pink but juicy meat with our fingers. There is no finer taste in this world than meat taken from a fresh kill and cooked while the animal is still being butchered. By the time we had finished and licked our fingers clean, the carcasses were slung across the backs of the sumpters we had brought and we were able to return to my home. As we rode, I told Robin of my plans to visit with Giovanni. If men were deserting for other companies then the best solution was to find another lucrative contract. Padua seemed the best opportunity.

Robin agreed, "Aye, we have not yet shown Venice, Verona and Mantua our skills. While you are away, I will recruit new archers. We have lost none to the other companies." He was right, it was the men at arms who had left us and they were, in the main, Italian, German and Hungarian. "I will easily replace the ones who have followed Michael. Our name still draws men from England as King Richard does not go to war and English archers need to draw their bows in anger."

I told Donnina what I intended and she was happy. It was not that she disliked me being in our home but when I was not there, she knew we were earning money and Donnina was keen to provide for our children in the future. I sent John to Pisa so that William would know that we had fewer men to pay as Michael and the men he was taking with him would no longer be White Company. It meant more money to invest. Gianluca prepared our mounts and sumpters for the ride to the north. We would not need to ride with anonymous cloaks. Our enemies were now to the north and west. Padua was, thanks to Giovanni, a friend. Bologna and Ferrara were neutral and we would be allowed free passage. I knew that at some time in the future there might be conflict with them but while there was peace, I would take advantage of my name. The defeat we had inflicted on the

Savoyards and the French had done nothing to harm my reputation. When we left, we wore my white livery and took the road north and east to Padua.

I had not warned Giovanni of our imminent arrival but then again, he and Francesco 'il Novello' di Carrara were busy skirmishing with the Veronese. I hoped that the conflict might induce the Paduans to hire the White Company. With Michael commanding Florence I knew that we would be allowed to take the White Company north. As we neared Bologna lands we were told, in the inn in which we stayed, that the Milanese now controlled the city. I had not heard how Galeazzo Visconti viewed me but I was taking no chances and after rewarding the helpful innkeeper we headed for Modena instead.

It was Verona itself that upset our plans. As we headed north, we heard of the escalation of the war on the borders of the two city-states. Wars, despite what those who write of such things might scratch onto parchment, are rarely fought as battles. Often it is a strategic game with marching and countermarching. Captains take and hold strategically important places. Farms and villages are raided for food. Such manoeuvrings are fluid and the front lines change regularly. When we reached Montagnana we heard that, a month since, a skirmish between Cortesia da Serego and the Paduans had taken place. My old friend Giovanni had thwarted the attempt to take the town and the Veronese had threatened Treviso in the north forcing the Paduans to shift defenders to that town. As we neared Rovolon we rode cautiously and it was as well that we did. The Veronese were building a bastida or field fortress. We were alerted by the banging of hammers and the noise of construction. The Veronese eyes were watching north and, as we sheltered in some trees that overlooked the small town from the south, we were able to see the temporary structure as it was built.

I rubbed my chin. Such structures were useful. It meant a small number of men could hold the bastida whilst others could ride forth and control the area. "We will need to go around Rovolon." I looked at Zuzzo who was our expert in such matters.

"There are two approaches. One is through Tencarola and the other over the ford at Brusenaga."

"Which is the quieter?"

"The ford at Brusenaga."

The Veronese would be more likely to use a bridge rather than a ford and that decided me. "We will ride to the ford."

Zuzzo said, "It is a longer route."

Gianluca added, "And we will get wet."

I laughed, "We are becoming soft. It will do us good to endure a little harder riding and to wet our boots."

We turned to head in a more westerly direction. Now my decision to wear my white livery became a danger for we were easier to see and identify. We had passed through the lands of neutral neighbours and now neared the Veronese. We were not enemies of the Veronese but I was known to be a friend to Giovanni and to Padua. If apprehended we could be held for ransom. We packed our white cloaks in our bags and donned plainer brown ones. We carried them as blankets for our horses and in case we needed to make hovels. Now they would disguise us. They stank, of course, and were dirty but my words to Zuzzo and Gianluca had been chosen deliberately. We were warriors.

We managed to find shelter for the night in the Abbazia di Praglia. It was a small monastery not far from the river Bacchiglione. The monks admitted us and took our payment for shelter but there was something in the air that made me suspicious. Zuzzo was well travelled and knew how to talk to people of all kinds. We had travelled together enough for a simple nod from me to set him on a quest for information. After we had finished our meal and while I spoke to the Abbot of our visit to Rome, he made the excuse that he had to see to the horses and disappeared. He did not reappear until he re-entered the large cell that we had been given as we prepared for sleep. There was just one bed but four palliasses provided a bed for the others. He held his finger to his mouth as he entered. He pointed to John who rose and went outside to make certain we were not observed.

Zuzzo waited a few moments and then spoke in a hushed whisper, "The Veronese are ahead of us. The abbot knows of this and that you are a friend of Padua. Antonio dell Scala plans on crossing the river by the ford and outwitting the Paduans who are to the west. They hope to surprise your friend who waits with his army on the other road."

I believed the intelligence but I was curious how my trumpeter had discovered the information, "How did you learn this?"

He smiled, "The monk who tends the horses is little more than a boy. I impressed him with a little magic to win his favour and when I showed him the trick it was simple enough to engage him in a conversation about travellers. The enemy warriors are just three miles ahead."

"Then they are not at the ford yet?"

"No, Sir John, only a fool would cross a ford in the dark and besides it is unguarded."

"Then let us be fools. We sleep for an hour and then rise. When the monks rise for Lauds, we will leave."

"And if they object?"

I looked to Gianluca and shrugged, "They are monks and not warriors. Even if they chose to send a rider to warn the Veronese then we would be ahead of them. Bring back John and then sleep."

Of course, I did not sleep. My mind was a maelstrom filled with military matters. When I had been in Padua, I knew that the main defence of the city was the gate to the south. The river and a canal protected the west. The city on that side had poorer defences as it relied on water for its defence. We had to get ahead of the Veronese. We would have to sneak through their lines. I was glad that I had four such professional men to guard me. They knew their business and the thought of riding through a large Veronese army would not discomfit them.

When the bell sounded for Lauds, I was already awake. We dressed and left our cell with alacrity. As I had expected the priests were not happy that we were about to depart. I smiled at the abbot, "I am sorry, Abbot, but the bell woke my men and once awake we could not return to sleep. This just means we leave earlier and we should have a clear road to Padua." I was giving the abbot the opportunity to confess that he knew the Veronese were ahead of us.

I saw in his eyes that he would deliberately lie to us and he made the sign of the cross and said, "Go with God." He expected us to be taken. The Paduans would take a dim view of the abbey that lay so close to their city colluding with their enemies.

John had the sumpter and so he rode behind Robert who was our solitary scout. Gianluca flanked me and Zuzzo brought up the rear. We did not gallop as that would have alerted our enemies as well as tiring out our horses. Instead, we walked along the road that had been built in the time of the Romans. When we neared the enemy camp, we slowed and Robert took us through the woods. We could hear the noise of an army waking up. The smell of the night watches' fires was augmented by the smell of food being cooked. We knew from the smell where the horse lines were and we wove a line through the trees to avoid either getting too close to the horses or the latrines.

Despite our care, we were spotted. I later deduced it was a patrol that had been sent to see if the ford was clear and they had ridden back, not along the road which twisted to the ford, but the more direct route through the trees. Robert was, by now, a very confident rider who was able to make quick and well-judged decisions. He spurred his horse and unobtrusively drawing his sword rode towards them. John followed his friend and, after a quick glance from Gianluca, I nodded and spurred my mount. My sword was also in my hand. I suppose the scouts must have known all the horsemen in their army for nobles would never be up this early and not recognising either the mounts or the livery shouted out their challenge. Their patrol outnumbered ours but we were better men. I saw Robert sweep and scythe his sword at the middle of the leader. He was plated but as he was drawing his sword, he exposed a slight gap beneath his breastplate. The sword sliced through the mail. It was not a mortal wound but it did incapacitate him. John had a tethered horse and he rode as close to his friend as he could get. The wounded noble's horse had veered off and Gianluca and I rode behind John to afford him some assistance. I smacked my sword to the left and was rewarded by a cry as my blade ripped into the upper arm of one rider. I had caught up with John for the sumpter was not cooperating and I was just in time to parry a blow to John's head. I twisted my sword in a riposte which managed to also rake down the man's face. A blade that close to an eye makes any man flinch and the Veronese warrior was no exception. Zuzzo was showing off for he rode his horse with his knees and was flailing both his arms at the same time. By the time we reached the last two men in the patrol five Veronese had been wounded or killed and the others forced away from us. We rode hard and this time headed for the road. We needed speed. Behind us, I heard the clamour of a camp filled with chaos. The sounds of battle were unmistakeable and da Serego had to wonder if his camp was under attack. He would need to wait for his patrol to reach him to know the truth. We could not waste that precious time.

It was still dark as we clattered along the road and then splashed into the ford. Thankfully, it was not deep and we did not need to swim but the current was strong enough to make us move further downstream than we might have liked. We had to force our horses to fight against the water to reach the other bank. We were still not completely safe but we could afford to rest our horses. We had not spoken since the attack. There had been no need. We were professional soldiers.

Once on the other side we shook ourselves dry and changed once more into our white cloaks. The mask of brown might be seen as threatening in a city that was surrounded by its enemies. The White Company would be welcomed in Padua. The stinking old cloaks were draped over the backs of our horses and we headed along the road to Padua. The rising sun told me that we had timed our crossing to perfection. Even now the Veronese would be starting their crossing of the river. We did not have long to warn the Paduans of the impending disaster of an invading army where they did not expect to find one. That there had been not a guard or a sentry at the ford told me that no one expected da Serego to attack from that direction. My fears were confirmed when, as the sun finally rose and we neared the outskirts of Padua, we came upon the first Paduan outpost. It was commanded by my old comrade in arms, Rodrigo.

He frowned when he saw us, "Sir John, I would say I was pleased to see you but your arrival at such an hour does not bode well."

I nodded. This was no time to sweeten my words with honey, "Your enemies are upon you, Captain Rodrigo. The Veronese are not far behind us and they are crossing the ford."

Some of the men at the barricade began to become agitated. Rodrigo snapped, "Are you men or mice? We all knew that they would come and that we would have to fight them. This is your land, is it not? If we do not bleed for it then who shall?" His commanding voice had the desired effect. He pointed to a youth, "Carlos, take Sir John to the city and say that I await orders."

"Yes, sir." The way the young man snapped to attention told me why Rodrigo had chosen him. The young warrior was eager and keen. He ran to his pony and mounted swiftly.

Rodrigo waved as we followed Carlos towards the Savonarola Gate, a mile or so up the road, "Thank you for the warning, Sir John. Padua will not forget it."

The gates were opened as we approached and seeing the young officer with us, we were waved through with alacrity. We galloped through a town that was just waking up but which already had streets heaving with more people than I expected. I knew immediately why. They were refugees who had fled the advancing Veronese. If this was a siege then belts would need to be tightened. I wondered, as we neared the city's palace, if my decision to come had been a wise one. I dismissed the idea almost immediately for we had brought a warning to an old friend and such bonds transcended the need for personal safety.

It was not Giovanni who greeted us when we reached the palace but Francesco il Vecchio da Carrara, the old leader of Padua. He recognised me and said, after I had bowed, "You bring news, Sir John?"

I told him the same as I had Rodrigo. The old man had led Padua for many years and was not discomfited overmuch by my words.

"I will organise the defence of the city." He turned to an aide and said, "Sound the trumpets to summon the militia. Carlos, take Sir John to my son and Captain Giovanni. I will bar the Savonarola Gate."

The words told me that we would not be able to return to Padua the same way we had left. We galloped back along the road through which we had just come. The echoes of the trumpets had men leaving their houses with an assortment of weapons, helmets and armour. They would soon be manning Padua's walls and I wondered how many of them would survive the attack.

The Paduan camp was a mile or so west of the city. Giovanni and il Vecchio's son, Francesco, were clearly planning on using the Brentelle canal and the River Bacchiglione as a defence against a Veronese attack. The clever crossing of the ford meant that the defences were in tatters.

Both my old friend and the young noble were clever commanders and realised immediately the futility of their position. Even as the banners of the Veronese appeared to the south of us the camp was struck and, once more, I retraced my steps. It was a race and my horse was wearying but it was a race we had to win. There was no time for words as we headed as quickly as we could for the south gate. That the Veronese did not pursue us told me that da Serego had a clear plan in his mind.

It was noon before we were able to speak to the two leaders of Padua and Giovanni. While my men attended to our weary mounts I was summoned to a council of war. I wondered if my military advice would be sought or was my invitation mere courtesy? I knew from the few words I had exchanged that both Giovanni and il Novello were grateful for my warning. With no defences to the south, the Paduan army would have been quickly destroyed by the vastly superior Veronese one.

"I have ordered the militia to be mustered. Captain General Giovanni, you are the commander of our army, how do you wish the men to be used? Do we man the battlements and await a fight?"

Giovanni glanced at me. This would be his fight and his decision but I knew he respected my opinion. I had had ideas but I would allow one of my oldest friends to make the first suggestions. I gave him a slight nod and the smile he returned told me that it had been the right thing to do.

"We cannot simply let them starve us out. As I saw when we returned here the city is overflowing with refugees. We do not have enough food to feed them." He picked up a wax tablet and drew a crude circle. He placed a cross close to the south gate. "We have six thousand militia in the town. I would have them leave the town with banners flying and march up towards the Savonarola Gate. That is more than half of the men at our disposal. I will take all the cavalry, all two thousand of them and we will head along the right bank of the canal. Captain

Cermisone da Parma will lead the eighteen hundred men on foot on the other side of the canal. The vegetation will hide us." I nodded my approval at the plan for I saw how it might bring an unlikely victory. The militia were bait. I did not think that the Paduans would have thought of such a plan. It took a condottiero to do so.

I saw il Vecchio frown, "This seems a foolhardy strategy for you are dividing our army into three."

I think that my old friend was reassured by my nod for he said, with a smile, "No, my lord, four. I will have the forty barges that lie moored at the southern end of the canal filled with our gunners and crossbows. They will give us a mobile fortress. The canal will ensure that they have an easy way to escape if my plan fails and they can also protect our dismounted horsemen and infantry."

Il Novello nodded, "I will come with you, Captain Giovanni."

Giovanni shook his head, "No, my lord. I need a da Carrara to lead the men of Padua. When the Veronese attack the militia, it will need a man of iron to hold them until we can attack."

His words were well chosen and the young noble swelled with pride.

I said, "And me, Giovanni, where would you like me?"

"You do not need to risk your life, Sir John. You have already given Padua great service."

I laughed and waved a dismissive hand, "And if you think that I will squat like a toad behind Padua's walls then you have forgotten much about me. I only have four men with me but we shall come with your cavalry. Perhaps I may be of some small service to Padua."

Il Vecchio had a mind that was still as sharp as ever and he said, "What brought you to Padua, Sir John?"

"To seek work for the White Company. This war between Padua and its enemies seemed to me one that we might influence."

"And when this encounter is over, Sir John, we will discuss such matters but until then every man draws a sword," he drew his own weapon, "even old men such as me!"

The gathered leaders all banged the table and their shouts of 'Carro, Carro!' echoed in the palace.

Chapter 18

My bodyguards, when I told them, showed disapproval on their faces. Their words did not but I knew that they were unhappy that I was putting myself in danger. There was a sound reason behind it. I knew it was a gamble which, if successful, would bring a healthy contract the White Company's way. We headed out of the south gate and headed due west. The noisy and ebullient militia headed north. They were marching before the walls of their families and I knew that they would march with confidence. That confidence, however, would be as thin as a piece of parchment if they were attacked. Giovanni had shown great skill in putting the young da Carrara at their head. The militia chanted 'Carro, Carro' as they marched. It was the war cry of the da Carrara family. Every Veronese eye would be drawn to them. They would have more than a mile to march and da Serego would be planning how to defeat them. Giovanni's plan had a chance so long as the militia marched north.

We, in contrast, walked our horses with no flags flying and we were, in any case, beyond the view of the Veronese. The gunners and crossbowmen had left first and would already be filling the forty barges. I thought it a particularly innovative way to use a weapon that was most vulnerable to cavalry attack. This way the missile men would have a mobile defence. The infantry marched on our right. When we reached the canal and the river then they would march to the east of the river and we to the west. We could easily cross it and yet the vegetation would hide us. Giovanni had told the assembled troops when we were assembled that double pay would be forthcoming. It was clever. The militia fought for their home but the provvisionati fought for pay and even though we would be outnumbered, I knew that the offer would have a beneficial effect and would influence the outcome of this battle.

I rode with my old friend. "I asked, before, where I was needed. Have you an answer now, Giovanni?"

He smiled, "I have some young nobles who are keen to show that they can win honour. There are just two hundred of them and had I not used Francesco to lead the militia then he would have commanded them. I know that your words will hold them back and they will not waste their lives. When we served together, I saw how you husbanded young warriors and allowed them to overcome their natural urges which, in turn, meant that they became better warriors. I am here to make all Padua into better soldiers as we did with Pisa."

"I will do as you ask but, as you know, the effect of our influence in Pisa did not last much beyond our departure. It is now waiting to be gobbled up by some predator, probably Milan."

"You may be right, Sir John, but we will do what we can."

When we reached the river and the canal it took some time for the barges to be loaded and that allowed us the opportunity to get ahead of them. The trees through which we marched were cooler than the road had been heading west. It was June and the noonday sun would bake the land and make marching in sweltering armour unbearable. Through the gaps in the trees, we could see the militia as they headed north and watched as da Serego marshalled his horsemen into blocks interspersed with infantry and preceded by crossbows. I did not underestimate the Veronese commander. His battle plan was sound. His only mistake, so far as I could tell, was his failure to guard against a flank attack. I smiled to myself. Perhaps it was only men like Giovanni and me who were able to see such things clearly. I always liked a surprise flank attack. I had found that if you could manage to do so from the enemy's right then while they had weapons with which to face you, they had no shields. Although plated men did not need shields, those with leather or mail armour did.

I was a detached observer as I watched il Novello place his men. They used some of the carts that they had travelled in to make a barrier behind which he put the crossbows and formed his men up. I heard their defiant cries of 'Carro, Carro' which were now augmented by the rhythmic banging of spears on shields. We did not mount our horses and that showed that Giovanni had great confidence in his plan. He knew that the longer our horses rested without plated men on their backs, the greater the chance of success.

I decided I wanted to watch the battle from a closer position and, after telling Giovanni what I intended, I went with my bodyguards and we swam our horses across the river. The water was refreshing and the horses as well as my men enjoyed its cooling effect. It also afforded me the information about the safety of fording the river when we made our attack. It was an easy ford. We joined da Parma's infantrymen as they watched the Veronese begin their attack. The carts behind which they sheltered gave the militia a sense of strength and they sent their crossbow bolts at the advancing enemy. When the exchange of missiles died down then two battles of horsemen charged the militia. That was the moment I expected the Paduans to break but il Novello proved to be an inspiring commander and they not only held the enemy soldiers but repulsed the first attack. A second battle of cavalry managed to push the militia back but they still held. When a huge block of Veronese infantry began their advance then I knew the militia did not have long and we swam back across the river.

"Giovanni, the militia and il Novello have done well but they cannot withstand a third attack."

He nodded, "I agree." He pointed to the canal. The barges were still making their way north. "They will be our defence. Mount!"

We had not dismounted and, once more we crossed the river. We arrived just as the Veronese drove a wedge through the centre of the Paduan line. The militia had done all that could have been expected of them and more. They fled, not south but east towards the Savonarola Gate. The carts and the wagons with their baggage were abandoned. I watched as da Serego ordered more of his infantry and his cavalry to pursue. The pursuit would be hampered by the abandoned carts. It also made the Veronese line less cohesive.

We heard the Veronese give their war cry, 'Scala, Scala!' They had victory in their grasp. I saw the Veronese leader detach a couple of men and they headed west. Was that for more men or, more likely, to tell Verona of their victory?

Giovanni nodded, "Just as I hoped, their eyes are on the prize and not on us. Form lines. Cermisone, use your men to block the escape west."

"Yes, Captain." He ordered his men into a column and they headed up the river to the northern ford.

We formed our lines and Giovanni pointed to the two hundred well-plated and brightly attired nobles awaiting me.

I nodded and rode over to them, "Young bloods of Padua. This day I have been honoured with the command of the hope of Padua. Follow me and obey every order and the commands from my trumpeter and we will win the day, win glory and live to tell the tale! If you do not heed my commands then your bones will bleach the plain before your city."

They all cheered. Gianluca rolled his eyes. We placed ourselves before the men who shuffled into two lines. We had acquired lances while in Padua but I had no banner to be carried by Zuzzo. Instead, we rode before the banners of eight of the nobles. We made a colourful sight. I also knew that we would attract the attention of the Veronese. They would see their chance of booty and riches.

Giovanni sounded the advance. It would alert the Veronese but that was immaterial as the men chasing the militia had lost all sense of order. More than half of the Veronese army was now committed to a pursuit that was already doomed to failure for il Vecchio had more militia behind the walls ready to repulse them. The ebullient Veronese would be of no use to da Serego who would have to face almost four thousand professional soldiers. He had many hundreds of wagons, camp followers and servants whilst most of his better soldiers were chasing militia. The nobles who remained with him were in for a real shock. We moved at the walk. Although it gave the Veronese the time to organise it was not a wasted effort for it enabled us to keep a straight line and to advance steadily. I waved my lance to the right as half a dozen young nobles began to spur their horses. I said not a word but my lance had the desired effect and they moved back. I had fought on horseback since the time of Poitiers and I knew instinctively when to speed up. The slight prick to my horse was enough to make him move faster and I prepared to lower my lance.

It was Giovanni who bellowed, "Charge" and his trumpeter sounded his instrument.

I said, over my shoulder, "Zuzzo."

The horn sounded and the young nobles began to chant 'Carro, Carro.'

The enemy had turned and tried to form lines to face us but they had been, in the main, unsuccessful. I lowered my lance and pulled the shield a little tighter. I doubted that I would need the shield for the mob of milling men ahead of us were not counter charging. However, a warrior who had survived battles as long as I had took no chances. I wanted to return to Florence and my wife and family, whole. I glanced, briefly, to my left and right. The line was not perfectly straight but then these were not the lances of the White Company. These were Paduan nobles who wanted to impress their wives and sweethearts watching from the walls of Padua. I had the time, as I pricked my horse once more, to see Venetian standards amongst the enemy ranks. The senior ally of Verona, Venice, had clearly intended to help the Veronese destroy Padua. The enemy horns now sounded a cacophony of commands. I suspected that da Serego was vainly recalling his men. Giovanni's strategy had clearly worked well and the flight of the militia had sucked the eager Veronese behind them. The trumpets caused more confusion amongst the men we were about to strike.

I pulled back my arm and prepared to strike at the horseman who rode a magnificent white horse and had a green and blue livery. He tried to urge his horse towards me but it was too little and too late. He was barely trotting when my lance smashed into his shield. He was not square on to me and the force of the blow and the power of my horse knocked him and his mount to the ground. I did not even have to pull my arm back for the next strike although the collision had slowed me. I punched at the head of the next man and his bascinet helmet fell from his head as his hand dropped his lance.

"I yield! I yield!"

Without turning I said, "John, take him and his horse."

"Aye, my lord. A fine pair of strikes."

The eager young noblemen I had led in the charge had not let me down. We had carved a hole in the centre of their line. The enemy threw down their weapons and surrendered. The best of the Veronese were chasing the militia. These were the nobles and had not expected to be attacked. My contingent apart, the rest were provvisionati. The men we had struck were not professional soldiers. They knew that they were outclassed and no one fought against condottiere and expected to win. We had taken almost half of their army, their wagons, treasure and camp followers. By any measure, we had a victory but it was not enough for I knew, as did Giovanni, that the whole army had to be destroyed.

He bellowed out his orders, "Captain da Parma, you and your foot soldiers can secure the captives. Horsemen of Padua, let us ride to the aid of our militia!" Cermisone had left men to guard the ford and then followed the horsemen.

There was a cheer and I shouted, "Form lines." Zuzzo's horn sounded the command and I saw that my young nobles obeyed me. They were flushed with excitement and the joy of victory but I think that they realised it was our discipline that had brought us the victory. They would all be better warriors in the future. I had done all that had been asked of me.

We rode purposefully towards the milling mass of men who were busy ransacking the wagons of the militia. So eager had they been to take treasure that the majority of the militia had made the safety of the gates and now joined the defenders on the walls. As our hooves thundered so the Veronese and their allies realised their perilous plight and men began to flee towards the river. They fled obliquely in a vain attempt to avoid our lances. Our long line simply wheeled. We were in the centre and as the nobles had the best of horses the manoeuvre was completed flawlessly. The loose line kept its formation. We drew closer to the backs of men who now discarded their booty as they fled for their lives. My lance had already struck men and I knew that it would not last much longer. I did not attempt to strike at men in plate for I knew that the river would take them. Instead, I struck at those wearing mail. In truth, they were the majority of men we encountered. Most of those on foot threw down their weapons and surrendered. I ordered Robert to take captive the first ten while the rest of us rode after the horsemen. Some of these were nobles. If I could take them then their ransom would be mine.

Many of the men were, however, wearing plate. I rode after one who had good back and breastplates but there was little protection to his side. I rode to his right and using the cantle of my saddle for support I thrust up and under his arm. He began to tumble, arms flailing and he hit the ground. The horse was a good one and a spoil of war. "Zuzzo, take the horse and the man if he lives."

"Aye, Sir John. Enjoy the sport."

I only had Gianluca with me but it could have been Donnina for no one was opposing us. They were a routed army and unlike our militia had no welcoming wall ahead of them. Instead, they had a wall of barges filled with crossbows and handguns. The puffs of smoke and the snaps of crossbows began to take their toll. Riders reined in and as we approached, I shouted, "You have lost, gentlemen. Sheath your weapons and surrender or you will surely die."

The majority of the men before us saw the wisdom in heeding my words and obeyed. The ones who did not, perished. Those who avoided the balls and bolts drowned in the river.

I was weary and I left others, under the command of Conte da Carrara, to secure the prisoners. I rode back to the city and we picked up Zuzzo, John and Robert along the way. We had more than a dozen prisoners and five excellent war horses. Thus it was that we entered the city along with Captain General Giovanni and the captured commander of the Veronese army, Cortesia da Serego. It would have been bad manners to make a comment to the Veronese general but I was able to compliment my old friend.

"Giovanni, a most excellent and complete victory."

He bowed his head, "Sir John, my time with you was not wasted. I learned from you and today those years as a student bore fruit. This victory was as much yours as it was mine."

Da Serego said, "Had I known that the White Company was hired by Padua then I might have been more cautious, Sir John."

I smiled, "General, I was not hired. These four men with me are the only members of the White Company. Today I led the young nobles of Padua."

Il Vecchio, resplendent in full armour, greeted us, and said to Cortesia da Serego, "You are bestowing on us a great honour with your visit, but our thanks and the merit for this go to our Captain General."

My friend beamed at the well-deserved compliment.

Da Serego shrugged and said, "Magnificent lord, it is but the practice of war."

The Paduan leader held up his arm for me to take, "And Padua owes you, Sir John, a debt of thanks. This night you and our Captain General shall flank me and we can speak of how that debt might be repaid."

I left Gianluca to see to our prisoners and Zuzzo accompanied me to our quarters. He chuckled as he helped me to take off my armour, "Even when we do not ride with the company we make money, my lord. By my estimate the ransom from the prisoners and the horses we have taken means that you have more than five thousand ducats."

"And as is my practice, Zuzzo, you and the others will share in that bounty."

"When I came to you, my lord, I did not need much persuasion for your reputation for fairness and the equitable sharing of treasure was well known. I also wanted to share in the glory that is Sir John Hawkwood. It is a far cry from my time as a jongleur."

"You, Zuzzo, are a warrior, through and through."

The celebratory feast was magnificent but it was only a foretaste of the one which was planned for the following week. I was bathed and shaved by Zuzzo and wore raiments that did not stink of sweat, horses and blood. I sat between il Novello and il Vecchio, father and son. Giovanni was on the other side of the elder statesman of Padua. It was the younger da Carrara who was able to tell us of the scale of the victory. "We lost but a handful of men and more than five hundred of our enemies perished at the river. We have, as prisoners, forty-eight senior and junior officers. We took ten thousand prisoners and we have more than six thousand war horses." He nodded over to the prostitutes who had been brought into the hall, "And there are two hundred and eleven women eager to serve us. You may take your choice, Sir John."

I shook my head, "I am beyond such dubious pleasures, my lord. Now if Sir Robin was with me, he might take half of the women as his share."

Giovanni laughed, "Aye, the old goat has an appetite for such women."

I turned to il Vecchio, "And della Scala?" The enemy had chanted the name of the Veronese leader when they had seen victory in their grasp.

Il Vecchio laughed, "Da Serego, it seems, thought that he had the victory and sent word to Verona that Padua was defeated. Della Scala was almost at the river with four hundred men ready to ride through our streets in a victory parade when he discovered the scale of his defeat. We will now use our Captain General to exploit our victory and then seek terms from Verona."

His son shook his head, "It is not Verona that should worry us, Father. As our Captain General showed today, we have the beating of Verona but more than five and half thousand of the enemy soldiers were from Venice. With Genoa defeated Venice now sees us as a tasty morsel to be gobbled."

The sobering words took the smile from the old man's face. He nodded and said, "Sir John, we shall be asking for nine thousand ducats ransom for Cortesia da Serego, I would use some of that money to hire the White Company." I bowed my head in agreement. "We would have, in particular, your archers."

"Of course. If you would let me know the details of the contract, I will know how many men I need to bring. When would you need us?"

"Our Captain General can use the autumn to finish off devastating the lands of Verona. If my son is correct then it will take until Christmas for our enemies to have recovered enough to face us in numbers. What say you bring your company in January?"

I did some calculations in my head. By that time I would have the ransoms paid and we would have the numbers we needed.

"That is satisfactory, my lord."

"Of course, if Venice and Verona sue for peace then your services will not be needed."

I smiled. I knew that Venice would not stop until they had a victory. "Yes, my lord, that is understood."

Il Vecchio was a cunning old man and he had offered any of the Veronese prisoners the opportunity to join Padua. Many took the offer and whilst that reduced the profit, it strengthened his army. The two most notable defectors were Facino and Filippino Cane. A furious della Scala had them hanged in effigy in Verona.

Condottiere

We left for home at the start of the next week with five fine warhorses and a line of sumpters laden with plate and weapons. Giovanni would send my ransoms when they were paid. My excursion to Padua had been more than successful. It had been one of the shrewdest decisions I had ever made.

Chapter 19

Donnina was not just my wife, she was my business partner and she was as delighted as I was with the turn of events. She had not been idle in my absence and she had used her network of relatives and friends to discover more about the wider world. We had learned that keeping abreast of events helped us to plan better.

"Now that my father is dead and my cousin controls Milan there are more plots and plans than in ancient Rome." I cocked an eyebrow. "Galeazzo has sent word to Verona that he sympathises with their plight and offers support."

"That is swift for the battle took place less than two weeks ago. How did you learn of this?"

She smiled, "I do not throw coins away without purpose my husband. I have friends in Milan who are loyal to my father and to me. I pay them a small stipend to keep me informed of all Milanese news. The messenger preceded you by one day."

I picked up her delicate hand and kissed the back of it, "Your father's greatest gift to me was you." She beamed at the compliment. "Do you think that Milan will give military backing to Verona?"

She shook her head, "He may throw coins Verona's way but he would rather achieve his ends through devious means than risking battle, especially with you. Is the news of the White Company's potential involvement known?"

I shook my head, "Father and son were keen to keep it secret while they are in negotiations with Verona. If the news of our contract was known then Verona might fear another attack and seek allies. I think, my love, that Padua hopes that our victory at Brentelle will result in peace and that they will not need to hire us."

"But you do not."

I shook my head, "If there was peace then Padua could pursue its claims to the Friuli and that would not suit Venice. Venice will push della Scala into war once more and even though we hurt them badly, so long as they have Venetian support they will have a constant supply of men."

"Then we must ensure that we are ready when the year turns. At least you have four months at home with your family. The girls are growing and they miss their father."

I was flattered by the attention of my girls and, to some extent, the toddler that was John, but I had never been the best of fathers and after a week I visited with Robin. The time had been when I would have also visited with Michael but he was now his own man. We had not fallen out but he was no longer a brother in arms. Robin was delighted with my account of the battle but a little miffed that I had not brought him some prostitutes.

I laughed, "Robin, you have more than enough here."

He sniffed, "A man like me has a large appetite and as I am likely to be away from my home next year then I need to plough while I can." I nodded and we drank our wine. "So, Sir John, you managed a victory without my archers. That is a first."

"It was not my victory, Robin, it was Giovanni's."

"We both know that you were the master and he the apprentice. Perhaps, that was his master's piece but he modelled it on you."

I still needed men and to that end, Donnina came up with an imaginative idea. I had a large estate sixty miles south of Florence, Montecchio Vesponi. I had acquired it two years earlier. There was a crumbling castle and it had not suited Donnina otherwise I might have occupied it as my home for it was easy to defend. At her suggestion, rather than let it crumble away to nothing, I had Robin move there. He took with him John Coe who had proved to be a great asset to the company. He was now a lieutenant and as he was popular with the English lances was a natural leader for them. With winter approaching and work for mercenaries in short supply, I told Robin to offer accommodation and food for any English and Italian warriors who wished to have shelter for the winter. It was not a purely altruistic move on our part. The men would, quite naturally, improve the buildings and the defences as well as provide me with a supply of soldiers for the coming campaign. Robin was happy to do as I asked, firstly because it would provide him with a fresh source of women and secondly, equally important to him, it would give him Englishmen with whom he could carouse. It was a mutually beneficial arrangement and showed me, once again, the cleverness of my wife. John Coe would train the lances and the two of them would be ready to lead our men to Florence when we went to war.

Michael did visit with me a month later and he came with a purpose. He too had information for me. After praising me for my part in the battle, he said, "I have heard that Galeazzo Visconti has offered an alliance with Padua against Verona."

My wife snorted, "Playing both sides off against the other. I pray that the Carrara family did not take him up?"

Michael laughed, "No one takes a snake to their bosom unless they are wearing plate armour."

I enjoyed the company of Michael although his new status changed our relationship. He still felt like my son but an estranged one. Had I been a sentimental man I might have been upset but I was a practical one and having the commander of the Florentine army as a friend was no bad thing.

In early September we heard that Giovanni's unopposed raids into Veronese territory ended when the Veronese captives had their ransoms paid and they were released. Giovanni degli Ordelaffi had been appointed to command a new Veronese army. Using Venetian money della Scala had hired German and Hungarian mercenaries and Veronese territory was being reclaimed. That news was second hand but in the last week of September, we had first hand news. Captain Rodrigo and an escort of six men brought my share of the ransom and the news, which he could not deliver without smiling, that the Italians in the Veronese army had fallen out with the German and Hungarian contingents. In the fights that ensued, half of the Germans had been slaughtered and the rest had defected to Padua. The lands they had recovered had been lost once more.

"Captain General Ubaldini told me to tell you that you will be needed as requested. Despite the words of il Vecchio, we know that war will continue."

The news in October confirmed Rodrigo's predictions. Lutz von Landau, alongside whom I had fought, had replaced Ordelaffi as commander of the Veronese army. I knew that he would not be so easy to defeat. I heard reports of how he fought his way from Treviso to Vicenza to join the Veronese army. He ravaged the lands and wrecked the grape harvest. He lost men but not as many as Giovanni might have hoped. I would be needed.

Alarmingly the campaign of von Landau proved to be successful. Despite the best efforts of Giovanni and the Paduans, von Landau destroyed the towers Padua used to guard its borders and then dammed a river so that Padua's mills could not be used. Things were looking desperate for Padua and I knew that we would be sent for. I was confident that in January the call for my contract would be issued. I sent John and Robert to visit Robin and tell him of my news. He and John Coe were to actively recruit the men who were with him at Montecchio Vesponi as well as send out word that the White Company was seeking archers and lances. I sent Zuzzo to Pisa to tell William of my plans. I had not felt welcome the last time I had visited with him. His wife did not like me. I had decided to use intermediaries in the future. He was, after all, just my bookkeeper and, increasingly, I did not need him. If I had a bank in Florence, I might have ended our contract but more than half of my money was in Pisa. I would let sleeping dogs lie.

It was in late December that I heard the most unexpected piece of news. Il Vecchio had offered von Landau ten thousand ducats to change sides. This was a clever move for von Landau had proved highly successful. At first, I feared that I would no longer be needed and would lose the contract. It was Rodrigo who brought me the news but he added the caveat that the offer was to take von Landau from Verona. In the end, it was della Scala who, inadvertently, solved the problem and cleared the way for the White Company to fight for Padua. When von Landau went to his employer to tell him of the offer, he was told to take it for it was winter and his services would no longer be needed. Della Scala was, foolishly, trying to save money. Von Landau's contract ended at the end of December. The condottiero simply walked away. I knew he was a good leader and would easily find work. He went to Milan where he found employment with the Lord of Milan and the field was clear for me.

Robin and John Coe brought the new recruits from my castle at the end of December. Winter in Tuscany was never as bad as in England and despite the mountains, the men were able to camp in the grounds of my estate. Donnina would have made a good quartermaster and understood well how to keep the six hundred men fed. Thanks to old age, disease, retirement, and Michael's poaching, I knew less than a quarter of the men who arrived at my home. The ones I did know lived close to Florence.

I had not seen Robin for some months and while he still looked like he could draw a bow he had aged. His hair had been thinning for some years and what there now was had more white than brown. I also saw the rheum of drink in his eyes and a paunch was developing. He saw my look and nodded, "Aye, I know, Sir John, I am getting old. My decision not to be in the fore might be a wise one. There are now archers who can send an arrow further than me. I shall use my wisdom rather than my strength."

We were old friends and I made no comment. It was not needed. I, too, was old. Few men my age went to war. "We have fewer men than we normally lead."

"More men would have been with us had we left earlier but the journey from England is perilous in winter. We have enough do we not? What is the contract?"

"We are contracted for three months. The amount we are paid is the same regardless of the number of men we bring."

He smiled, "It is Sir John Hawkwood that il Vecchio wants." I shrugged. "I have some interesting recruits. There is an Italian I would like you to meet."

I was intrigued, "Lead on."

He nodded to his servant, John, "Have my war gear taken to my chamber." Carlo was waiting to allocate Robin his chamber and he waved an arm inside the hall.

"I have with me a young man who, despite his youth, has many skills. His grandfather, Guido, was a condottiero. He died before we came to Italy but Tedesco has inherited his grandfather's skills. His father, Marco, also had skills but he preferred to be a farmer and live on the profits his father made."

"Tedesco?"

"A nickname that was given to him by the men he brought. There are six of them and they are a tightly bound band. His full name is Giovanni Tarlati da Pietramala." The camp was a busy hive as the men saw to their beds and their horses. I heard the clash of steel and saw two men sparring. Robin nodded, "That is Tedesco and his man at arms Stephano."

One of the men was young, younger than Michael, while the other looked to be of an age with Gianluca. The young man looked so slight that it seemed a slight breeze would take him away. I realised that was an illusion for they were not wearing armour and the young man's skills were evident. The one referred to as Stephano had the grizzled look of a veteran with all the skills and experience that imbued but Tedesco was handling him with ease. I realised after just a handful of passes that the only man I knew with quicker hands was Zuzzo.

Tedesco riposted and disarmed his man at arms. Rather than being upset Stephano laughed and shook his head, "Your hands get quicker each day while mine slow. Well done."

The young Italian bowed and saw us watching. He bowed, "You are Sir John Hawkwood, Giovanni Acuto?"

"I am and you have skills, Tedesco."

"Thank you, my lord. I take that as a great compliment. I have long wished to serve you but I wanted my apprenticeship to begin when I could show you my potential. I would be a condottiero." In one so young that might have seemed arrogant but I saw that his men agreed with his own estimation. "I would learn from the best."

I nodded, "Before he becomes old and senile, eh?"

"I did not say that and your reputation is still intact. There are few men who still lead companies after so long. He used his fingers, "Sterz, Malatacca, Thornbury, Baumgarten, all are dead or retired and the only one who comes close to you in skills, Lutz von Landau, was defeated by you already. I come here not for the pay, although that will be more than welcome, but education in the ways of war."

Robin was right. He was a malleable young man with great potential and I liked him from the first. "Then have your lance stay close to me when we head to Padua." I smiled, "I will have other matters on my mind and will not be able to give you advice. That you will have to see for yourself."

One advantage of the smaller number was that we had enough horses for all of them to be mounted. Tedesco's lance had brought enough animals but some of the archers, especially those who had travelled from England, had none. Our success in war meant we had plenty. That evening I dined with just Robin and Donnina. My bodyguards were in the camp mingling with the men. It was important that the company knew the men who were close to me. Zuzzo would teach them the signals he would sound and the others tell them of the formations I liked to use. I now wondered how I had survived without the four men to guard me.

"So, Sir John, what is the plan?"

"We ride north to Monselice. Rodrigo's man told me that Giovanni is camped at Cerea where he raids Veronese lands. I will ride to Padua and confirm the contract with il Vecchio."

Robin frowned, "It is not yet signed?"

"The message I had from Giovanni was that the old man wishes us to serve him. I know that a verbal contract is worth nothing and so I will ride to Padua. I will use your new man Tedesco as an escort. You will command the rest of the company."

As ever Donnina was thinking about the coins we would accrue, "And the payment?"

Smiling I said, "Do not fret, my sweet, it will be safely brought to our home." Donnina had ordered the building of a secure building in the grounds where she could store money. It was not the bank I had at Pisa but we controlled this one and, increasingly, William Turner was left out of the negotiations. He would continue to oversee our investments and keep a tally of the men and what was owed them but our close relationship had ended with his marriage.

It took some days for the sumpters to be prepared and the war gear that we would need to be collected. I could have used wagons but that would have slowed us up. Instead, we used horses to carry what we needed. I would wear plate but only when we were fighting. I had decided not to wear a helmet for I had no intention of getting too close to swords and lances. Robin and Donnina were both right. There were others who could do the fighting. What none could do but me was use my mind. We might be taking fewer men to war than normal but Sir John Hawkwood would still lead the White Company and I was not arrogant enough to believe that every action would be successful. The past had shown me that things could go awry and my carefully crafted plans thrown into disarray by events beyond my control. I would need to be detached from the fighting and now that I had a good bodyguard I could do so without fear.

Donnina also had a servant prepared to accompany me. Jack was the son of a man at arms, John of Worcester. John had died and Jack was brought up by his Italian mother. When she had died the youth had been given the job of helping my steward and had proved so skilful that Donnina had seen his potential and over the last three years she had groomed the young man so that now, aged eighteen, he would see to my food and my clothes whilst on campaign. It would be he who led my laden sumpter. He would be the one who polished my plate. I would still see to my own weapons. A good warrior always sharpened his own sword and lance. Even when I had enjoyed a squire, I had used my own whetstone. Jack could cook and had been shown how to trim hair and beards. That he had few skills as a warrior was immaterial. If the day came when he had to draw a weapon to defend himself then that would be the day that my bodyguards and me all lay dead.

The horse I would take was one taken at the Battle of Brentelle. I had named him Ajax for I liked the name. Old Ajax had died peacefully. Caesar was also getting old. The new warhorse was young and I would not need another in the time left to me. He was a grey but, in truth, was the whitest horse I had ever seen. It was vanity I suppose for with my white livery and polished plate I would stand out on the battlefield. I wanted the enemy to know that Giovanni Acuto was on the field of battle. My bodyguards would also ride greys. I also had Blackie, a second warhorse. I would use him if I needed to don a black cloak and ride in disguise and he would be a good replacement should anything happen to Ajax. The other servants we would be taking would take care of the horses. They were all men who had been warriors but were now past their prime. The men of the White Company had to be the best but even the old ones were not forgotten. They would be paid and paid well. They could still defend the baggage but they would not be the ones waiting for my orders to charge and seize victory. They would be my eager young dogs of war and not the arthritic old hounds.

Chapter 20

We had almost one hundred and forty miles to travel and whilst the first part was in the relatively safe lands of Florence, we would have to pass through the lands of the Duke of Ferrara, the Este family. Rodrigo's man had assured me that our passage would not be barred but just to be sure I sent Zuzzo, John and Robert ahead to confirm the fact. I was pleased that I did so when they returned as I was told that whilst we could pass through Ferrara, we were not allowed to pass through their towns. We would have to skirt them. I did not mind although it would add ten miles to our journey. Every lord would be suspicious of a mercenary company passing through their lands. It took four days to reach Monselice. This was Paduan land and Robin and my company were welcomed.

I left with my bodyguards, Tedesco and his men, as well as Jack. It was not a long ride and we reached Padua within a few hours. While my men saw to our animals, I was taken to il Vecchio. "Ah, Sir John, you have come at the right time."

I nodded, "You said to come in January and, despite the inclement weather, I have brought my company. All that is now required is the actual contract." I smiled to take the sting from my next words, "As von Landau recently discovered, such matters are important." I was pleased that a look of guilt crept over the Paduan's face. Had von Landau accepted the offer from da Carrara then there might have been no contract for me.

He waved over a scribe, "Here it is, and the amount is ready for you to take." I read it and both the wording and the amount were satisfactory.

"And who is to command?" It was a blunt question and I locked eyes with the old man.

He gave as blunt an answer as was possible, "Giovanni d'Azzo degli Ubaldini is the Captain General and my son, Francesco is also there."

I frowned, "So does Giovanni command or your son?"

"There is no disagreement between the two men, Sir John. They are in perfect accord." I did not like the vague words.

"As you well know, my lord, a divided command on the field of battle is one that is doomed to failure."

The old man stiffened and I knew that he had taken offence at my words. I wanted one commander and that would be either me or Giovanni and not a young noble, no matter how well connected. "Your company, Sir John, is there to serve Padua. There will be no freebooting."

I shrugged, "My company have never been guilty of such acts but so long as it is quite clear that I am there to follow orders and will not be responsible for any failure in this war against Verona then I accept the contract."

"We will not fail." He coloured as he began to lose his temper.

I kept my calm, "Your arrangements do not guarantee success."

"And making you Captain General would do?"

"I am just saying that one man should command. Giovanni is a good general."

"And the implication is that my son is not."

"I have not yet seen your son command an army, my lord. I know Giovanni. I was at Brentelle."

"When my son did all that was asked of him."

"And yet it was Giovanni's plan which worked."

I saw his face as he wrestled with my words. Eventually, he nodded, "I will have my son meet you at Monselice. Perhaps the two of you need to work out a way to cooperate and lead my armies to victory."

"Perhaps."

We had time to visit the markets in Padua and I went, after the meeting, to buy supplies that we could not get in Florence. Padua was closer to Venice and the merchants of Padua, despite the animosity between the two city-states, were able to buy things that could not be obtained in Florence. I bought medicines, spices and herbs as well as honey and vinegar. This was winter and we needed medicines more than ever. I also bought, and I know not why, an interesting object. I think it was a narwhal horn or a similar part of a sea creature. The man who offered it for sale had it secreted amongst other weird and wonderful items. It was almost as long as Jack, my servant.

He tried to sell it to me as a unicorn's horn, "It is magical, my lord, and I believe it makes a man more potent in bed." He gave me a lascivious look.

Shaking my head I said, "I am over sixty years of age and have children enough. I need no magic to help me but as this is just a seaside trinket then I think I will pass."

Zuzzo laughed, "As if the bone from an animal or fish could help a man." He wagged a finger at the man, "I was a jongleur and know of these tricks. You cannot fool Sir John Hawkwood."

His eyes widened, "You are Sir John Hawkwood? Giovanni Acuto?" I nodded. "Then accept my apologies, Sir John. You may have this trinket for whatever you decide." I cocked my head to one side. He smiled, "I will dine out on this story, my lord."

Deciding to test his words, I took a copper coin out and handed it to him.

He beamed, "Thank you, Sir John." He handed me the strange object.

As we headed back to our rooms Robert shook his head, "Even a copper coin is too much, my lord."

I laughed, "To you and I, perhaps, but children are young enough to believe that it is the horn of a unicorn. If you were a child would not such a gift please you?"

He smiled, "It would and, as such, is worth more than a copper coin. You are indeed Giovanni Acuto, my lord."

As we rode back to Monselice, Tedesco rode next to me. He was eager to learn. "Sir John, you do not command the army then?"

"I trust Captain General Ubaldini, my young friend, and I know that he will heed my advice."

"And what will be your battle plan?"

"First, we have to reach the Paduan army and that is at Cerea. We will need to cross the Adige and the Veronese will have defenders at the fords. I do not wish to lose men before we reach the Paduan army. My company is too valuable to waste."

He had a bright mind. "Then if you do not intend to use the fords, how will you cross?"

I waved an arm at the men around me, "As you can see my company is all well mounted. Better that we swim horses across an icy river than risk losing men attacking a bastide. As you will learn, my company is well trained and they obey orders. Those who have ridden with me for a long time know that I protect my men for as long as I can and when they are risked, they know that victory is at hand."

"And how do you know when that is, my lord?"

I smiled, "A good question and one to which I cannot give an answer that you will understand. I have been at war since I was barely a youth and what I have learned is in my head. I know the right time to stand and loose arrows and when it is the perfect time to launch lances. You are young. Learn from men like me and Giovanni. You need make no decisions in this war. It is a three-month contract and if you use that time well then you will be on your way to becoming a condottiero. Just be patient. I have seen too many men given the challenge of leadership and make a fatal mistake."

I meant every word I had said and Tedesco nodded, sagely, and then said nothing for the last few miles to our camp. Once there I arranged for men to take the treasure back to Florence. The ten men I chose were all veterans. Once they had delivered the gold to my wife, they would meet us at Cerea. A company might have to fight to reach Cerea, ten men could hide.

The fact that it was just a three-month contract pleased most of my men. Many of them were new and the shortness of the contract would allow them to get to know each other. Robin had promised them more work in the future. Although that had been a little bold of him, I was confident that we would find more contracts. Our new castle gave us the space to train and to knock the rougher edges from the men.

"So we wait here for il Novello?"

I nodded, "Aye, we do and that is no bad thing. Firstly, we are paid from this day and secondly, the young noble knows the ways to reach Giovanni. Our friend has made a bold move to raid deep into Veronese territory. We cannot afford to lose men for we are few in numbers."

When Francesco da Carrara did arrive, he brought with him a small escort of Paduan nobles. I recognised a couple of them from the men I had led at Brentelle. It boded well.

"It is good that you have come, Sir John. With your archers and the White Company to augment the Captain General's men and the men of Padua, we will wreak havoc in the heartland of Verona."

"And how do we reach Captain General Ubaldini?"

"Fear not, I shall be your guide and deliver you swiftly to our army."

We left the next day and it was clear, from the direction we would take that he intended to cross the Adige by the ford of Castelbaldo. I knew that there was a bastide nearby and our crossing could be contested. While I did not think we would be bested we might lose men and I did not have enough to be profligate. As we neared the river I reined in. "What is amiss, Sir John?"

"This is foolish, my lord. The ford is defended. There are Veronese there and they have a bastide. We will ride further north and cross the river by swimming our horses across."

He shook his head, "I do not intend to ruin my clothes by a dousing in the river." He raised his head and pointed due west, "Your company is paid for by Padua and I command you to follow me."

My heart sank. When the White Company went to war, I usually led the army. I was quite happy to defer to Giovanni but not this young cockerel. "My lord, we will ride north."

"If you ride north, I will take that as a refusal to obey the orders of Padua and the contract will be null and void. We will demand the return of our gold and we will defeat Verona without your help."

I should have headed north but I knew we needed this contract and I did not want to lose new men by a refusal to fight. I reluctantly nodded.

Having won the verbal encounter il Novello grinned, "Fear not, my lord, when the Veronese see the banners of the White Company, they will fall back to their bastide and cower behind its walls."

I was not so sure and I had Robin order the archers to take their bows from their bow cases and for the men at arms to arm themselves with their lances. The Paduan shook his head at such caution. "I had expected more steel of the White Company."

"My lord, there is a reason that my company has lasted longer than most other mercenary bands. We are cautious and we do not take unnecessary risks. You can order us to cross the Adige but the manner in which we do so will be my decision."

The next miles were travelled in cold and uncomfortable silence. Robin's scouts reported that the ford appeared to be unguarded but I knew that could be an illusion. Il Novello took it the other way. He and his escort of nobles boldly approached the ford and began to cross it even as my archers dismounted to string their bows. I waved Tedesco to lead his lances and an advance guard of twenty men to follow il Novello, "Keep an eye on our young friend, Tedesco."

"Aye, my lord."

The young warrior showed that he knew what he was doing for he spread his men out in a long line and although they wore no helmets. they had their arming caps and coifs about their heads. Il Novello and his nobles were bareheaded.

Robin nudged his horse next to me, "I like this not, Sir John, while we can avoid the bastide," he pointed at the small fort that had been constructed a little way from the ford, "we know not how many men it holds nor if they are defending this river by other means. We should have scouted it out and crossed at dawn."

I nodded, "I know but we have our orders."

"Who commands here, Sir John, the cockerel or Giovanni?"

It was a low point for me as I had no real answer to give to my friend. The archers were ready and they stood at the ford's edge with loosely nocked arrows awaiting the command. Il Novello and his nobles had reached the other side and Tedesco was halfway across when the handguns belched foul-smelling smoke and the crossbows cracked. There was a hidden ditch beyond the ford and it was manned. The Veronese had been expecting us and it was filled with men, more men, in fact, than I led.

Robin spurred his horse and shouted, "Loose! Loose!"

The range was extreme and the targets hidden, wreathed in smoke but as three of the nobles tumbled from their saddles the arrows of the White Company descended into the smoke. Arrows would be wasted but it was all that we could do. Tedesco and his men raised their shields as the Paduan survivors fled back across the river. There was little point in making a comment to il Novello as the white-faced Paduan galloped past me. There was no need. The three dead nobles were a testament to the foolishness of the plan. I would give the orders until we reached Cerea.

"Zuzzo, sound the order for lances."

"Aye, my lord."

I was already formulating a plan. The swirling smoke hindered my archers but it also restricted the view that the Veronese enjoyed. The men in the bastide might be able to see us but they had no way of communicating with their comrades in the ditch.

The men at arms lined up alongside me. Tedesco and his men, having successfully effected the escape of the Paduans, joined us. We had two lines. Jack handed me a lance. Robin rolled his eyes but wisely said nothing. I know that I could have stayed at the river's edge but I had a point to prove to il Novello.

"Zuzzo." The horn sounded again as arrows continued to fall into the ditch. We moved into the river. The guns were still blasting and the bolts still cracked but they were sent blindly. The greatest danger was to our horses. I was just glad that Ajax was with the baggage. Once we reached solid ground I shouted, "Charge!"

The horn sounded and we thundered across the open ground towards the Veronese defenders. Bolts and balls cracked against metal and I saw men fall. Then I heard a joyous sound. From the west came the sound of a different horn. It was too far away to be the defenders and, unless it was a force of Veronese horsemen, suggested help was coming our way. The handguns had stopped and the smoke began to clear. I spied in the distance the banners of horsemen and they were in great numbers. I hoped they were friends but I could not be certain. When the defenders of the ditch began to run towards the bastide then I knew the truth. They were allies.

I knew, even as I reined in and gave the command to halt, that if il Novello had been close to me he would have insisted upon a pursuit. I had no intention of losing another man. There was no point. We could not take a bastide without a great loss of life.

We had been lucky and as a soldier, I knew that you took that luck and did not push it.

Giovanni raised the visor to his helmet and beamed, "Sir John, we came to escort you the last few miles to our camp and, it seems, we arrived just in time."

I clasped his proffered arm, "And this was timely, old friend. Let us not tarry here for the cold is eating into my old bones." The crossing of the river had been icy and we had not had time to change. The wind made the cold worse and the sooner we reached the fires of Cerea the better.

"What made you cross here, my lord? That is not like you."

I gestured behind me with my thumb, "Your young commander ordered me to. I hope that it is you who commands here and not il Novello."

A frown fell upon his face, "This is not Pisa, my lord. The da Carrara family see themselves as Caesars." He shook his head, "We will talk later."

I turned to Robert, "Have the archers and the baggage brought across. John, see to the wounded and the dead."

In the end, we lost no men although the five who were wounded would need at least a month to recover. It was not a good start. We buried the Paduan nobles before heading west to Cerea. There was a chilly silence between Francesco da Carrara and me. The young nobles who had followed me at Brentelle clearly blamed their leader for the debacle at the Adige and he rode with just his squire for company. He glowered at me whenever our eyes locked. For some inexplicable reason, he seemed to blame me for the disastrous decision. I put it from my mind as I needed to speak to Giovanni.

"So, my friend, what is your strategy?"

"We have a short time, Sir John, to win this war. Venice is sending men and I am sure that Milan will exploit the situation. We raid the land around Verona and hope that they sue for peace. In that peace we will gain lands and our borders will be protected." I was silent and Giovanni nodded, "I know, it is winter and there will be little for us to take." He shrugged and said, a little more quietly, "Father and son are in agreement on this matter. They want our victory at Brentelle to be exploited."

I used my thumb to point back at the river, "If the raid had been to secure the crossing at Castelbaldo and the bastides at Castagnaro and Castelbaldo then the border would be secure and we would not fear being trapped. The back door is now firmly locked and unless we take Verona we will have to battle to return to Padua."

He nodded, glumly, "I know, Sir John, but what can I do? I do not command a company as you do. I serve Padua and I obey the orders given to me by the da Carrara family. You are lucky that you have no such restrictions. You and the White Company can leave whenever you wish."

"I cannot, my old friend, for we have never yet reneged on a contract. For good or ill I will have to make this work." I smiled apologetically, "Sorry, Giovanni, we will have to make this work."

"Then we will have to use what we have to the best effect." In illustration, he waved forward one of the knights who had better armour. "This is Antonio Pio and one of my Paduan captains."

The knight bowed his head, "It is an honour, my lord, to serve you."

I smiled, "Captain Pio, we both serve Padua; you as a noble and me as captain of a free company but we shall need to work together to do so. What can you tell me about your fellow Paduans? I have led your young nobles but the older ones, the veterans, what of them?"

He looked around to see that he was not overheard and said, quietly, "When we followed il Vecchio, the elder da Carrara, we enjoyed some success. Il Novello is a brave man, that is clear to all but he can be reckless. He has many friends who are loyal to him. My fear is that in the heat of battle, they might follow their hearts and not their heads." His eyes widened, "I hope I am not being disloyal. I have said nothing that was meant as an insult. Courage and bravery are to be applauded."

"You have said nothing that could be so construed and it is important that the Captain General and I know the mettle of the men we lead. Courage and bravery will be needed but so will cold and clear minds."

For the rest of the road to Cerea, I ran through the cloth of battle I had before me. I would need to cut it very carefully. I knew that Giovanni was in command but I also knew that he would heed my advice. Our long-standing friendship had stood more severe tests in the past. My advice would be heeded.

There was a mighty cheer as we entered the Paduan camp. Giovanni was popular as was il Novello. I also knew that the sight of the White Company would bring hope to the Paduans as we had won more battles than we had lost.

We ate hot food and slept in the houses from which the Veronese had been evicted. The next day il Novello called a council of war. It was an ominous order as it told me who was really in command. The most senior Paduan officers attended, including Antonio Pio and Francesco da Carrara's uncle, Arcoano Buzzacarino. Clearly, il Novello was still in a foul mood following the embarrassment of the crossing of the Adige and he began by berating the army. Although his words suggested that all in Cerea were at fault his eyes constantly lighted upon Giovanni. "Your men are doing nothing here and we should be threatening the very walls of Verona. This army showed at Brentelle that it could win a great victory. If we allow the Veronese to be reinforced then the men we lost that day will have died in vain."

Silence fell. I wanted to take il Novello by the scruff of the neck and shake him for this was not the way to encourage men. Every head, including Giovanni's, was hung. I said, "Captain General, will you not answer these words?"

Giovanni had been seated and, in answer, stood and taking his baton of command addressed il Novello, "I will not answer such words before allowing Sir John to speak even though I hold the baton of command of your Carrara army." Bowing his head he held out the baton to il Novello. "Sir John should command this army. I am the apprentice and he is the master."

I still do not know what Francesco thought but when Pio and Buzzacarino shouted that I had to take the baton, he nodded. I took it. My reasoning was simple. I would not allow myself to be bullied by il Novello and if I had command then we had a better chance of winning. "I accept joint command with my old friend, Captain General Ubaldini." That brought a cheer from everyone although il Novello's was muted.

That done I set about organising the men to make raiding more effective. I spread my archers and men at arms around the companies. I allowed men like Pio and Buzzacarino to command but in most cases, I had one of my men as the one who would lead. Tedesco and John Coe were used judiciously. I needed discipline and I feared that the Paduans might not be as disciplined as my men. Verona was an ancient enemy. We had to raid, take supplies and get back to Cerea intact without loss of life. I knew my men and I could trust them.

We pushed on to Verona and, at first, had instant success. Perhaps they thought that Giovanni was a cautious general, but with the White Company pushing them the Paduans took towns, villages and farms. We had a week of undisturbed raiding. It yielded less than il Novello had expected. It was winter and the animals we took were less than we hoped. It was turnips and beans that we took and precious little treasure. I thought this was a futile activity. I consoled myself with the fact that we had less than two months of the contract left and then we could go home. We did not even have the opportunity to take battlefield loot.

That changed ten days after our raids began. Della Scala sent two of his generals, Polenta and Ordelaffi to engage us. It was annoying rather than damaging. It happened to be the column I led that first encountered them. I had fifty archers and fifty lances when we raided Bussolengo, a town to the west of Verona. We had found and slaughtered one cow when my archers reported horsemen approaching from the east. Leaving three men to butcher the animal, I rode with my lances to meet them head-on. My archers infiltrated the narrow streets. They would ambush the Veronese while we engaged them. We were wearing mail and not plate to save our animals. As we galloped through the square so they came in the opposite direction. We did not carry lances. They were unnecessary. Drawing swords we rode at them and, as my archers rained death upon them, they fled. Only six of them died but they had wounded with them. We took six horses, one of which was injured. We would add his meat to that of the cow and have the semblance of a meal.

That evening, as I sat with Robin and Giovanni, il Novello liked to sit with his nobles, I told them what the encounter had shown me, "Firstly, we have to be on our guard for more such attacks but, equally, the Veronese whom we met were weaker than I would have expected. None had plate, few had mail and most wore padded jackets or leather jacks."

Tedesco was with us and he frowned, "Surely that means that Verona is ripe for the plucking, Sir John."

"No, my friend, the very opposite. Della Scala is sending out men merely to slow us down and he is not sending his best men. After Brentelle he had to begin rebuilding his army. That army is in Verona and if we were foolish enough to attack it then we would fail and the Paduans would lose their army. It is not a large army and I am convinced that the Veronese will have a much larger one. No, Tedesco, we continue to do as we have been doing and then, when our contract is almost over, we will suggest a return to Padua." I smiled at Giovanni, "And then you can resume command."

"Believe me, Sir John, I am coming to believe that it is a poisoned chalice. I will be sad beyond words when you return to Florence."

A week later an emissary came to us from della Scala. He came under a flag of truce accompanied by three priests as a sign of good faith. I was sceptical from the first but I played della Scala's game. Egidio Palione came from the prominent Colonna family who ruled Palione. I learned he was illegitimate but I did not hold that against him. He was incredibly clever and that became obvious in the way he spoke and how he acted. He had been sent as a spy. Il Novello did not see the plot but I did. Palione was there to find our weaknesses and he wished to assess our numbers. Thanks to my tactic of sending out small groups of men he would fail in that.

He said he had an offer of peace but when I pressed him the details were like a mist on a river. It was hard to see clearly. He was clever but I was cleverer. I learned that all the messengers sent by il Novello to his father asking for more men had been captured. Palione blurted it out and I saw him mentally berate himself for the slip. We let him go and I explained to il Novello what it meant.

"My lord, they know we do not have enough men to take Verona. They know we are short of food and they have yet to send an army against us. I think it is time we left and headed back to Padua before we are trapped here with a starving army and surrounded by enemies."

He looked at the Paduan nobles and Antonio Pio nodded, "I agree with Sir John. The men are not only starving, but they are also becoming rebellious. I had to have two men whipped the other day for refusing to obey an order. They deserted and three others went with them. This will happen more and more."

When the others nodded their agreement then il Novello said, "Very well. We shall leave."

We left but the trap had already been sprung. Our journey back to Padua would not be an easy one. I did not know it at the time but the greatest challenge of my military career lay ahead of me.

Chapter 21

The only ones with any order or control on that retreat from Verona were the provvisionati of the White Company and the men paid by Giovanni. The senior Paduan nobles tried to keep discipline but there were desertions along the way and any farm or house that was not guarded by my men was looted. I had men flogged for rape and I feared that when we reached the river all order would end. The situation was exacerbated by the fact that thanks to the intercepted messengers, della Scala knew our predicament and he had planned for our flight. Cerea was seen as a haven for it had been our base. When we reached it, we discovered that the water and the wine vats had been polluted by the enemy. The first ten men who reached the water and wine fell writhing in agony. We had counted upon the supplies there keeping us going until we reached the Adige. Even il Novello fell into a deep despair and there was mutinous talk.

I spoke with Giovanni, Robin and my inner circle. For the first time in my career, I had a problem that seemed insoluble. While my White Company protected us from the mutinous mob that seemed to blame me, we wracked our brains for some solution to the problem. Robin came up with part of the solution. "The water, Sir John, is merely polluted. We can make it drinkable with the addition of vinegar. It will not taste pleasant but it will be drinkable."

"And the wine?"

Tedesco smiled, "I was brought up in wine country and know viniculture. The men who drank the wine had bad stomachs. We put aquae vitae in the wine vats and add honey. It will sweeten the drink and take away some of the poison." He shrugged, "I will not drink any of the wine but it may assuage those who are desperate for a drink."

Zuzzo said, as I nodded, "And we can make it appear magical." We all stared at him, "Sir John, we are in danger of losing this army. We are deep in enemy territory and they are already breaking apart. We need to give them a show to make them believe in you. Remember that narwhal horn we bought?"

"Aye, the present for my children. What of it?"

"We tell the men that it is a unicorn's horn and has the ability to purify both wine and water. We do as Sir Robin and Tedesco suggest and you explain to the camp what it is that you intend. We make a great show of using the horn. You then drink some of the wine to prove it is safe." I was dubious and it showed in my face. "Sir John, I worked as an entertainer for many years. Fear not. I will have a goblet of fresh and untainted wine for you. Let me do the prestidigitation and you shall be the magician. It is not far to the Adige. Your company and the men led by the Captain General can do without. It is the mob who must be satiated."

He was right for we had our own supplies. It was the Paduan infantry that needed the wine and the water. They had not husbanded our meagre supplies.

"Very well. See to it and I will go to the camp with the horn. Let the distraction begin."

I went to my bags and fetched out the narwhal horn. It did not look like that of a unicorn. I had with me just Gianluca, John and Robert. I looked at it dubiously. Gianluca said, "Men are superstitious, my lord. They believe in dragons and the like. Say that you found this in a cave where St George slew the dragon. You link the two stories and that will add credence to the myth."

Robert nodded, "Aye, my lord, every man wants to believe these stories. It is not Christian but they are exciting tales. Who knows, far to the east there may be unicorns."

Gianluca added, "Zuzzo told us of a four-legged armoured beast from Africa that has two such horns. Perhaps it is a unicorn."

"Very well. Wrap the horn in the silken cloth I bought for Donnina. Gianluca, you carry it as though it was a piece of Christ's cross and you two guard him with drawn swords."

Zuzzo's influence helped us make a dramatic entrance to the noisy camp. Our solemn faces and the processional nature of the four of us made the camp silent as we walked to the fire at the centre. The Paduan nobles were noticeably absent, not risking the wrath of the mob. I stood in silence and then turned a full circle as I spoke.

"I know that many of you are unhappy at the recent turn of events. You are hungry and the food that was promised has not been forthcoming. This latest treachery, the poisoning of the water and the wine is a heavy blow to bear. I did not wish to do this but I have no choice." I gestured to the silken cloth and the hidden horn. "I am an old man now but I have travelled far in that life and when I was younger, I travelled to the east where I found the cave in which St George slew the dragon. I found his bones but I also found this." I did not reveal the horn but touched, reverently, the silk. "It is the horn of the unicorn that fought alongside St George and was slain by the dragon. It has magical powers. I use it only rarely. I believe it can purify the water and the wine yet I am loath to unleash its magic. I leave it to you. Should I use the power of the unicorn's horn to save the water and the wine?"

There was a moment of silence. It was the sort of silence that precedes a clap of thunder. Suddenly they erupted with a collective, "Aye."

I walked over to the cloth and unwrapped it as though it was something that might bite. The light from the fire added to the dramatic effect. My three bodyguards had all adopted a reverent look. They appeared like priests from some ancient religion. I took the horn and made my body stiffen. As I lifted it in the air, so that all could see, I gave a dramatic shout as though the power of a real unicorn filled me. The silence seemed to deepen for those closest to me recoiled. I kept an awed expression on my face as I turned and, with my three men surrounding me, marched to the water butts and the wine. I walked slowly to afford my men more time to complete their task. Gianluca handed me a tool to grate the horn. As we neared the poisoned drinks, I saw that my men had disappeared. It made it all seem surreal.

I went first to the water butts and dipping the horn in the trough that lay beneath the tap I said, "I call upon St George to make this water pure." I then slowly grated some of the horn into first the water butt and then the wine vats.

Zuzzo had appeared and stood with my bodyguards. His arrival went unnoticed. He was dressed in the same livery as the others. I saw in his hand the two coistrels, the leather cups we used on campaign.

I then went to the wine vats. I turned the spigot and let the wine flow over the horn. "I call upon St George to make this wine whole again."

Turning I faced the mob and I feigned licking the wine-covered horn. In reality, I licked the back of my hand but the darkness hid that from the mob. I turned and handed the horn to Gianluca. He played his part and almost winced as I gave it to him.

"Zuzzo, bring me a goblet and let us see the power of the unicorn."

Zuzzo went to the water butts. He placed the coistrel carefully on the ground and then pretended to fill the already full coistrel. The mob never questioned why he might have had two coistrels. He walked over to me and handed me the coistrel. I lifted it to my lips and drank, ensuring that some spilt out. I knew it came from Zuzzo's waterskin and I downed it all and then held it upside down to show that it was empty. The mob waited for me to fall down dead.

"Zuzzo, let us try the wine."

He did the same there but this time allowed the wine from the vat to pour over his hand. The wine was from our wineskins and I drank it all.

I held the two coistrels up and the mob cheered. "Men, the magic has worked but, to be sure, let us all sleep this night and then drink on the morrow."

Their faces showed joy for they had been entertained and they had seen what they viewed as a miracle. They began to filter back to the camp. As they did Zuzzo said, in my ear, "Sir John, when you tire as a condottiero then we five can travel the country and earn coins by entertaining. You are a natural performer."

John said, "You know, Sir John, he is right, I almost believed it myself."

"We will break camp before dawn. They are at peace now and if we leave early, they may forget their thirst. I would reach the Adige in one day."

That night my prayers were longer than usual. I prayed that God would forgive my blasphemy and that St George would still continue to be on the side of the English.

Only a few of the men tried the water and the wine. None died and none were ill. I do not think that the taste of either was totally pleasant but the trick had worked and they obeyed their officers.

We hurried the few miles to the Adige and when we reached the river we found that the bastide at Castelbaldo was occupied but such was the size of our army that, as we approached, the garrison fled. The pontoon bridge had been rebuilt by the Veronese and the river was crossed more easily. I knew what would happen and I said to il Novello, "Stop your men from entering the bastide, my lord. The supplies that are there will keep us safe until we reach Paduan land."

The next lord of Padua hesitated and that proved fatal. The Paduans raced for the bastide. It was well stocked and there was both wine and water. Once inside they gorged themselves and refused the commands of their officers. We had lost the majority of the army. All we had left were the nobles and the professional soldiers. In the case of the nobles it was that they were too slow to reach the bastide before their men.

Shaking my head I said to Giovanni, "Let us camp close to the ditch where I was held before you rescued me. We will have a defence at least."

"Aye, Sir John."

The only ones who had not occupied the bastide were the White Company, Giovanni's company and half of the nobles. We made a cold camp on the damp ground which had been soaked in the recent rains. We had a spartan meal of a watery soup made from the last of the rotting meat and vegetables we had taken in Cerea. It was my lowest point.

The next day we could still hear the carousing from the bastide. In effect, we had less than two thousand men on whom we could rely. That they were the best was immaterial. I had wanted to push on to Padua with the supplies from Castelbaldo to keep us going but those plans were now in tatters. We held a council of war.

"We might only be thirty or so miles from Padua, Lord da Carrara, but it might as well be the moon we were trying to reach. If the Veronese choose to cut us off and attack us on the road then even the arrows and the lances of the White Company will not save us."

Il Novello's face showed that he agreed. The handing over of the baton of command from Giovanni to me merely meant that this disaster would be laid at the door of Sir John Hawkwood. I would no longer be Giovanni Acuto.

Giovanni had left local scouts to watch the Veronese and at noon two rode in to tell us that Antonio Della Scala, at the head of a huge army, was a day away. It gave me little comfort to know that I had been right and Antonio della Scala had kept his best men safe. He had a huge army and, unlike ours, they were not starving.

"My lord, we need your men from the bastide and we need the food. They are Paduans. They need a leader." I suspected, as I said my words, that any further contract from Padua would be unlikely. Diplomacy was never one of my strong points.

Realising that I was right, il Novello, with Captains Pio and Buzzacarino, walked over to the bastide. It was almost a mile from our camp and, as we waited to see the outcome I spoke with Robin and Giovanni. "No matter what happens we fight here. This ditch will slow down the enemy and we can anchor the line at the river by those trees. Can your archers use them, Robin?"

"Aye, Sir John, but without the Paduans, we cannot hold them."

Giovanni pointed to the Castagnaro Canal, "And even with the Paduans we do not have enough men to make a line to the other canal. We can be outflanked."

"We could just leave and head back to Florence." I turned to look at Robin who, as usual was honest and blunt. He shrugged, "This is down to il Novello and his Paduans. You have done all that you could, Sir John."

"We have never deserted yet and I will not begin now. Have your archers make the woods defensible."

Captain Pio returned from the bastide and he looked despondent, "Sir John, if you send men with me, we have salvaged a little of the supplies but that rabble have devoured ten days' worth of food."

"Where is Lord da Carrara?"

"He is guarding the food and trying to persuade them to rejoin the army."

I sighed, "Giovanni, arrange it."

They had barely left when our scouts galloped from the north. They were led by Guglielmo Curtarolo, one of il Vecchio's chosen men. He reined in and his red face told me that the news he had to impart was dire, "Sir John, Lord della Scala approaches. He has with him more than four times the number of our men." He looked around and saw the handful of men working on the ditch. "Where are the rest?"

I pointed across the river to the bastide, "Il Novello is trying to rally them. The numbers, my lord, I need the numbers."

"Almost fifteen thousand men, Sir John."

My heart sank and I waved him to ride to il Novello. We had twelve hundred men on whom we could rely: mine and Giovanni's. There were twelve hundred nobles led by da Carrara. Cermisone had twelve hundred infantry made up of spears and crossbows and then there were the two hundred cavalry led by Antonio Pio. I would need God's help to win this day. The majority of our army, the Paduans, would be of little or no use.

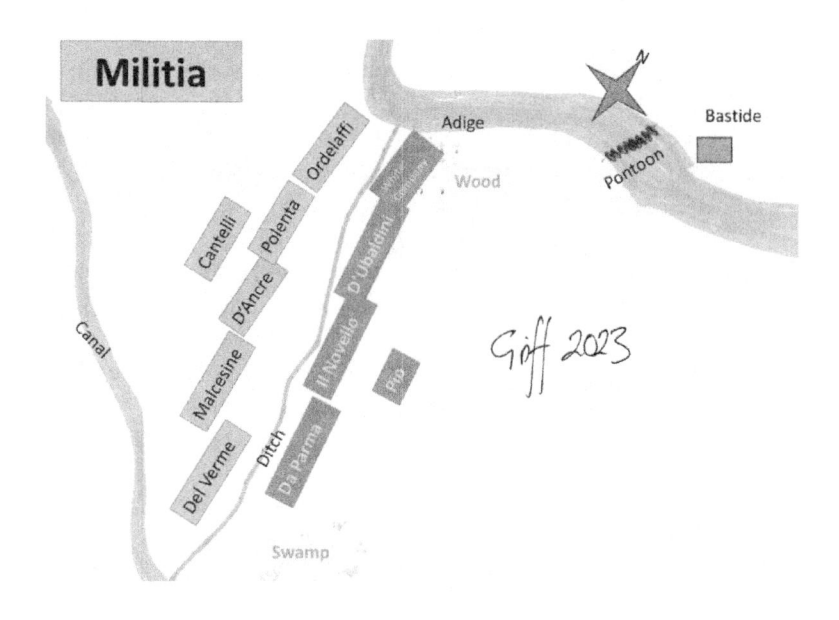

"Sir Robin, Giovanni, here! Zuzzo, sound officers' call."

I waved to Robert to bring my horse as Zuzzo sounded his trumpet. I needed height and I needed to be mobile.

Antonio Pio and Bartolomeo Cermisone da Parma also followed. They were both dependable men and the best that Padua had to offer. I mounted Ajax and used the baton of command to confirm my orders. "Bartolomeo, I want your men on the extreme left of our line. Use the swamp to your left for protection. Have your pavesiers make a barrier behind the ditch."

"Aye, Sir John."

He waited while I gave the rest of my orders and that showed what a good leader he was. He knew that if he understood all the orders then we would have a better chance of victory. It was still a slim chance but I would not surrender until all hope was gone.

"Captain Pio, your two hundred men are our mounted reserve. If our line is breached then use your lances to seal it. If any men break through you stop them." I saw his face and I smiled, "I know that I give you an impossible task but my hands are tied. We are fettered to this ditch. To move would be fatal. We have to hold and you are the one who can plug the gaps."

"Yes, Sir John."

"Captain General, you and Lord da Carrara will form the centre of our line. You will hold at the ditch and use your lances to prevent the enemy from crossing. You hold and that is all. If we win this battle, and *if* is a mighty word, then it will be the archers who win it for us." They all nodded. "Robin, I want the archers in the woods and our lances on the extreme right. Our lances will protect you and your arrows will whittle down their numbers and draw in their reinforcements."

Giovanni said, "We fight dismounted?"

I nodded, "Della Scala had this ditch dug. Let us hoist him by his own creation. Now hurry. I want our line in place before the enemy appears."

I turned as il Novello appeared at the head of a couple of hundred men. I shook my head. While the men in the bastide had proved that they were not reliable, they were, at least, a physical presence that would make us appear a little stronger than we actually were. Banners flew from the walls of the bastide. It was an illusion for the men were both drunk and cowardly but only we knew that.

"I have heard the news. Guglielmo is attempting to rally the men in the bastide." He saw my look and shrugged, "It is why we pay you and the Captain General, Sir John. Where do you want me?"

"I will anchor the extreme right. Da Parma the left. You and Giovanni will have your dismounted lances to hold the middle."

His head bowed, "Perhaps this will be a glorious end for us."

I snapped, "This will not be a defeat! We may not win but I do not intend to lose. All you have to do, my lord, is hold the enemy at the ditch." I pointed to the skies for it had begun to rain. "Perhaps God will aid us with rain and make this into a bog but whatever happens, I want every man to obey the horn of Zuzzo."

"Is that your plan? We simply hold."

"For the present, aye. As you say, my lord, you pay my men to fight and me to plan. I have not yet seen the enemy battle. When I do…" The truth was I had no idea how we could win.

Leaving him to organise his men and to don his plate I headed for Robin. "John, fetch my armour." As my man at arms headed to my tent, I spurred Ajax. The rain was not heavy. In one respect that was good for it would not dampen the bow strings but in another it was bad. I needed heavy rain to soak the ground.

I dismounted and Robin joined me. The archers had made barriers between the trees by using fallen timber and cutting saplings to embed into the soft ground much as we had at Poitiers. Behind such defences, they would send arrows to weaken the enemy's resolve. I saw Tedesco and John Coe helping to organise the dismounted lances. The two of them would earn their promotions this day. The archers had given some sharpened saplings to the lances which were now being embedded and they would help to slow down an enemy.

"Gianluca, I want our horses fetched and tethered out of sight behind the wood."

As he rode off Robin said, "You plan to flee? That is not like you, Sir John."

I snorted in derision, "You, of all people, should know that I will not run. I want the option of using horses if we can and the closer they are to us the better. This wood is the only cover on the battlefield. I want della Scala in the dark for as long as possible."

He nodded and pointed his bow at il Novello, "He is the weak spot. He is hot-headed and the enemy will come for him. If they break…"

"Then you and your archers will need to hurt whoever fights against him, will you not?"

He turned and then paused adding quietly, "I think, Sir John, that this will be my last battle. Today, I feel old. I want my home and my women. Is that wrong of me?"

I smiled, "You and I have done all that we could and if you wish for retirement then good. I wish you well but I know there are still battles to be won and I will be the one to win them."

As he left, I turned to view the apparent chaos as men formed battle lines. The contrast between the professionals and the Paduans was clear. The White Company and Giovanni's men moved purposefully and calmly. I could hear the banter as men who had fought together before joked with one another. The Paduans rushed, banging into each other and the clattering of metal on metal made it seem even more chaotic. Da Carrara was not helping as he screamed out orders. He had lieutenants and sergeants who could marshal the men more effectively. It was then, from the back of Ajax, that I viewed the Veronese as they came from the northwest through the gap between the river and the canal.

"Gianluca, ride as close as you dare and identify the units. Take no chances. I would know their numbers and their formation."

"Aye, Sir John." He galloped off.

"Zuzzo, wine… preferably untainted!"

He laughed and said, "Today will be a good day, Sir John. I can feel it in my bones."

Left with my two Englishmen, I said, "Today will be a day for calm. Deliver my orders as though you are asking your grandmother for a honeyed cake, with a smile and with firmness."

"Aye, Sir John."

More men were coming from the bastide. I knew that not all would but the ones who remained in the bastide would be the ones I could not rely upon. Better to have fewer men but ones who would stand and fight.

Our battles were almost formed when Gianluca returned. I had seen for myself the banners of some of the leaders: della Scala, da Polenta, Ordelaffi, the Count d'Ancre, Malcesne and Cantelli. They were good men. I knew that d'Ancre bore a grudge against Giovanni and I guessed where he would oppose the Captain General. I also saw the banner of Francesco Visconti. He was close to della Scala who would, I knew, direct the battle from the rear. I would be with my White Company.

Gianluca was calm as he gave me the bad news. "There are more than five thousand horsemen, my lord. Behind those are seven thousand foot soldiers, the militia under Dell'Ischia. I know him. He is a good man." He waved his arm. "If there is good news, my lord, it is that his artillery and powder weapons still labour along the roads and are behind the militia."

Zuzzo returned and we held out our coistrels for him to fill. I used my men to sound out my ideas. "If their five thousand cavalry charge then we will win."

Gianluca nodded, "The ditch will stop them and we have lances at the fore. What if he dismounts his men, Sir John?"

"He still has the ditch to cross."

John said, "My lord, I see a wagon and it looks to have fascines in it."

I looked and nodded, "You have good eyes. That means they can fill the ditch."

"It will be an unsteady platform, Sir John."

"It will, Zuzzo, and I will take any hope that you can find." I dismounted. "Zuzzo, help me don my armour. You three prepare for war. I want you all well protected this day."

Fitting mail and then plate armour took time. "Will you need your helmet, Sir John?"

I shook my head, "I need good vision and my intention is not to have to engage in close combat. This day needs the mind and not the sword of Sir John Hawkwood."

By the time I was ready, the enemy had formed up. Della Scala showed that he was no fool by keeping his militia as a huge reserve. I saw that he had kept a reserve of a thousand cavalry behind his main battle line under the command of Lodovico Cantelli. I shook my head with a wry smile. My enemy had a mounted reserve as did I. The difference was that his was five times the size of mine. The enemy dismounted, apart from his cavalry reserve. His men began to edge forward to fill the ditch with the bundles of wood, the fascines.

"John, tell Sir Robin it is time to spur the Veronese to attack before he can bring his artillery to bear. Our men will stand but the Paduans will flee when the air is filled with the stink of gunpowder."

"Aye, my lord."

Robert asked, "You want them to attack us, Sir John?"

"It is vital that they do. I want them to bleed on our lances and for our archers to whittle down their numbers."

"There are many of them, my lord, and we have but five hundred archers."

"I know, Robert, but we do what we must do and pray to God for help."

Just then it began to rain for a second time. I knew that my archers would have dry bowstrings beneath their hats. They would be able to manage at least ten arrows before they would need to change strings. I did not worry about my archers. Robin could handle them. My fear was il Novello.

Zuzzo said, quietly, but I heard him, "The arrows will draw them to us."

Robin did not shout his order but used a visual signal and the enemy were unprepared. Robin's arrows caught the Veronese unawares and those with just mail or ill-fitting plate fell. Shields were raised but still men fell and the Veronese trumpets sounded the advance. Shouts of 'Scala! Scala!' filled the air.

Our men began to shout, 'Carro!' but some of the voices made it sound like 'Carne!', flesh.

The order was given and Ordelaffi's men moved forward to attack my White Company. Zuzzo's prediction had materialised but as they moved across the slippery ground, they held their shields to their left and that made them move not at my men but Giovanni's. As Count d'Ancre and his men moved forward so the pressure on Giovanni increased. The range grew closer so the arrows had more effect and bodkins bit into flesh. It forced the enemy away from the archers and closer to Giovanni. They were, however, the professionals and his company and mine were holding the enemy. We were provvisionati. It was then that da Carrara and his kinsman Buzzacarino were assaulted by the centre battles which had been reinforced. It was hard fighting. It sounded like blacksmiths hammering metal. The long cavalry lances poked and prodded over the ditch. We were holding the enemy and while my archers, their rate of arrows somewhat slowed now, began to take their toll, we had a chance. We could weaken their left and if my men and Giovanni's could hold, we might be able to break their will.

It was then that il Novello made a mistake. He crossed the ditch to get closer to his enemies and his men, led by Buzzacarino, followed. He was immediately attacked. He showed courage and skill and his jupon was soon slashed and cut. He continued to fight but Arcoano Buzzacarino fell. What happened next surprised me. The battle around il Novello stopped and Arcoano was helped from the ditch and taken to the surgeons before the battle recommenced. The truce allowed me to see that on our left da Parma and his infantry, although wearing less armour than their opponents, outnumbered them and they were holding. Della Scala had committed Cantelli's reserve to try to turn our flank. He still had his militia but he would not commit them until the battle was as good as won.

"Come with me." I led my bodyguard, first to Giovanni. "I am going to view our lines. Can you hold?"

"Aye, Sir John, so long as Robin can keep up this rain of death." The arrows were still falling although the rate had declined. Robin was nursing his men to ensure they could keep sending arrows as long as possible.

We headed to the centre of our line. Francesco da Carrara was still furiously fighting. His bodyguards lay dead or wounded. I turned to my men. They had lances, "Extricate il Novello."

The three with lances rode through the Paduans, who parted and jabbed their lances into the faces of the Veronese. Zuzzo's sword cleaved skulls and the Veronese fell back. My men used their horses to protect il Novello.

He raised his visor and said, "What do you want?"

"I want you across the river in Castelbaldo. You draw the enemy like flies to horseshit." I know now that my words were ill-chosen but I was angry.

He shouted back at me, "I will not leave, even if it means that I die!"

I lost my temper. I had never done so before but my tantrum was borne out of frustration. I took the baton of command and hurled it into the ditch, "Everyone, return to the battle."

I rode with my bodyguards for the right flank. The centre would fall for, as I moved back, I saw that Ordelaffi had ordered his men to attack il Novello and they were pouring across the ditch. It was only a matter of time for the enemy had seen the weakness of our centre. Lances were now shattered and it was hand-to-hand combat with swords, maces and axes. The ground was becoming bloody.

I then spied hope for Ordelaffi's order had drawn men from the left flank. It was now empty and as the woods masked our movements, I could try an attack with a handful of men. Desperate times call for desperate measures. "Gianluca, pull as many of our company as you can from the fray and tell the Captain General that he has to hold on with fewer men."

"Aye, my lord."

We had a small reserve of men and I shouted to them, "Mount your horses, we will cross the ditch close to the woods."

"Aye, my lord."

Gianluca brought about a hundred men including John Coe and Tedesco. It was a tiny number but they were the White Company and, as such, the best of warriors. "Mount your horses and follow me."

"We ride to glory, Sir John?"

I smiled, "No Tedesco, such things are the province of poets and writers. We ride to snatch the victory from the very jaws of defeat." As we passed around the edge of the woods and the river I shouted, "Robin, keep up the arrows."

"Aye, Sir John."

It was eerie for as we crossed the ditch the only enemy before us were the arrow struck dead. I raised my sword. I did not want Zuzzo's horn to warn the enemy. We would use a visual signal and I would trust to my men. We hit the rear and left of

Ordelaffi's men so suddenly and with such force that two hundred died before they realised. Giovanni saw the ripple of death along the line and he and his men crossed the ditch. Attacked to their fore and their rear the Veronese left simply crumbled.

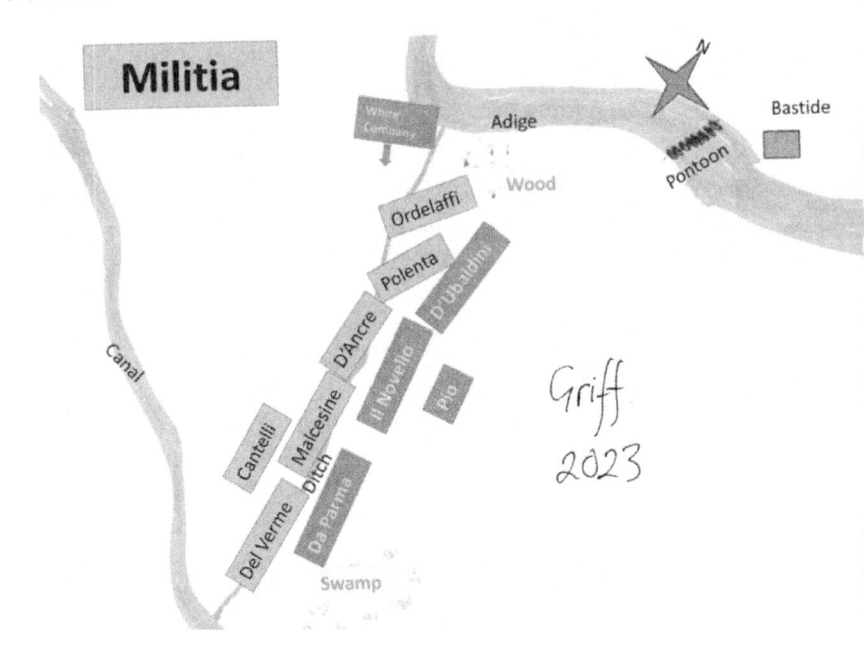

"The standard!" I spied della Scala and forty or so men around the standard that was carried by a young noble. Eager to be there at the kill they were so close to the rear of Ordelaffi that they would not be able to see my sudden charge. Some of my men were still engaged in the rolling up of the Veronese left but I had my bodyguard and the lances of Tedesco as well as John Coe and his men. Della Scala would not see us until it was too late. "Zuzzo, keep my banner safe!"

"Aye, Sir John."

I ignored della Scala and instead rode at the standard bearer. He had the reins and standard in his left hand while he tried to fight me with the sword in his right. He stood no chance. I had been born with a weapon in my hand and forgotten more about swordplay than the standard bearer would ever know. While John Coe disarmed della Scala I used my sword to batter the weapon from the standard bearer's hand. I then grabbed the standard. He fought to hold on to it but I had been an archer and, wrenching it from his grasp I hurled it to the ground. The already panicky Veronese were now in utter chaos. Many, those who could, found their horses and tried to flee when they saw their standard fall and their leader taken. Francesco da Carrara, having seen that victory was in our grasp had mounted his men and they were now pushing back the Veronese. We were crushing the Veronese between giant metal pincers.

"You have lost, my lord, surrender."

John Coe's Italian was a little imperfect but della Scala understood the reality. He held out his sword and said to me, "I will surrender to you, Sir John, for you have shown this day that you are without peer."

Il Novello and his men rode up, "I thank you, Sir John, but I will now end this battle." With the Carrara battle standard waving from the standard bearer, the heir to Padua led our men to Dell'Ischia and the waiting militia.

In terms of numbers, they were evenly matched. Giovanni, Filippo da Pisa and Ceccola Broglia were chasing the Veronese cavalry and the men who advanced on the militia were on foot. They were, however, plated, mailed and better armed. Ensuring that our prisoners were closely guarded we followed il Novello and were close enough, as the sun began to set, to hear his offer to accept Dell'Ischia's surrender. It was refused and the slaughter began. As the men at the fore fell so those on the flanks took to the river or tried to flee. It was a forlorn hope. The ones who survived were saved by darkness and the weariness of men who had fought for many hours. The fighting ended when the sun set and men were too weary to fight any longer.

The dawn that had suggested a defeat ended, at dusk, with a victory, some men said my finest; the Battle of Castagnaro.

Epilogue

Florence November 1387

The real winner of the Battle of Castagnaro was the Lord of Milan, Galeazzo Visconti. We did not know it the day after the battle as we looted the dead and my men's purses swelled, but it soon became clear that without even sending a single man to fight on either side, he had managed to gain more than Padua. There was, perhaps, a hint, when il Novello led the triumphant Paduan army back to Padua and an agreement between Visconti and il Vecchio was reached. By the start of April it was clear that Verona was doomed for Milan, her neighbour to the north, was sharpening its claws. My friend Giovanni had given me the baton of command and I had thrown it away. Il Novello kept away from the two of us and when Visconti made an offer to Giovanni to join Milan, my oldest friend agreed. I could not blame him. Padua had bankrupted itself with the war. With my men to the southeast, Milan to the north and west and Padua to the northeast even the redoubtable Antonio della Scala could do little to fight his enemies. It was agreed between the two allied leaders that Milan would receive Verona, and Padua would take the prize that was Vicenza. I told men like Antonio Pio that I thought the alliance was a mistake and I discovered that his loyalty to the da Carrara family was greater than to me. Il Vecchio threatened to have me executed for my words. It was il Novello who came to my rescue. Before the order could be confirmed, he ended my contract a week or so early. The White Company headed home and I was glad. I could see the way things were going even if the stubborn il Vecchio could not. He had discarded his only hope of survival. Giovanni had gone and I was dismissed.

The long ride back to Florence was a happy one. Despite the ill feeling of our departure I knew that we had done well. We had saved Padua and put the city in a safer state of affairs than we had found it. We were all in a good mood because financially the company was in profit and as the men had all taken coins, armour and horses from the enemy, they were also well off. Many had taken enough to be able to do as Robin planned and retire. My leaders and I had ransoms. I had shared mine with my bodyguards. I knew that I would not have survived had they not followed me so closely. They were an investment and I would care for them.

Donnina, of course, was delighted both with the outcome and my safe return. The hall had been enlarged in the three months we had been away and she had plans for our profits already. Robin stayed with us for a week and told Donnina of his decision to retire. She had smiled and nodded, "But of course, as you will still live in my husband's castle you will continue to recruit and train archers for him?"

My wife was a force of nature and Robin's wry smile told me that he understood the arrangement, "Assuredly, my lady."

When he left I realised that I was now without any of the men who had helped me to make a name for myself. Michael served Florence, Giovanni Ubaldini, Milan, and Robin had retired. There were new men like John Coe and Tedesco but they were younger than my first born. When next I went to war I would do so not with greybeards and veterans but children.

As the summer passed and the crops grew, I watched the political machinations that revolved around Padua and Verona. The new emperor elect, Wenceslas, tried to broker a peace but such was the cunning of Visconti that it never came to anything. He played both sides off against the other. It was in his interest for there to be no peace. Giovanni led the armies of Milan and they took the city of Verona in October. Della Scala was defeated again. If the da Carrara family thought that they had Vicenza they were wrong for another Milanese army took that town and refused to hand it over to Padua. Il Vecchio and il Novello could do nothing. Visconti's words had been a veil to hide his true intentions. The one man who might have been able to forestall it, me, had been dismissed. They had lost Giovanni who might have saved it and as Castagnaro had shown me, il Novello was more of a liability than an asset. For the moment Padua remained free but the predator that was Milan would take time to digest Verona and then when its appetite returned, the mangled corpse of Padua would be swallowed.

As Christmas approached and my wife and I sat and discussed the year, we both agreed that once Milan had taken Padua then the greedy eyes of the behemoth that was Milan would turn to the other jewel that it wanted for its crown, Florence. My company and I were still in the pay of Florence. One day I would go to war for Florence and this time would be against the Visconti family. My fate and that of the Visconti were irrevocably intertwined. My career was not yet over and I had no intention of hanging up my sword, not just yet, at any rate.

The End

Glossary

Battle- a military formation rather than an event
Bevor- metal chin and mouth protector attached to a helmet
Brase- a strap on a shield for an arm to go through
Brigandine- a leather or padded tunic worn by soldiers; often studded with metal and sometimes called a jack
Canaglia – the bulk of Italian city-state armies. It translates as the rabble
Centenar- the commander of a hundred
Chevauchée – a raid on an enemy, usually by horsemen
Cordwainer- Shoemaker
Cuisse - metal protection for the thigh
Dodici – the council of 12 nobles who ruled Siena
Faulds - a skirt of metal below the breastplate
Feditore-an Italian warrior
Gardyvyan- Archer's haversack containing all his war-gear
Ghibellines – The faction supporting the Holy Roman Emperor against the Pope
Glaive- a long pole weapon with a concave blade
Greaves- Protection for the lower legs
Guelphs- the faction supporting the Pope
Guige strap– a long leather strap that allowed a shield to hang from a knight's shoulder
Harbingers- the men who found accommodation and campsites for archers
Jupon – a shorter version of the surcoat
Mainward - the main body of an army
Mêlée - confused fight
Noble- a gold coin worth about six shillings and eightpence
Oriflamme – The French standard which was normally kept in Saint-Denis
Pavesiers - men who carried man-sized shields to protect crossbowmen
Perpunto- soft padded tunic used as light armour during training
Pestis secunda – second outbreak of the Black Death in 1360-62
Poleyn – knee protection
Provvisionati – professional soldiers

Rearward- the rearguard and baggage of an army
Rooking - overcharging
Spaudler – shoulder protection
Shaffron – metal headpiece for a horse
Spanning hook- the hook a crossbowman had on his belt to help draw his weapon
Trapper – a cloth covering for a horse
Vanward- the leading element of an army, the scouts
Vintenar- commander of twenty
Vambrace – upper arm protection

Canonical Hours

- Matins (nighttime)
- Lauds (early morning)
- Prime (first hour of daylight)
- Terce (third hour)
- Sext (noon)
- Nones (ninth hour)
- Vespers (sunset evening)
- Compline (end of the day)

Historical note

John Hawkwood was a real person but much of his life is still a mystery. At the end of his career, he was one of the most powerful men in Northern Italy where he commanded the White or English Company. He famously won the battle of Castagnaro in 1387. However, his early life is less well documented, and I have used an artistic licence to add details. He was born in Essex and his father was called Gilbert. I have made up the reason for his leaving his home but leave he did, and he became an apprentice tailor. It is rumoured that he fought at Crécy as a longbowman and I have used that to weave a tale. It is also alleged that he was knighted by Prince Edward at Poitiers.

The problem with researching this period is that most of the accounts are translations and the interpretation of the original documents leaves much to be desired. In one account the battle of Rubiera occurs in 1372 whilst in another in 1370. All I know is that von Landau was defeated and captured by Sir John and that the battle came about because he was still fighting for the Visconti family. As this was the last time he fought for the Visconti for some time and was employed by the pope to fight against Milan and Florence in 1371, I have had to adjust what I know. The dates might be open for debate but the battles and the outcomes are not. Until I manage to get a time machine this will have to do.

The massacre at Cesena happened. Sir John was ordered by Robert de Genève to massacre the population. He was acting on the pope's orders. Sir John saved many of the population. He was always, it seemed, trying to get payment for services and that explains his freebooting activities. There is no doubt that he acted like a warlord. He captured and kept castles in lieu of payment. There were many occasions when the employers of the White Company failed to pay them for their services. The White Company proved to be very loyal as it was Sir John Hawkwood who paid them from his own purse. That made him different from other condottiero.

I know that Hawkwood's marriage when he was in his fifties to a girl who was just 17 will make some people uncomfortable. However, it happened many times in the Middle Ages and to be fair to them they stayed together and appeared to love each other. Donnina bore him children and seemed an equal partner in the marriage. She was a strong woman and, unusually for the time, took charge of his finances.

Hawkwood's battles against Louis of Anjou and the Sienese were more skirmishes than battles. In both campaigns he used almost guerilla like tactics. King Charles of Naples and Pope Urban were allies. I made up the visit of Sir John to Sorrento but the conspiracy of cardinals and King Charles did result in the ending of the alliance, the torture of the cardinals and the excommunication of King Charles.

Padua went from being an ally of Venice in her war with Genoa to a city to be gobbled up by the greedy Venetians. The Battle of Brentelle was Giovanni Ubaldini's victory and Sir John was not present. I had him present for the sake of continuity in the story. The conversation between il Vecchio and da Serego was documented as were the number of captives that were taken. Da Serego was held for ransom and languished for more than a year. When he was ransomed his freedom did not last long and he died soon after gaining his freedom.

Giovanni Ubaldini did hand over his baton to Sir John. Ubaldini was a good commander, but he knew that Sir John was a better one.

There are many strange events around the Battle of Castagnaro. Firstly, it was the pinnacle of Sir John's career. He was an old man and yet he clearly outwitted his enemy. The chanting of 'carne' is documented as is the hurling away of the baton. Il Novello did refuse to retreat from the ditch and the battle for the ditch was paused when Buzzacarini was wounded. The incident at Cerea with the poisoned wine and water is less easy to explain. The Veronese did poison both the water butts and the wine vats. As the Paduan army was on the point of mutiny Sir John had to do something. He produced the horn of a unicorn and grated it into the water and the wine. Clearly, he did not have the horn of a unicorn and the grating of an animal horn would not remove poison from either liquid. My theory is that not all the wine and the water were poisoned and he might have used a natural antidote. It was theatre and it did work but until we have a time machine to travel back and see the master performer at work we shall never know.

I have used the words spoken whenever possible - the exchange between da Serego and il Vecchio is one.

Griff Hosker
June 2023

The books I used for reference were:

- French Armies of the Hundred Years War- David Nicholle
- Castagnaro 1387- Devries and Capponi
- Italian Medieval Armies 1300-1500- Gabriele Esposito
- Armies of the Medieval Italian Wars-1125-1325
- Condottiere 1300-1500 Infamous Medieval Mercenaries – David Murphy
- The Armies of Crécy and Poitiers- Rothero
- The Scottish and Welsh Wars 1250-1400- Rothero
- English Longbowman 1330-1515- Bartlett and Embleton
- The Longbow- Mike Loades
- The Battle of Poitiers 1356- Nicholle and Turner
- The Tower of London-Lapper and Parnell
- The Tower of London- A L Rowse
- Sir John Hawkwood- John Temple Leader
- Medieval Mercenary: Sir John Hawkwood of Essex – Christopher Starr

Other books by Griff Hosker

If you enjoyed reading this book, then why not read another one by the author?

Ancient History

The Sword of Cartimandua Series
(Germania and Britannia 50 A.D. – 128 A.D.)
Ulpius Felix- Roman Warrior (prequel)
The Sword of Cartimandua
The Horse Warriors
Invasion Caledonia
Roman Retreat
Revolt of the Red Witch
Druid's Gold
Trajan's Hunters
The Last Frontier
Hero of Rome
Roman Hawk
Roman Treachery
Roman Wall
Roman Courage

The Wolf Warrior series
(Britain in the late 6th Century)
Saxon Dawn
Saxon Revenge
Saxon England
Saxon Blood
Saxon Slayer
Saxon Slaughter
Saxon Bane
Saxon Fall: Rise of the Warlord
Saxon Throne
Saxon Sword

Medieval History

The Dragon Heart Series
Viking Slave *
Viking Warrior *
Viking Jarl *
Viking Kingdom *
Viking Wolf *
Viking War
Viking Sword
Viking Wrath
Viking Raid
Viking Legend
Viking Vengeance
Viking Dragon